ONE FINAL TURN

ALSO BY ASHLEY WEAVER

THE ELECTRA McDONNELL NOVELS

A Peculiar Combination

The Key to Deceit

Playing It Safe

Locked in Pursuit

THE AMORY AMES MYSTERIES

Murder at the Brightwell

Death Wears a Mask

A Most Novel Revenge

Intrigue in Capri (ebook short)

The Essence of Malice

An Act of Villainy

A Dangerous Engagement

A Deception at Thornecrest

ONE FINAL TURN

An Electra McDonnell Novel

ASHLEY WEAVER

MINOTAUR
BOOKS
NEW YORK

First published in the United States by Minotaur Books, an imprint of St. Martin's Publishing Group

ONE FINAL TURN. Copyright © 2025 by Ashley Weaver. All rights reserved. Printed in the United States of America. For information, address St. Martin's Publishing Group, 120 Broadway, New York, NY 10271.

www.minotaurbooks.com

Designed by Omar Chapa

The Library of Congress Cataloging-in-Publication Data
is available upon request.

ISBN 978-1-250-35093-0 (hardcover)
ISBN 978-1-250-35094-7 (ebook)

Our books may be purchased in bulk for promotional, educational, or business use. Please contact your local bookseller or the Macmillan Corporate and Premium Sales Department at 1-800-221-7945, extension 5442, or by email at MacmillanSpecialMarkets@macmillan.com.

First Edition: 2025

10 9 8 7 6 5 4 3 2 1

For Clare Oldham,
the reader who became a friend.
Thank you for loving Ellie as much as I do!

ONE FINAL TURN

CHAPTER ONE

LONDON
FEBRUARY 1941

No one could ever say I'd lived a dull life. I was, in fact, a biographer's dream. I'd been born in prison, the child of a man murdered before my birth and the woman convicted of killing him. Raised in a loving family of criminals, I'd grown up learning to pick locks and crack safes and spent my formative years breaking and entering. The drama of all of this, however, seemed to pale in comparison to what had happened in the past six months of wartime.

Since the war had begun, I'd been repeatedly shot at, nearly been poisoned, and fought for my life against killers and spies. I'd survived months of bombings that shook and rattled and destroyed my city. I'd uncovered a hornet's nest of secrets about my family's past, fallen in love, and faced heartbreak.

Life had been so much simpler only a few short months ago. The woman I had been then would be incredulous at who I was now, at everything I had lived through. I sometimes felt like an entirely different person.

It was not uncommon these days for me to reflect on this change of circumstance, and it was no different as I traveled with

Uncle Mick to do a locksmithing job. That was our trade, or part of it: locksmiths by day, lockpicks and safecrackers by night. However, since being drafted, so to speak, into using our specialized skill set in working with military intelligence, we'd been keeping to the straight and narrow. For the most part, anyway.

One side effect of the Blitz was that there were a good many things that needed rebuilding. And buildings needed locks. So Uncle Mick had been quite busy. I'd helped him on several jobs over the past week, which had been a merciful distraction.

Despite the tumult of my mind and emotions, I was doing my best to cherish this bit of normalcy with my uncle while it lasted. In a few days' time, I would be embarking on another adventure, another chapter in the ever-evolving saga of the life of Ellie McDonnell. I would be traveling to Lisbon, Portugal, to try to find my cousin Toby, who had reportedly escaped from a German prisoner of war camp.

Toby had been missing since the Battle of Dunkirk in June of the previous year. Though we'd tried to keep hope alive, it had gotten weaker with each passing day without any news of him. As far as we could tell, the Germans had rounded up tens of thousands of our soldiers after the battle, but his name had not appeared on any of the lists of captured prisoners. I wouldn't voice my worries to my family, but, secretly, I had begun to fear that he was dead.

It was only when Major Ramsey, the military intelligence officer with whom I'd been working, had come to me a few weeks ago with news of a POW escape route through the Pyrenees to Lisbon and intercepted communication about an escaped prisoner presumed to be Toby that I had really felt hope again.

Now I was about to travel to Lisbon to find my cousin. He would have information about the escape route that British military intelligence could use to streamline the escape of prisoners out of occupied Europe. Prisoners who would, naturally, be a vital source of information.

I was thrilled at the prospect of finding Toby and bringing him safely home. And, of course, I was happy to do anything I could to help the cause. There was, however, a sense of uncertainty I couldn't shake, because I would be traveling out of the country for the first time and would also be working under a different officer. My employment on this mission would be overseen by Captain Archie Blandings, an officer based in Lisbon who I'd met on my last job with Major Ramsey.

The change of command was because, at the end of our last mission, Major Ramsey had dismissed me, effectively ending my career in intelligence work until Captain Blandings recruited me for this job. Ramsey would also be coming to Lisbon to assist in the mission—he had played too integral a part in the lead-up to this to be left out—but he had made it very clear that his involvement changed nothing between us.

Getting sacked by Ramsey had been a heavy blow. Partly because I loved the work I was doing, and I was good at it. Until my work with military intelligence, nothing had compared to the electric thrill of midnight burglaries. Now I had found that using those same skills on the side of right—to do something that made a difference in the world—gave me purpose and a bigger rush than thievery ever had. What made losing this even worse was that I'd fallen in love with Ramsey, a devastating truth I had realized only after I lost him. And so that relationship, both personal and professional, had ended in sorrow.

"A penny for your thoughts, Ellie girl," Uncle Mick said.

I realized suddenly that he had been speaking to me. I looked up at him and smiled apologetically. "I'm sorry. I was woolgathering."

He gave me a gentle smile in return. "So I assumed. Want to tell your old Uncle Mick your troubles?"

Uncle Mick was my father's brother. He'd stepped in to raise me alongside his own two motherless sons. He'd loved and supported me as well as any parent might have, and he understood me better than almost anyone in the world. I knew he could sense my inner turmoil, and I wanted to reassure him.

"I'm all right," I said. "I just have a lot on my mind. You asked for the strike plate, didn't you? I'm sorry." I looked down at the array of tools and parts on the floor and picked up the correct piece, handing it to him.

I loved working with Uncle Mick. There is something awe-inspiring about observing a master at their craft, and I always felt that way when I saw my uncle with locks in his hand. It was as though he were a magician. Even knowing the tricks as I did didn't make the execution any less impressive.

For those few hours when we worked together, I could put everything behind me and concentrate on the job and nothing else. At least theoretically. It hadn't stopped me from slipping into abstraction today.

He said nothing as he continued his work, but I knew he hadn't forgotten the exchange. I was proven right as we left the building and prepared to walk to our next job.

"You don't have to do it, you know."

I knew he wasn't referring to this locksmithing appointment.

Uncle Mick was always careful to give me his unconditional support without pressing me too far about my feelings, so the fact that he was doing so now meant he was truly worried about me and my upcoming trip. I felt a stab of guilt to add to all the other emotions that had been assailing me.

"I'm going to be fine, Uncle Mick," I said, meeting his gaze. "Really. I . . . You know things didn't work out so well between Major Ramsey and me, but I still want to do what I can to help the war effort."

"He's a fool to let you slip through his fingers, Ellie girl." Uncle Mick's green eyes, the exact same color as my own, held understanding and sympathy. He always did have a way of cutting straight through to the point.

I smiled wanly.

"You're special, and he ought to have realized it. I thought he did." He sighed. "I suppose sometimes a man fights a thing even when it isn't his enemy."

"Thank you," I said, unable to help the tears that sprang to my eyes. "That's sweet of you to say."

"It's no more than the truth." He put an arm around my shoulders and pulled me into a hug. "Just know that whatever may come, you can always turn to me."

I nodded, unable to speak.

Our jobs for the day completed, I was glad to retreat to my flat, a small building behind Uncle Mick's house that he had gifted me when I'd reached adulthood.

I closed the door quickly behind me to keep the brisk wind from blowing inside. This had been one of the coldest winters I could remember. As though war and the Blitz hadn't tried us enough, Mother Nature had decided to give us a wallop as well.

Tossing my coat and muffler over the back of a chair, I went to the kitchen to put the kettle on. First things first.

Burglar, the calico kitten I'd rescued a few weeks ago from the rubble of a bombed-out house, brushed against my legs, meowing plaintively.

"I haven't forgotten you," I said, reaching down to rub his head. He immediately began to purr.

I took a bottle of milk from the fridge and poured it into his saucer on the floor. He set about lapping it up as I made myself a cup of tea.

My sugar ration was nearly up for the month, so I put a sparing amount in my tea, lamenting the fact it wouldn't be as sweet as I liked. My sweet tooth was my biggest weakness, and, though it was a very minor thing amongst all the horrors of war, the rationing of sugar was a sore trial to me.

I took my cup and saucer back to the sitting room and sank onto my sofa. I was tired. It seemed I was always tired as of late. Whenever I tried to sleep, however, I found myself tossing and turning. I'd developed dark circles under my eyes that I'd been doing my best to conceal with cream foundation.

None of this was so unusual, I told myself. I'd been in near-constant danger the last few months, forced to fight for my life on multiple occasions. It wasn't just night after night of Luftwaffe bombs that shook the ground and reduced the city to rubble and ruin. It was the work I had done, the death I had seen. Seeing the man I loved almost die before my very eyes, though I hadn't acknowledged I loved him then. Losing him anyway.

All of it felt like a weight that grew heavier and heavier with each passing day, a crushing load that sometimes made me feel as though I couldn't draw a good breath. I had to believe that if I were able to find Toby alive, it would take a great deal of the weight off.

If not, I feared I might suffocate.

And so I had taken up my other source of distraction, in addition to helping Uncle Mick, as I waited for Captain Blandings to arrange the details of our trip to Lisbon: the tangle of family secrets I was working to unravel.

My mother had been sentenced to hang for killing my father, but before succumbing to influenza instead, she had protested her innocence with every breath. I had been working on proving it.

Shortly before my career in intelligence had been shot all to blazes, I'd made contact with her closest friend, Clarice Maynard, who had revealed a piece of the puzzle that had changed how I viewed the mystery: my father had been spying for the Germans in the last war. I had set out to discover if this was true, and, if so, whether it had been connected to his violent end.

In the trunk of my parents' things in the cellar, I had found a book on Greek mythology. Under the chapter heading "Electra," there had been a letter written in code. The letter, once deciphered, had revealed the name of a particular flower shop. My visit there had not given me much information, aside from the suspicious way the shop woman had acted when I'd mentioned my father's name.

Then there had been the assailant who had come at Ramsey and me with a knife and told us to "mind our own business." It had seemed unrelated at the time, but Ramsey had later caught the man, who'd confessed it was me he had been trying to warn away.

By then, however, Ramsey had dismissed me, and I had fallen apart at the seams for a bit. I'm not proud of it, but one's first real heartbreak can sometimes consume all else. I had denied knowing anything about it to him, and we had not spoken since.

Perhaps, since it was my only lead, I should return to the Chambers Flower Shop and see if I could learn anything else before I left for Lisbon. It might be a bit foolhardy to go back, considering I had been warned away, but I didn't think there was any other choice. If I wanted answers about my father, I had nowhere else to go.

"What do you think, Burglar?" I asked the kitten.

He meowed in response, blinking his pale green eyes at me.

"That's just what I was thinking."

I finished my tea and went to put my coat and boots back on.

As I took the Tube toward my destination, I was aware of the potential danger in visiting the Chambers Flower Shop. This was the sort of imprudent activity the major would have chided me over. Truth be told, it was the sort of activity that had gotten me sacked. Ramsey's reason for my dismissal had boiled down to the fact that I was too inclined to act on my own, to ignore instructions. He didn't feel he could trust me, he'd said, not when I was forever keeping secrets and doing things as I saw fit.

Well, I didn't have to answer to him now. I didn't need to worry what he would think.

Besides, I didn't intend to go inside. Not yet. I just wanted to watch the place for a bit, observe the comings and goings. If this was still some sort of meeting place for German spies, it was likely there would be unusual activity—people entering and leaving without flowers, for instance.

Once in the neighborhood, I joined groups of pedestrians moving along the street and walked toward the flower shop. There were quite a few shops in this part of Finchley, and it wasn't difficult to blend in with people carrying sacks from the greengrocer or butcher. The warm scent of fresh bread from a bakery somewhere nearby floated in the air, and my stomach growled.

From across the street, I came up parallel with the flower shop and stopped suddenly, the man behind me plowing into my back.

"Beg pardon," he said, even as I muttered my own apology. He went on his way, and I moved out of the flow of foot traffic to observe the building. It was closed. Not just for today, it seemed. There was a FOR SALE sign on the boarded-up window.

I felt a moment of despair.

It was one of my last leads, and now I had lost it. Evidently, my previous visit to the place had alarmed them enough to go underground.

I sighed. I shouldn't be surprised to meet another dead end, but it was disheartening all the same.

A thought occurred to me then. It was, perhaps, a risk, but I had to try something.

I took a piece of paper and pen from my coat pocket. Luckily, they had been left there after I'd tallied up the receipts for Uncle Mick's customers. He was terrible at bookkeeping and left the task to me if at all possible.

I thought for a moment about what to say. Then I jotted the note on the paper.

My name is Electra McDonnell. My father was Niall Mc-Donnell, who was murdered on 12 October 1915. I believe he had some connection with this shop. If you would be so kind as to contact me, I also have valuable information to share.

I left the number of the post office box I had only recently engaged in order to keep any correspondence such as this from being noticed at home.

The note finished, I read over the words. It was just vague enough to be intriguing, I thought. They would wonder what I knew, what I might possibly be able to tell them—or tell the authorities. Perhaps this would do the trick.

I glanced around to be certain there were no suspicious characters loitering about. Then I crossed the street and slipped the note under the door of the flower shop. If anyone connected to the shop came back, they would find it. Perhaps they would contact me.

It was all I could do for the moment, so I would have to be satisfied.

Wrapping my muffler more tightly around my neck to ward off the cold, I turned toward home.

CHAPTER TWO

The final days leading up to my trip seemed to both drag on and move much too swiftly.

I got a book on the history of Portugal from the library and read it cover to cover. It was a prewar edition, of course, and I knew things would likely be much changed. But never let it be said that Ellie McDonnell didn't do her research.

I packed and repacked my luggage, going over the lists I had made and doing my best to find additional clothing items I might need with a combination of my small savings, my ration book, a bit of luck, and Nacy's skill with a needle.

Nacy Dean, a distant relation of ours, had come to help Uncle Mick raise the boys and me a few months after I was born. She had been with us ever since, a stalwart presence in our household and the glue that held us all together. She had always been like a mother to me, and she hadn't given up her mothering now that I was grown.

"Are you sure you're feeling all right?" she asked me as we worked together on alterations one evening. "This dress fit you two months ago."

Leave it to Nacy to notice my weight loss. She had already

noticed my lack of appetite. I hadn't craved food for months, to be honest. Learning that one's father had been an enemy spy in the last war coupled with the stress of wartime living and the strain of heartbreak will do that.

She no doubt attributed the majority of my melancholy to my failed romance. Though I hadn't been able to tell her all the details, she knew that the major and I had parted ways, both professionally and personally. She had comforted me as only a mother figure could, embracing me while I cried and fussing over me as though I were ill and not just heartsick.

She didn't know the full truth of it, however, and I wasn't at liberty to tell her. I hated this war. I hated that it built walls between me and the people I loved and trusted the most. I missed the days of free and open conversation between myself and my family. It was just one more personal casualty of war to add to the ever-growing list.

"I'm fine," I assured her. "I'll be back home soon, and you can go to work fattening me back up."

"A fine thing this is, his coming here to ask for your help after he dismissed you as he did," she huffed, stabbing the fabric with her needle. "Having you gallivanting across the world in the middle of a war."

It wasn't the first time she'd said it. In fact, she'd said it repeatedly since I told her that I would be going to Lisbon.

She had always been rather fond of the major and had made no secret of the fact she hoped something romantic would develop between us. But her loyalty was all on my side in the matter, and she was a bit miffed at Ramsey and not altogether pleased that I was going to be working with him again.

I hadn't told Nacy or Uncle Mick that I was going to Lisbon to look for Toby. I didn't want to raise their hopes or make them unduly worried about my journey there. They were worried enough as it was. Neither of them liked me going far from home. Once the baby of the family, always the baby of the family, it seemed.

"Lisbon is relatively safe," I said. "And Captain Blandings has lived there a long time. He knows the lay of the land, and he'll look after me."

"I still don't like it," she said, as she had said often these past few weeks. "We've never even met the man."

She was relieved of this complaint, at least, the next afternoon when Captain Archie Blandings arrived with my travel documents and a few last-minute details.

"We'll be leaving Friday," he said.

I felt a wave of excitement mingled with a tinge of anxiety. That was two days away. The time had finally come.

"I have a contact that we'll want to speak to as soon as we arrive," Archie said. "He won't, I'm fairly certain, know the escape route himself, but he will likely be able to tell us who does. If we can be put in contact with the person who usually receives the escapees in Lisbon, he will likely be able to give us any information concerning your cousin's whereabouts."

I tried to tell myself not to get my hopes up too high. Even if Toby had escaped and was making his way to Lisbon, the journey would be fraught with danger. He would be hunted, hungry, and cold, and the mountain crossing would be a difficult one. Any number of things could go wrong.

This thought would send the hope pendulum swinging back toward despair. Then I would remind myself that Toby was smart and strong and resourceful. If anyone could give the pursuers the slip, it was him.

And so I went back and forth between optimism and worry. More than once I had to remind myself what Uncle Mick always said: *Focus on what is*. It was the smartest way to live one's life, but certainly not the easiest.

Archie and I talked for a few moments of final preparations, and then I asked him to stay for dinner so he might meet Uncle Mick and Nacy.

"I'd love nothing more," he said, and I was glad of it.

Though I knew it wasn't necessary to run Archie past my relations, I also knew they would feel better if they'd gotten to meet the man who was to escort me out of the country.

Archie was as charming as always as we sat down at the dinner table together, complimenting Nacy on her cooking and talking knowledgeably with Uncle Mick on a variety of subjects. Archie had clearly come from a very different walk of life—his accent and manner hinted at posh origins—but there was not the least bit of loftiness in him. He seemed very much at home sitting in our cozy dining room.

"You'll look after our Ellie, young man?" Uncle Mick asked when the meal was over.

I half expected Archie to offer a smile and a cheeky assurance, but his expression was solemn as he nodded. "I'll protect her with my life, sir. You needn't worry."

Uncle Mick looked at him for a long moment and then nodded. "That's good enough for me."

Nacy, her eyes suspiciously bright, rose from the table to bring out the warm, spicy cake she had contrived to make despite the stingy rations.

"I trust him," Uncle Mick said to me when Archie had gone. High praise indeed.

"I do, too," I said. "I haven't known him for long, it's true, but I think he's very intelligent and competent."

"I'm glad you'll be in capable hands," Uncle Mick said as he lit his pipe.

There was a second part of that sentence unspoken, I knew. *But I still wish I could be there.*

I knew he would have liked to come along. He wasn't an

overbearing sort of guardian, but it was difficult for him to let me go to another country in wartime. After all, his two sons were already fighting this war. I was, in every way that mattered, his daughter. And now he had to surrender me, too.

I felt a swelling of compassion as I realized the sacrifice he was making. "I'll be home soon," I said. "Please don't fret."

He smiled. "I have every confidence in you, Ellie girl. I know, whatever you're doing, you'll show the Germans what we're made of."

"I certainly intend to give it my best."

Friday arrived with me feeling as prepared as I was ever going to be. We were to take an early train from London to the airfield in Bristol. The recently formed British Overseas Airways Corporation (BOAC) was still operating commercial flights from Bristol to Lisbon, and it was on one of these flights that Archie had booked us passage. This airport was, I knew, one of the few civilian airports in the country that continued to schedule regular flights.

Archie was waiting for me at Paddington station and helped me with my luggage. He was wearing civilian clothes and looked handsome and dapper in his dark suit, though his strawberry-blond hair was, like my own black curls, defiant of any constraints put upon it. I thought the wayward lock that insisted on falling down over his forehead gave him a youthful air.

It might, under other circumstances, have been uncomfortable traveling with a man I had only recently met, but there was an easiness between us that I'd always found rare in new acquaintances. I felt as though I had known him for ages, and I was glad he would be my companion on this daunting adventure.

We found a seat on the train and settled in for the ride. Archie read a newspaper while I mostly stared pensively out the window at the landscape flashing past indistinctly in the gray predawn light.

"We're lucky," Archie told me at one point, as he followed my gaze out the window. "The clear weather looks to hold. This wretched winter has thrown the flight schedules off more times than I can count."

I was glad for clear skies, too. I was nervous enough about this flight without the threat of bad weather.

There was a car waiting at the Bristol station to take us to the airport. Archie had arranged everything very neatly. Once we were at the airport, Archie took charge of the luggage and then shepherded me in the right direction to present our papers. It was an entirely new process, and I was glad to have a seasoned professional to show me the ropes.

It all went incredibly smoothly. Archie had the sort of brisk efficiency that befitted an army officer and a skilled diplomat, but it was all done with that boyish smile and coppery forelock softening the edges. I noticed how easily he charmed drivers and porters and the girls behind the airline desk.

It wasn't just me, then, with whom he could establish an easy rapport. It was an excellent talent, I reflected: that ability to cause people to lower their guard. No doubt it had benefited him in intelligence work as well.

Once things were settled, we had only to wait until we were called to board.

I elected to pace rather than sit. We would be sitting for several hours once we were on the plane. Besides, I wanted to burn off some of my anxious energy. I was not at all certain I was going to enjoy flying.

Though my cousin Colm had often hung around the Hendon Aerodrome, learning all he could about planes and occasionally finagling a ride in one, I'd been content to keep my feet flat on the ground. The recent bombardment of enemy aircraft hadn't made me any fonder of the machines. They were now associated in my mind with death and destruction, and I didn't relish the thought of being trapped inside one.

Archie came up to me, his expression slightly concerned. "Is everything all right?"

I was inclined to put on an act of bravado, but I knew I wouldn't be able to maintain it during takeoff.

"I've never been on an airplane before," I confessed.

"I've been on dozens of flights," he said. "Nothing to be worried about."

"No," I said, not quite convinced. "I'm sure there isn't."

"I was a bit uneasy the first time," he said. "But all went well. They make this flight safely several times a week, you know. You needn't be worried. The Luftwaffe has been very sporting about commercial flights to neutral countries."

Thus far, I thought, though I didn't voice this grim opinion aloud.

Why I should be so nervous about this when I'd been in much more life-threatening situations, I didn't know. Then it came to me: I was about to relinquish complete control over my life. In every other dangerous situation I'd entered, I knew I could rely on myself to get out of it. I had a better chance of surviving when I could think on my feet—and my feet were about to be far off the ground.

Well, as Uncle Mick always said, when there was nothing else left to do, one just had to hope and pray.

Finally, the call was made. Archie came and took my arm, and I found myself glad of the support as we walked through the door and out into the cold morning air.

"It's a de Havilland Albatross," he said as we walked across the tarmac toward the plane. There were a few others making the trip with us, most of them men who appeared to be unaccompanied. I wondered how many of them were, as we were, traveling to Lisbon with hidden motivations and objectives.

As a grim reminder of the seriousness of all of this, I saw the pitted ground off to one side, a reminder of the German attack on the airport in December.

I went up the little staircase ahead of Archie. Before entering the doorway, I took one last glance at the solid earth of my homeland.

Onward and upward.

CHAPTER THREE

I entered the plane, and I was surprised to see it was comfortably appointed, almost in the style of train compartments, with sets of two upholstered seats facing each other on each side of the aisle.

Archie, a gentle hand on my elbow, guided me toward our seats, in the second compartment, and I took the seat nearest the window, though it technically wasn't a window anymore. It had been blacked out with paint, presumably to keep spies from seeing anything important from the air. The upholstery was dark and sturdy but still rather cozy, with a padded cushion behind my head. If I closed my eyes, I could almost imagine I was sitting in Uncle Mick's favorite chair in the parlor. Almost.

It was getting more and more difficult to conjure up the feeling of home.

Suddenly I missed my cousins, missed them so desperately there was a lump in my throat as I fought down tears. What I wouldn't give to have them with me now. Clever Colm, who could tell me all about what was happening in the engine, who could make it seem possible—even reasonable—that a giant piece of metal with twenty souls inside should be able to hurtle through the air at incredible speeds. Or Toby—brave, cheerful Toby—who would tease me about my nervousness and make me forget that we were risking our lives, not just by taking to the skies but by trusting that honor in our enemy would keep them from firing upon us.

As I always did when the absence of my cousins felt like a weight too heavy to bear, I allowed myself hope in the future. The boys and I would be reunited—one day soon, if I had any say in the matter. I was, after all, going to Lisbon to look for Toby. It wouldn't be long before the three of us were together again. I had to go on believing that.

Of course, when I managed to push away thoughts of my family, I realized that part of the ache in my heart was for Major Ramsey. That was a different kind of pain, sharper and fresher than missing my cousins.

The devastating realization that I was in love with Ramsey had come about only after I'd lost him. Exactly how and when it had happened, I wasn't sure. I only knew that it was the sort of hopeless love people wrote tragic songs and plays about. Time after time, we had fought the attraction, and then, finally, we had to acknowledge it. We had shared a few passionate kisses that had set my body and mind ablaze with silly hopes for the future. For a few beautiful moments, I had thought happiness might be possible, that we might find some way to reconcile the vast differences that lay between us.

Then he had dismissed me from my job with the intelligence service and dismissed me from his life just as easily.

It was my fault; I could admit that now. I had acted recklessly and betrayed his trust. But some part of me still felt that, if he truly cared about me, he would not—*could* not—have sent me away so easily.

Well, what did it matter now, anyway? Perhaps I would be shot down by Messerschmitts in the next few hours and he would be left to mourn what might have been.

I realized my thoughts were spinning wildly out of control and tried to rein in my racing imagination. I looked over at Archie. He seemed to sense my nervousness and smiled reassuringly.

I drew in a slow, steadying breath through my nose. As the plane began to ascend into the sky, I clenched my teeth and gripped the arm of the seat. Archie looked over at me and then reached over and set a warm hand on top of mine. My hands had gone to ice, so I appreciated the gesture all the more.

When the plane leveled off and we began to fly in what seemed a relatively stable manner, I let out a breath. It did not feel much different from riding on a train. All the same, it was a strange experience to know I was up here in the air. I wasn't entirely sure I liked it. It was, however, marvelous that such a great distance could be traveled in so short a time. In a few hours, I would be on the other side of the Continent.

"All right?" Archie asked.

I nodded. "I think so. Thank you."

He removed his hand and settled into his seat, and I tried to relax. It was going to be another several hours before we reached Lisbon, so I might as well make myself as comfortable as possible.

That also meant not thinking too much about the job that lay ahead. I was confident we could do it, but thinking about the mission while flying high above the sea made me dizzy.

"You're going to enjoy Lisbon," Archie said. "It's a beautiful city, and there's a lot to see and do."

I knew what he was doing. He was trying to set me at ease. I appreciated it immensely because my thoughts were in a whirl.

We talked for a while about the sights he wanted to show me and the various restaurants and shops he thought I would enjoy.

Once we'd been in the air for some time, I grew a bit more comfortable. Despite the fact that we were barreling through the air at an incredible speed, I didn't feel at all sick, so I thought I would try to distract myself with reading.

I reached into my bag and pulled out the mythology book I'd found amongst my father's things. I'd always loved mythology, my interest in it piqued as a child by the fact my mother had named me Electra. In Greek myths, Electra had sought to avenge her murdered father, Agamemnon. Was it, I had long wondered, a hint from my mother that I should find my father's killer?

This link seemed even more important when I had discovered the book with the coded letter tucked away under the chapter heading "Electra." I felt that my name had been a message to someone, but the book had thus far given up few secrets beyond the indication of the flower shop connection.

With a strong sense of the potential relevance, I opened the book to the chapter on Icarus and began to read.

A slight drop in the plane made my eyes pop open. Before I could let out a gasp of alarm, however, my brain told me we had leveled off again.

It was then I realized I had drifted off to sleep. I was surprised I had managed it on the flight, especially considering I'd barely managed it in my own bed as of late. I was even more surprised to find that I had been sleeping on Archie's shoulder.

I sat up quickly, my hand going to my hair to tidy it. "I'm sorry," I mumbled. "How very rude of me to fall asleep on you."

"I'm glad you were able to rest," he said with an easy smile. "We've just begun descending."

"Oh. Good," I said, trying to neaten my appearance. I could feel several pins coming loose in my hair. I took a compact out of my handbag, confirming that my hair looked a mess and my expression spoke of just having woken up. There was a slight marking on my cheek from the seam of Archie's jacket.

My mythology book had slipped from my fingers to the floor, and I reached to pick it up.

The heavy reading had done the trick in relaxing me, it seemed.

Considering I had not slept much the past few nights, perhaps it was not entirely surprising.

The plane began a noticeable descent, and I wished I could look out the window to catch my first glimpses of Portugal. Archie had told me we would be landing in Sintra, a principality to the northeast of Lisbon. A car would be waiting to take us to the city center.

There was another bump, and I grabbed the arm of my chair.

"This is common when landing," Archie told me. "It's likely to be a bit bumpy when we touch down, too. The airstrip is grass here, and the weather affects the surface of the field."

I was immeasurably glad he had accompanied me to Lisbon rather than having me meet him there. I was game for adventure and as daring as the next girl, but to have taken this first flight alone would have been daunting in the extreme.

Thankfully, after a few more uneasy moments, we made the landing in one piece.

"Not so bad, was it?" Archie asked.

I shot him a look that said I didn't agree, but one did have to admit that the speed of air travel was a benefit. Who would have imagined, even a few decades ago, traveling to a distant country in the space of mere hours?

A few moments later, the airplane door was opened, and we alighted onto the landing strip. I blinked against the bright light, then looked around, eager to form my first impression. The airport was unremarkable, but, in the distance, I could see a rocky mountain range dotted with colorful buildings. And, though I couldn't see it, I could smell the sea.

I took in a deep breath of the fresh, salty air, glad to set foot on firm soil again—or, at least, on somewhat soggy grass.

It was warmer here than in London. After weeks of bitter cold, it was nice to feel the sea air, which was cool and refreshing rather than frigid.

I took Archie's arm as we moved away from the plane, the wind ruffling my hair. I felt the excitement of a new adventure.

We had arrived in Portugal.

Let the adventure begin, I thought.

CHAPTER FOUR

There was a car waiting for us, and Archie introduced me to the man who was standing beside it.

"Ellie, this is Simon Woods. He's my driver, bodyguard, and sometime nursemaid. Simon, this is Miss Ellie McDonnell."

Mr. Woods smiled. "Pleased to meet you, Miss McDonnell."

"Nice to meet you, too, Mr. Woods." He was a young man, in his early twenties, at a guess. His dark brown hair was cut short, and his blue eyes were warm.

"Been holding down the fort, Simon?" Archie asked.

"Yes, sir. As well as I'm able."

"Good man."

Archie opened the car door for me as he directed the porters with our luggage in Portuguese, and then we were off, driving toward the city.

I stared out the window, trying to take it all in. I supposed it seemed rather gauche to a man like Archie, my gaping at the scenery as though I had never seen a beautiful view. But I had been out of London only a handful of times, and never out of England. Despite everything, I felt the exhilaration of seeing a foreign land for the first time.

In the distance, on a hilltop, I saw the towering form of what looked to be a castle. "What's that?" I asked, pointing in its direction.

"The Palácio da Pena," Archie said. "It dates back to the Middle Ages, though it's been renovated frequently since then. It's rather an interesting mix of architectural styles. Well worth a visit."

"I'd love to see it."

I looked then at the landscape stretching out before us. Even now, in the winter months, it was beautiful and much greener than England was at present. There were rocky promontories and areas of verdant forest and clusters of pale buildings with red clay–tiled roofs nestled amongst the green trees, all of it set against the vibrant blues of sky and, in the distance, sea. I drew in a breath at the sight of it.

"It's lovely, isn't it?" Archie said, obvious pride in his voice. "I don't know if I'll ever go back to living in England full-time. A part of my heart shall always long to be in Portugal."

"Lovely indeed," I replied. "I can't wait to explore as much as possible."

Lisbon, too, was a sight to behold. My eyes drank in the sight of the colorful buildings with those distinctive red roofs and bright tiled murals. Everything seemed so clear and vibrant.

"The Tagus," Archie said, nodding toward the distant river. "It flows into the Atlantic here."

As we drove farther into Lisbon, the streets became thronged with cars and pedestrians. As we passed cafés and restaurants and little shops, I saw how crowded and busy they were. Lisbon was teeming with life.

In some ways, I realized, one big city was very much like the next. I wasn't sure what I had expected of arriving in a different country, but it had been naïve to assume that it would present itself as something totally outside my experience. I would be as comfortable walking down these streets as I would Oxford Street.

It occurred to me that something seemed to be missing, however.

Then I realized how unaccustomed I was to driving along roads un-
blemished by German bombs, with no craters to avoid or rubble in
sight. The realization brought a pang of sadness, but it was also heart-
ening to know there were places in the world still unscathed—at least
physically—by the war.

Archie didn't talk much on the drive. Occasionally he pointed
out a few places of interest, restaurants we might like to eat at or
shops I might stop into when I had time. He spoke as though I were
here on holiday—perhaps for the driver's benefit; I wasn't sure how
much Simon Woods knew about why I was truly here—but I hoped
I would indeed have a few spare moments to explore the city. I already loved it.

Finally, we pulled up in front of a magnificent structure. I let
out a low whistle. "That's the hotel? It looks like a palace."

"It is, in fact, called the Avenida Palace," Archie said with
a smile. "Once the luggage is unloaded, you can go back to the
consulate, Simon. I'll get Miss McDonnell settled, and then I have
another appointment."

"Yes, sir," Woods said.

"Thank you for the lovely drive, Mr. Woods," I said as I got
out of the car.

"My pleasure, Miss McDonnell."

Archie gave the bellboy instructions about our luggage in Portuguese before taking my arm and leading me toward the gleaming
front doors.

"I'm not entirely sure I can afford this place." I was only half
joking. I wasn't quite certain where this mission fell on the line
between personal and professional. I had agreed to do it mainly
because I hoped to find Toby, and that was understood by all
parties. How much of the bill I was expected to foot was a little
less clear.

Archie, however, laughed off the remark. "My office keeps a
few rooms in reserve here. It's often difficult to find rooms in Lis-

bon, what with the influx of refugees and . . . other visitors. We've found keeping the rooms has been useful to us. And you're in luck. I believe the vacant rooms are the ones with balconies."

The doorman opened the front door, and I stifled a gasp. The lobby was just as magnificent as the exterior of the hotel would lead one to believe. Tall columns led to a domed ceiling high above. The furniture was luxurious and elegant, the floors gleaming marble. I thought of all the windows that did not have to be boarded up because of bomb threats. And not a blackout curtain in sight.

There were a great number of people milling about, and my practiced eye told me that most of them were wealthy. Of course, this hotel was expensive, and no doubt even more so when places to stay in Lisbon were in high demand.

If I'd been in the business of pickpocketing, there would have been any number of opportunities here. A great many of the ladies were wearing more than the usual amount of jewelry. And I imagined most of the men had very fat wallets. When one was fleeing one's home, one had to keep one's valuables close, after all.

Luckily for all of them, I was not in the pickpocketing business.

As I stood back a bit, taking it all in, Archie sauntered up to the front desk with the practiced ease of a man at home in these environs. It was a different persona than the one I had seen thus far, and I wondered if he had put on the more relaxed and amiable temperament for my benefit or if this posh routine was the act. Perhaps he was a bit of both.

After a quick exchange in Portuguese with the clerk, he accepted a key and turned back to me. "Allow me to show you up to your room."

We took the lift, and he led me down the long, carpeted hall, stopping in front of a door. He unlocked it and opened it for me.

"I hope this will be suitable," he said as we went inside.

"It's much more than suitable. It's gorgeous." The room was, as the lobby had been, elegantly appointed. Tall French windows let in the sunlight through filmy curtains. Beyond them, the balcony. I could faintly hear the noise of the street below.

"I'll give you some time to rest and unpack," he said. "I'll call on you for dinner, shall I? We can discuss our plans in more detail then. There's a very nice restaurant within walking distance, if that suits you."

"Yes, that sounds perfect."

"All right, then. I'll come by at seven o'clock."

Though I was curious about Major Ramsey's whereabouts, I didn't want to ask, and Archie seemed to realize it.

"I don't quite know when the major will arrive," he said. "He did not confide his plans to me, but I imagine he'll be here within a few days."

"I think we'll manage just fine without him." I smiled to lighten the words, but I saw the slight flicker of his eyebrows that told me he hadn't missed the undertone of rancor.

I knew Ramsey had told him I'd been dismissed. Ramsey had admitted to me that Archie had gone over his head to the major's superior officer in order to employ me on this job. That meant, then, that Archie was aware there were certain tensions. Good. I didn't intend to hide them.

He looked as though he were debating whether he wanted to discuss it, so I decided to change the subject. "I am registered under my own name, I assume? I traveled under it."

"Yes. There's the possibility that my movements were monitored in London and, in the course of that, they might have determined your identity. If that's the case, it's better that they don't see a different name on the flight manifest. That would only draw attention and create suspicion."

I nodded. "And I suppose McDonnell isn't such a unique name that it would be immediately linked to Toby."

He smiled. "A lot of Irish and Scots with the name McDonnell." He reached into his pocket then and withdrew a small card, handing it to me. "These are the numbers at which you can reach me, should you need to do so."

"Thank you."

He took his leave then, and I closed the door behind him, making sure it was locked out of habit.

Then I stood near the door and took stock of the room. It was larger than I had expected. The walls were papered in dark green, and there was a big bed with a gleaming headboard of dark wood, plus a sitting area composed of a chair and settee and an artful scattering of small tables with lamps and vases. A large wardrobe and a standing mirror took up another corner.

There was also a door that appeared to connect to an adjoining room. I made sure it, too, was locked.

Then I went and, pushing aside the filmy white curtains, opened the French doors, stepping out onto the balcony. I stood against the iron railing, first raising my face to the sun for a few moments and then looking down at the street below. I could see the cars and pedestrians moving with purpose, each of them no doubt on some important errand of their own.

The city had seen an influx of refugees since the Germans had begun rampaging their way through Europe, I knew. A great many people had come here seeking safety and, if possible, a way off the Continent.

There was something of that in the atmosphere, a watchfulness in the gazes of many of the people who walked down the streets. A look of the haunted or hunted in the eyes of people I had seen in the lobby, though they tried to mask it. Numerous people in this city had no doubt experienced much worse than I had these past few months.

I drew in a breath of the cool, faintly salty air and thought that it was good to have moments like these, to recognize that my story was just one of millions, my problems small in comparison to many.

Everyone is fighting some battle of their own, Uncle Mick always said. I would do well to remember that.

I looked down again at the street, and it was then I noticed a man on the pavement opposite looking up at me. For an instant, our eyes met, and then he turned and disappeared around the side of the building.

There had been something purposeful in his gaze. I recognized it instantly. He was no passing pedestrian who happened to notice me standing here on the balcony. Either he'd been watching this room, or he'd been watching me.

I wasn't sure which might be more alarming.

CHAPTER FIVE

Archie came to my door to collect me for dinner. He looked smart in his dinner jacket.

Before coming to Lisbon, I had scraped together the funds to buy three new evening gowns, besides the serviceable two I owned and the burgundy velvet one that had been purchased for me on an earlier escapade with Major Ramsey. Tonight, I was wearing the black evening gown I normally wore out dancing with Felix Lacey, my dearest friend and a former beau, of sorts. In other words, not the nicest of my evening gowns but not the shabbiest either. It was a few years old, but, as I didn't spend many evenings out on the town, it was still in very good condition.

"You look lovely," Archie said as he helped me on with my coat.

"Thank you," I said, smiling. "So do you."

"I don't think, of the two of us, I'm the one to whom the eyes will be drawn."

His gallantry was endearing, but my smile faded a bit at the words. Because they suddenly made me remember those dark eyes that had met mine from across the street.

I told Archie about the man I had seen watching me. I had wondered if he would dismiss it as my imagination, but he didn't.

"It could be any number of people," he admitted. "There are eyes everywhere in Lisbon just now. But I don't think there's cause for alarm as of yet. Just be on your guard."

I nodded, slightly relieved. "I will."

We went downstairs. The lobby was even livelier than it had been that afternoon. People were milling about, many of them in evening dress, and the air was filled with the scent of mingled perfumes and cigarette smoke.

Music was coming from somewhere, and there was the murmur of conversation and laughter and the tinkling of glasses from the bar. Despite myself, I felt excited to be going out on the town in such a vibrant city.

We went out onto the street, and Archie offered me his arm as we walked. The evening was lovely, so much milder than the frigid cold we had left behind in England. I certainly didn't miss the biting winds cutting through my clothes. Here I wore my coat unbuttoned over my gown.

"Have you ever had Portuguese cuisine?" Archie asked, as we walked.

"No, but I'll be delighted to try it. I want to play the tourist as much as I possibly can."

He grinned down at me. "I'm glad to hear it. I'm eager to show off my adopted city. You're going to love Lisbon. It's such a beautiful place, with an incredibly rich culture dating back to the Romans."

"I'm thrilled to see something of the world," I said. "I've always wanted to travel."

"Then perhaps you've fallen into the right sort of work."

We reached the restaurant, and the waiter led us to a table in the corner. I found my long-absent appetite piqued by the delicious scents wafting through the place.

"Anything in particular you prefer to eat?" Archie asked. "Or prefer not to eat?"

"I'll try most anything once," I said. "I shall leave the ordering in your capable hands."

"You must try *bacalhau* for your first Portuguese dinner, I think," Archie said, perusing the menu. "It's a salted cod that is used in many dishes here."

The waiter returned, and Archie ordered what sounded like a large amount of food. I hoped I could manage to eat some of it.

"Are they rationing here?" I asked when the waiter had gone.

"Yes, but, being neutral, it's a bit less tight than in England. So far, at least."

We were served a plate of olives, cheese, and some sort of warm, flat bread to start. Next came steamed clams and then what Archie informed me was an octopus salad. Seeing the suction cups amongst the vegetables gave me pause, but I gamely tried it and found I enjoyed the flavor, if not the texture, of the dish.

We then had the cod, served with cheesy potatoes, which was as delicious as Archie had described. I managed to acquit myself nicely.

Just when I thought I couldn't eat another mouthful, the waiter brought out a dish very like crème brûlée. *Leite creme,* Archie called it. And I found it within myself to eat a few more bites.

The food was wonderful, and I greatly enjoyed Archie's company. He set me at ease in a way that I hadn't been for some time. He was clever and very amusing, and I found myself laughing more than I had in months.

He flirted with me in the way of charismatic and sociable young men who enjoyed the company of women, and, knowing there were no strings attached, I managed to respond in kind. If he knew my heart was not in it—and he surely did—he was gracious enough to behave as though he found me witty and charming as well.

I also discovered once again how ably he could smooth out a troubled situation when the couple at the next table tried, in frustrated French, to tell the angry waiter that there was something amiss with their bill.

It wasn't until Archie interfered that the couple was able to communicate. With easy assurance, Archie calmed the irate waiter, and, in a few minutes, the couple had been sent on their way without having to pay anything.

"You bend people to your will with no effort at all," I said to Archie when he returned to the table. "I'd never have thought that waiter would agree, much less give them their meal for free."

He grinned. "I've found I'm rather a wizard at working things out. It helps in the diplomatic service. Besides, I enjoy the challenge of solving problems."

"I shall remember that next time I'm in a bind," I said with a laugh.

It wasn't until I pushed the final plate away and Archie was drinking an after-dinner brandy, which I had declined, that he changed the subject to business.

"I was able to arrange to meet my contact tomorrow," he said. "He'll be able to give us information about how we might link up with the escape-route network, or at least point us in the right direction. These things have been kept very tightly under wraps. Almost immediately following the Battle of Dunkirk, people on the ground here began organizing routes to attempt to evacuate soldiers out of France and back to Britain. They're even busier now, with downed pilots and resistance workers who have been compromised and need to get out."

I felt a sudden pang—a strange mingling of fear and sadness and loneliness—as I thought of Felix. He was in occupied France now, working, I assumed, with some resistance organization there. He had not been able to give me any details, and it had been a tearful goodbye when he'd set off. I knew how dangerous the work was, what would happen to him if he were caught.

Felix, however, was like a cat; he always landed on his feet. If anyone could survive, even thrive, beneath the noses of the Germans, I was confident he could. I prayed for him every day and hoped that it wouldn't be long before he was sitting on my sofa with me, drinking tea and listening to concerts on the wireless.

I brought my attention back to what Archie was saying. "As you know, the last communiqué we received gave intelligence that a group of three POWs had escaped from a German prison camp roughly a month ago. They were making their way south."

I had always assumed, with France being so close, that if Toby had managed to escape, he'd come north, directly home. I had recently, however, come to understand the error in my thinking. There was no easy way across the Channel under German observation. And if he was being held farther inland in France, the safest bet would be to get to a neutral country and find his way back from there.

"It takes a good deal of time to cross the Pyrenees, as you might imagine," Archie went on. "Forty days on the low end, if they're all in good health."

There was a lot riding on that phrase, I knew. *If they're all in good health.* What were the odds of that? After six months in a German stalag, there wasn't much chance they'd be hale and hearty. And that wasn't counting if they'd been injured or on the receiving end of German brutality.

I felt my stomach tensing at the idea of all the things that could go wrong. But I reminded myself that Toby was strong and smart. He had Uncle Mick's knack for improvisation and ingenuity, and all the things Nacy had taught us about foraging and first aid. If anyone could do it, Toby could.

"What makes you think he'll come to Lisbon rather than try his luck in Spain?" I asked.

"We have informants who work the various escape routes, and this one has connections in Portugal. It's much more likely the escapees will be directed via this route and, as such, will eventually arrive here in Lisbon."

"So, if all goes to plan, he may be here within a week or two," I said.

Archie's eyes searched my face. "If all goes to plan," he said. "But don't be alarmed if he's not here by then. It may be longer."

I nodded. "Yes. Yes, I know."

"Our hope is that we will be able to get more information about this route and reinforce assistance for those attempting to escape. We would also like, of course, to make contact with as many POWs as possible to get information about what is happening in France."

I knew this was why they had involved me. Because Toby trusted me and would therefore trust the people to whom I introduced him. It would smooth the road, as it were. It was why Archie had risked Ramsey's wrath to get me involved.

"The man we will meet tomorrow knows a great deal of what goes on in Lisbon and well beyond. He will, I think, be able to give me the name of the person or persons in this city who are most likely to receive your cousin when he arrives."

When he arrives. It was such an optimistic phrase that I felt my chest clench with the sheer faith of it. I had tried, in these long months since Toby had gone missing, not to hope too much. I had never given up believing that we might find him; I could not bring myself to do that. But I had known, in the back of my mind, there was a good chance he would not come home. Now hope—a very real hope—was once again within our grasp, but I was a bit afraid to reach out and grab it just yet.

I thought of the thousands of families who, when this war was done, would never know where the graves of their sons, husbands, and fathers were. How many men had died in the past months, would die in the months to come, and would be hastily buried or—even worse—left unburied on battlefields?

When looked at with a wide lens, the devastating impact of war was almost unbearable. I tried to be brave, to carry on with a stiff upper lip and my shoulders squared, but sometimes I didn't have the energy.

Archie must have seen something of that feeling in my expression, for he reached out suddenly and covered my hand on the table with his. "We'll find him," he said.

"Yes," I said, pushing back the darkness once again. "Yes, I'm sure we will."

CHAPTER SIX

Archie and I ate breakfast together in the hotel restaurant the next morning. He was, I was becoming convinced, in league with Nacy to fatten me up. Either that or it just felt that way because of how delicious I found the Portuguese food.

The only problem was that they always tried to serve me coffee, which I detested. I didn't know how people could go about drinking great quantities of it when, to me, it tasted like fireplace ashes. But to each their own.

We set out on foot after breakfast to meet Archie's informant, Melik Suvari.

"You'll like him," Archie said as we walked arm in arm. "He's an interesting fellow. He's a Turk but has lived all over the world, speaks six or seven languages, and he always seems to know things a little before they happen."

"He sounds like a valuable informant," I said. "And you think his information is reliable?"

"It always has been before."

We reached the end of the street and Archie paused. With a hand on my elbow, he guided me down a side street. It was done so naturally that, at first, I didn't realize what he was doing.

"What's the matter?" I asked, when it occurred to me that I'd been steered away from our original destination.

"I recognize the man standing outside the café," he said. "He's a fellow called Velo who sells secrets to the highest bidder. He'll know me, and I can't be seen talking with our informant."

"I'll talk to Suvari alone, then," I said. "If you think he'll trust me without you."

He looked down at me. "I don't like sending you in alone, and something tells me Ramsey wouldn't like it either."

"Ramsey isn't in charge here," I said, dismayed to hear the edge in my voice that I'd meant to hide.

The corner of Archie's mouth tipped up. "No, he's not. You're sure you don't mind speaking to Suvari alone?"

"No. I'm willing to do whatever I need to do to find my cousin," I said. "How will I know him?"

"He'll be wearing a carnation in his buttonhole."

I laughed. "Will he really? I thought they only did things like that in films."

"It's just his way," Archie said with a grin. "A personal sartorial touch. Look for a big man. Dark, with a grand mustache. We worked out a sort of signal when we first met; I'm sure he'll remember it. Go to his table and tell him that you're hoping you can find a good cup of English tea. He'll reply that he prefers strong coffee."

My nose wrinkled in distaste, and Archie smiled.

"He'll offer you a seat," he went on. "And then he'll pass on whatever information he has while you enjoy your beverages."

I nodded. "It sounds simple enough."

"You're sure you're comfortable doing this?" Archie asked.

"Yes, I'm sure." Truth to tell, I was rather thrilled at the prospect. I supposed a lot of people engaged in espionage work during this war had to adapt to the threat of danger, but I'd grown up with it. Coming from a family of thieves, I knew what it was to live life on the edge of discovery, the vital importance of preserving secrecy and discretion. In so many ways, I was ideally suited to this work.

"I'll wait for you at the end of this street, then," Archie said, pointing in the direction he meant. "There's a little courtyard with a fountain there. If at any time you get uncomfortable, leave the café and come back at once."

I nodded and then turned and moved out of the side street and toward the café. I was enjoying working with Archie. It was nice to be trusted to do the job. As much as I felt the absence of Ramsey, I had to admit that things were easier without his overbearing presence when it came to missions. Still, my traitorous heart missed him.

Velo, the man Archie wanted to avoid, was still standing outside the café when I passed him. He was short and thin, with a mustache and glittering eyes that lighted on me for a moment before moving past me. My instincts were good, and they told me he was a dangerous man.

The café was crowded and smoky. The smell of strong coffee and pastries wafted through the air.

As in the restaurant last night, there were people from several different countries, the languages blending together in a colorful mélange of cultures. Nearly every table was full, and the place seemed to buzz with life and energy.

I felt as if this sensation was something that could grow addictive, as though experiencing other parts of the world might become a thrill that I would crave for the rest of my life.

How likely was it that I would be able to travel the world, if there was no telling how long this war might last, and when the war was done, there was no telling what would be left of the great cities of the world? The thought was a depressing one.

I would just have to enjoy this experience as much as I could, then.

Looking around the room, I tried to find the big, dark man

with the carnation in his buttonhole. I wished that there were some way he could recognize me, but I had no carnation.

I had been afraid that it would be difficult to remain inconspicuous on this venture, but there were so many people that no one appeared to be paying attention to me. This was a city full of the displaced and the desperate; my movements were of little interest to most of them.

Finally, I spotted a big man with a black mustache who sat smoking a thin cigarette as he read a newspaper at a table near the wall. The red carnation in his buttonhole was a nice accent to his pinstriped suit.

Drawing in a deep breath, I moved toward his table.

"Excuse me," I said, flashing a smile at him. "But do you know if I can get a good cup of English tea here?"

His dark, assessing eyes moved up to my face even as he rose from his chair. "I would recommend the coffee, mademoiselle. It is much better here. Very strong."

He towered over me as he moved to pull out a chair so I could join him.

"Thank you."

He motioned the waiter over and ordered a cup of coffee for me. I did not protest, though I had really hoped for the cup of tea.

When the waiter had gone, the man turned to me. "I was not expecting a woman alone."

"Captain Blandings was not able to come in. He saw someone he knew and didn't wish to be recognized."

The man nodded. The watchfulness of his dark eyes belied his aura of easy leisure.

He offered me a cigarette, but I declined. "You are new to Lisbon?"

"Yes, but I am very much enjoying the city already."

He talked to me lightly of things I might want to see until the waiter brought my coffee. I took a polite sip and fancy I managed to keep from grimacing.

"I'm afraid I have bad news for you," he said when the waiter had moved away.

I felt my heart sink, but I made sure to keep my expression pleasant, as though I were merely chatting with an old friend. "What is it?"

"The man you need to speak with has been discovered. Or, at the very least, he is suspected. He's gone to ground, and you will not be able to find him."

I hid my disappointment at the words. "Do you have any idea where he may be? Perhaps if we search . . ."

He shook his head. "You will not find him, believe me."

I would take his word for it.

"There is, however," he said, "someone else who may be of use to you."

He reached out a hand on the table, and I looked down at it then back up into his face. He raised his brows ever so slightly, and I slid my hand into his. I ought to have realized what he was about. As our fingers touched, I felt the piece of paper he was slipping me. He gave my hand a little squeeze.

He leaned forward slightly, as though we were deep in a heartfelt conversation. "This man will have the information you want, but he will probably be difficult to find."

"We'll try our best," I said.

"I wish you luck."

He released my hand, and I moved it back down into my lap. Though it had never been a part of our trade, I had a bit of a knack for pickpocketing, so it was easy enough to slip the paper into my pocket without drawing any notice from anyone who might be watching.

"Thank you. I appreciate your help."

He lifted his cup to me in a salute. "I would beg you to stay and finish your drink, but someone else is coming to meet with me in . . ." He glanced down at his wristwatch. "Ten minutes."

I had taken two or three sips of the coffee out of politeness, and my mouth tasted terrible, so I was not at all offended.

"You're a busy man," I observed as I reached for my handbag.

He shrugged. "I find idleness bores me. And please do not insult me by trying to pay for the coffee."

"Thank you," I said, rising.

He rose with me, reaching out to squeeze my hand. "Be careful, mademoiselle. It is not always easy to know who to trust in this city."

"I will," I promised, and then we parted ways.

I made my way back down the side street and found Archie where he had indicated he would be, sitting on the edge of the fountain in the courtyard. He was smoking and flipping through a magazine he had apparently acquired from a nearby newsstand. He dropped his cigarette when he saw me, grinding it beneath his toe and tucking the magazine under his arm as he rose.

"Was the meeting a success?" he asked when I reached him.

"Yes and no." I related to him what Mr. Suvari had told me about his contact having gone to ground. "There's something else, though. He slipped me a piece of paper with the name of someone else who might help us."

I pulled it from my pocket and opened it. A small photograph was tucked inside. It was apparently taken from a distance without the man's knowledge. He was short and slim, wearing a fedora pulled down partway over his face.

There was writing on the paper, too. It contained a name: *Fernando Estrada*.

"Do you know him?" I asked Archie.

He leaned over my shoulder to look at the photo and then shook his head. "No. He's not familiar to me."

"Well, at least Mr. Suvari has given us a lead," I said.

"Yes. I'll see what I can find out about Estrada. In the meantime," he said, smiling down at me, "let me take you out dancing tonight. There's nothing else we might do until we find out where Estrada might be, and I want you to enjoy Lisbon."

"All right," I said. "That sounds lovely."

I took Archie's arm, and we walked back in the direction of the hotel.

We had just reached the main boulevard when I heard a commotion. I looked in that direction and saw something was happening in front of the café I had just left.

A group of people was hovering around a figure on the ground, talking in a babble of excited voices. My stomach dropped. It was Mr. Suvari lying on the street.

CHAPTER SEVEN

I took a step in his direction, but Archie caught my arm. "No," he said softly. "We can't."

"But . . . but we might be able to help."

He shook his head, his expression grim. "He's beyond help now."

"What . . . ?" I began.

As if on cue, I heard someone from the crowd yell in English, "He's been stabbed! Someone call the police!"

I turned to Archie, horrified. But he wasn't looking at me. His eyes were moving around the street, cool and assessing.

My gaze traveled back to the still form lying on the pavement. I caught sight of his carnation on the ground before it was trampled under someone's foot.

I felt suddenly sick to my stomach and had to clench my teeth against a wave of nausea.

"We need to go, Ellie," Archie said in a gentle voice, his hand on my back.

This was not the first death I had seen—not even the first murder victim—but I felt just as shocked as I had the first time. The sudden, violent end of life was incomprehensible. It was almost impossible to believe that the vibrant man I had been speaking to moments ago was gone. Those warm, flashing dark eyes, and the vast intelligence behind them, dimmed forever.

"Ellie . . ." Archie said again.

I turned away from the scene of the tragedy, and Archie put an arm around my shoulders, shepherding me back down the side street from which we had just come.

He didn't say much as we walked.

We took a long route back to the hotel, stopping every so often in doorways and stepping into side streets. Even in my somewhat dazed state, I realized that Archie was making sure we weren't being followed.

Did he think that Mr. Suvari's murderer might be after us? The thought was chilling.

At one point, I bumped into Archie and felt the hard object beneath his jacket. He was wearing a gun in a shoulder holster, I realized. I wondered if this was a special occasion or if he normally wore one. I hadn't noticed any difference in the way he carried himself, so I was inclined to think being armed was not an unusual occurrence for him.

As I had before, I found myself adjusting my ideas about Archie Blandings. He gave the impression of being young and rather harmless, but some part of me suspected there was a more dangerous layer to him that he kept well concealed.

His eyes met mine, and I knew that he understood I had detected the weapon. He offered me an almost apologetic smile but said nothing.

"Who killed him?" I asked finally.

"I don't know, but rest assured I'm going to find out."

"You don't have any idea?"

He let out a slow breath—not quite a sigh, but close enough to worry me. "In addition to working with us, Suvari also had some Gestapo connections. I've been told the Germans have begun to worry he was passing too much information in our direction."

"But wouldn't they have taken him in for questioning?" I asked. "To murder him like that . . . He couldn't be of use to them dead."

Archie glanced at me. "It might have been not so much what he knew but what they did not want him to find out and pass along."

"Oh," I said. The information he would pass on to us. We needed to be careful, then, that we didn't attract too much interest.

I remembered something else. "He said he had another meeting in ten minutes when I left him. Whoever it was must have murdered him."

"I'll send someone to speak to witnesses," Archie said. "I should be able to discover something."

"That man you recognized at the café," I recalled. "Velo. Do you think he might have done this?"

"I don't think so. But I'll look into it, nonetheless. And I'm afraid our dancing date will have to wait. I'll need to go to Porto this afternoon after what's happened. I have a contact there who may be able to give me some more information."

"Yes, of course," I said vaguely. Dancing was the last thing on my mind.

We got back to the hotel, and Archie brought me up to my room. I would be glad to have some time to myself, to quiet my mind. I knew very well that violent death was a risk in this job, but I also knew that I would never get used to witnessing it.

"Will you be all right alone tonight while I'm in Porto?" Archie asked as I opened my door.

"Yes, of course."

"You should be safe here, but I'll send Simon along to sit unobtrusively in the lobby with a newspaper for part of the evening, just to keep an eye on things."

"You needn't worry about me."

His honey-colored eyes searched my face. "I know what you saw today was dreadful. It's a shocking thing to be at the scene of a murder, and sometimes the shock takes hold of one when least expected."

I felt tears spring to my eyes. For some reason, I was not uncomfortable shedding them in front of Archie. "It was a dreadful thing. But I'll be fine. Really."

I'd seen worse, after all.

He reached out and squeezed my arm, his hand staying there for a moment. "Suvari was a good fellow. We'll find out who did this."

I nodded.

"I know you don't want to be cooped up, but I'd feel better if you dined in the hotel tonight and didn't go out."

"All right," I agreed. I certainly didn't feel like another night on the town anyway.

He made his farewells then and left, and I shut the door behind me, locking it.

I had known this trip was not a holiday, but it was already off to a more harrowing start than I had expected.

After a pot of tea and a nap, I felt I at least had the energy to go down to the hotel dining room for dinner. I was dispirited and a little afraid after what had happened today, but my stubborn streak would not allow me to hide away in my room.

Besides, Archie had been careful to ensure we weren't followed, so I didn't think there would be any danger in my eating downstairs.

As I walked across the lobby toward the dining room, I glanced around for Simon Woods but saw no sign of him. Perhaps he had already come and gone. Or perhaps Archie had instructed him to come later in the evening.

At the hotel restaurant, I had some sort of very good chicken dish, though I found my appetite had once again all but disappeared, and my eyes darted around the room, wondering if anyone here might be an enemy.

Get hold of yourself, Ellie, I chided myself mentally. *Now is not the time to go to pieces.*

I was glad when the meal was over. I took the lift upstairs and walked down the empty hallway to my room, ready to get back into my bed. Perhaps tomorrow things would not seem quite so harrowing.

I had just reached my door with the key in hand when I stopped dead in my tracks. My gaze narrowed on the lock plate, a cold chill running down my spine. It wouldn't have been noticeable to most people, but I had been raised by Uncle Mick, one of the best lock-picks in London.

The door to my room had been tampered with.

CHAPTER EIGHT

I hesitated at the door, considering what I should do. I stooped down to look more closely at the lock. The pick marks were subtle, likely indistinct from ordinary wear made by many people staying in the room, carelessly scraping their key against the plate. But I had grown up observing the doors I entered, making mental notes of the locks and their conditions. These scratches had not been there this morning.

I couldn't tell from the plate whether the intruder had gotten into my room. It might have been that they were sloppy yet still successful. The last thing I wanted to do was walk in on an intruder.

On the other hand, I had been in the dining room for an hour, and no doubt they would have tried to be in and out as quickly as possible. It was unlikely they were still in the room.

Drawing in a deep breath, I slipped my key into the lock, unlocked the door, and flung it open.

There was no sound of movement, no dark figures I could see. I reached out and switched on a lamp. Everything appeared as I had left it. If someone had been inside, they hadn't wanted to alert me to the fact.

I made a quick search of the room. There was nothing missing, and, so far as I could tell, nothing had been moved. It seemed they had not been able to get inside. Even if they had, I reflected, they would have been disappointed. There was nothing here for them to find.

My careful search completed, I went to the telephone, prepared to ring Archie at the number on the card he had given me yesterday. And then I remembered he was in Porto. I could not reach him, and I knew no one else in Lisbon.

I could, I supposed, go downstairs and speak to the hotel employees, but what could they do? Simon Woods might still arrive at some point, but I was probably safer in my room than lingering in the lobby waiting for him.

Well, Archie would be back in the morning, and I thought I would be safe enough in the meantime.

To better secure the room, I put a chair under the doorknob. It wasn't intruder-proof by any means, but it would at least give me notice if someone tried to get in—and a head start at defending myself.

Having done the best job I could of it, I changed into a pair of flannel pajamas and got between the luxuriously soft sheets.

I was roused some hours later from a fitful sleep by the sound of someone trying to enter my room.

I sat up, listening. There was the scraping of a key in the lock and the rattle of the knob, though I didn't hear the lock disengage and the door didn't open. To my ear it definitely sounded like a key. Had they come back with skeleton keys since picking the lock hadn't worked?

Another rattle of the knob. They weren't even trying to be quiet about it now. Did they know I was here? If so, had they come to harm me? Surely they wouldn't have been so clumsy about it.

I slipped from the bed and moved to the door. Silently, I slid the chair away from the doorknob and, glancing around the room, picked up an empty and very heavy vase that rested on a nearby table.

Holding the vase by the lip in my right hand, I turned the lock and flung open the door with my left, ready to strike.

Major Gabriel Ramsey stood in the doorway.

I froze.

It was hard to catch him off guard, but his brows rose half an inch at the sight of me.

"Good evening," he said.

"What the devil are you doing?" I demanded, deciding to bluster my way through the awkwardness of this encounter. "It's the middle of the night."

"I've just arrived," he said, his tone mild. "The clerk gave me this room number, but the key doesn't work."

We both glanced at the room number on the open door, as though we expected it to answer for the confusion.

"They must have gotten them switched," I told him after a prolonged pause. "Archie told me he keeps these two rooms in reserve. You're next door, I assume."

"Ah. That makes sense."

We stood there for a moment. His eyes swept briefly over me, and it was then I realized I was wearing my pajamas with no robe, my feet bare, my hair no doubt curling wildly in every direction, a chinoiserie vase hanging limply from one hand.

He, meanwhile, looked as impeccable and polished as ever, even after a long day of travel. His navy-blue suit was spotless and unwrinkled, his fair hair neat, his posture perfect. Only in the handsome lines of his face, the slight creases around those violet-blue eyes, did I detect, perhaps, the faint hint of weariness.

"I apologize for having disturbed you," he said when it became apparent no explanation on my part was forthcoming. "I'll ring Blandings in the morning and we can meet up."

"Archie's gone out of town overnight," I said. "To meet with a contact."

"Then perhaps you can catch me up to speed," Ramsey said.

"Would you have breakfast with me at . . ." He glanced at his wristwatch. "Perhaps nine hundred hours?"

"Of course," I replied politely.

Another pause. "Very well. I'll see you in the morning, then. Again, I'm sorry to have disturbed you."

"No trouble."

He watched me for another fraction of a moment, then gave a slight nod and turned away.

I closed the door, locking it. I didn't bother with the chair this time. Now that Ramsey was next door, I knew I'd have backup in case of another attempted intrusion.

I could hear the faint sounds of his entering the room next to mine, the key giving him no trouble at all in that door.

As I set the vase back on its table, I glanced at the door that adjoined our rooms. I had locked it when I'd arrived, but, really, it was a moot point. Ramsey would never darken the threshold—and I certainly wouldn't be tiptoeing into his room. That might as well be a brick wall. An impenetrable boundary to match the invisible one that existed between us personally.

With a sigh, I got back into bed. It was a long time before I fell back to sleep.

I dressed carefully and professionally the next morning. I wanted to look nice enough, hopefully, to erase the hoydenish image of myself he'd seen in the middle of the night, but not enough to give Ramsey the impression I was taking special care with my appearance for him. I chose a flattering blue dress and pulled my hair into a neat chignon. After debating about it for too long, I put on a swipe of lipstick.

I gave myself a final look in the mirror, decided I was presentable, then left the room and went down to the hotel dining room.

I was early, but Ramsey was already there. He had selected a table in the corner of the room. He caught sight of me as I approached and rose to pull out my chair for me.

"Good morning," he said.

"Good morning," I replied as I sat.

He took his own seat again, and I waited. I was a social creature by nature. I had developed Uncle Mick's propensity for chatting easily with all sorts of people, and I enjoyed making conversation. I felt the urge to do so now, but I repressed it.

Major Ramsey and I weren't friends; he had made it abundantly clear that he wanted nothing to do with me. Under those circumstances, I was determined to keep things strictly professional.

"I took the liberty of ordering tea for you along with my coffee. You'll have to let the waiter know what you'd like to eat."

"Tea will be fine," I said. "Thank you."

My appetite was gone again this morning, and without Archie here to coax it back, I didn't want anything for breakfast.

"How do you like Lisbon?" he asked after a moment of silence.

"It's lovely," I said. "I hope to see much more of it."

The waiter arrived with my tea and the major's coffee then, mercifully sparing us from having to continue our stilted small talk. Ramsey ordered his breakfast, and, when I declined any, he ordered a plate of pastries that I supposed were meant to entice me. I hoped he was prepared to eat them.

When the waiter had gone, I looked across the table at Ramsey. He was looking back at me in a way I couldn't quite interpret.

"What were you going to do with that vase?" he asked suddenly.

I remembered the vase I had picked up as an impromptu weapon when I opened the door to him last night.

I focused on pouring my tea, stirring a bit of sugar into the porcelain cup with the silver spoon. "I was going to bash you over the head with it if you were an intruder."

"That was your first assumption, was it?"

I looked up at him. "Someone had tried to get into my room earlier in the evening. There were scratch marks on the door."

The hint of amusement that had been in his eyes disappeared. "Are you certain?"

"Yes."

"Was anything in your room taken or tampered with?"

"Not that I could tell. I'm fairly certain they didn't succeed in getting in."

He considered this, his gaze growing thoughtful.

"You hadn't had any more trouble in London?" he asked at last.

I didn't have to ask him what he meant. He was thinking of when we had been accosted by the knife-wielding assailant who had given us a warning. I was, of course, still disinclined to tell Ramsey anything about my quest to find my father's killer after the way things had ended between us. Nor was I going to tell him about the Chambers Flower Shop and its potential ties to my father's death. I had been close to confiding in him once, but that ship had sailed. Sailed and sunk. A U-boat couldn't have done a better job of it.

"No," I said simply. "Nothing ever came of that."

He clearly didn't believe me, but nor were we on good enough terms for him to press this personal issue.

I decided to put the conversation back on track. "I do wonder if the attempted break-in of my room might be connected to the murder yesterday."

Ramsey fixed me with that cool gaze of his, and I realized he had not yet spoken with Archie and knew nothing of Mr. Suvari's murder. "Perhaps you had better start at the beginning."

I related to him my meeting with Mr. Suvari and his sad death in front of the café. My tone, I was glad to note, was succinct and professional. I let none of the emotion I had felt yesterday seep into the retelling.

"Who was the man Suvari referred you to?" Ramsey asked.

"Someone called Fernando Estrada. There was a photograph of him inside the paper with his name that Mr. Suvari passed to me, but Archie didn't recognize him."

"And the photograph was still in your room when you returned last night?"

I paused to consider. It had been in the pocket of my jumper. I hadn't thought to look there after I'd seen the scratch marks on my door.

"I don't know," I admitted. "I'll look when I go back to my room."

I thought, for an instant, that he would suggest going there with me to look for it, but he seemed to sense the suggestion would not be well received.

"And you didn't notice anyone following you back from the café?" he asked instead.

"No. Archie was very careful about making sure no one followed us back."

Ramsey was wearing his displeased expression, though I couldn't be sure which part of the narrative in particular annoyed him.

"You said Blandings went out of town. Where did he go?"

"He's gone to Porto," I said. "He has a contact there he thought might know something about Mr. Suvari's involvement with Gestapo agents."

He lapsed into silence for a moment, apparently thinking things over.

"And what are your instructions for today? You're to wait for Blandings to return?"

"I have no instructions," I said. *Unlike you, Archie does not command me like a king* was implied. "I plan to go out for a while today."

"To do what?"

"Just to enjoy the city," I replied. "Archie took me out in the evening, but I would like to see some of the city by daylight."

I could tell from the look on his face that he wanted to tell me this was unwise, to instruct that I stay at the hotel. But he was no longer my commanding officer, nor was there any personal relationship between us. He had no right whatsoever to interfere, and he realized it.

"You'll let Blandings know I've arrived when you hear from him?" he asked stiffly.

"Certainly."

"And you'll let me know if anything comes up in the meanwhile?" It was couched as a polite request, but I recognized it for what it really was. Major Ramsey was too used to command to hide it well.

"Yes, if anything comes up, I'll let you know."

The waiter arrived then with his breakfast, setting a plate of food before Ramsey and the plate of pastries before me.

"Will you have something?" Ramsey asked, unfolding his napkin.

"No," I said, rising and forcing him, in his unfailing courtesy, to do so as well. "Thank you for the tea. I'll leave you to your breakfast."

Before he could reply, I turned and walked out of the dining room.

In the privacy of the lift, I pressed a cold hand to my hot face. That had gone about as badly as I'd imagined it might. I had wanted to be cool, indifferent. Instead, I had been frosty and tight-lipped, which no doubt showed how much he had hurt me, how much it hurt still. Ah, well. At least our first encounter was over and done with.

Back in my room, I gathered my handbag and coat. I was going out for a while, if only to a few of the nearby shops. I could not be cooped up in this hotel with Ramsey on the other side of my bedroom door.

I was just preparing to leave when I remembered my intention to look in my jumper pocket. I had left it over the back of a chair when I'd taken it off, and it was there still. All the same, I would make sure.

I went over to it and slipped my hand into first one pocket and then the other. A second search produced the same result.

The photograph was gone.

CHAPTER NINE

So they had gained entrance to my room, after all. And the only thing they had taken was the photograph. Was that what they had come for? Surely not.

But the fact remained that I could see nothing else that was missing. Everything was where I had left it; only the photo had been taken from the pocket of my jumper.

I considered alternative explanations. Was it possible it had simply fallen out? I didn't think so. The pockets were deep, and I often put things into them without concern for their safety.

No, someone had taken it from the pocket. That was the only explanation.

I wondered if I should relate this to Ramsey. He had told me to let him know if I discovered anything. I wasn't sure what he could do, but it seemed to me that the man in the photograph might be in danger now that his face and name were known to our enemies.

It was just then the telephone in my room began to ring.

I moved to answer it, wondering who might be calling me here. "Hello?"

"Hello, Ellie. It's Archie."

"Oh, Archie," I said, a feeling of relief washing over me. "I was just wishing to talk to you."

"Is everything all right?"

"Well, Ramsey has arrived." He could draw his own conclusions about whether that was all right or not. "But I wanted to tell you that the door to my room was tampered with when I was out last night."

I heard a muffled curse on the other end of the line and decided that was a sufficient enough reply to continue.

"Nothing was taken, except the photograph of Fernando Estrada that Mr. Suvari gave me."

"The photograph?" Archie repeated. "Why would they take that?"

"I don't know," I said. "Potentially to identify whatever Mr. Suvari had given me? But even with his name and photograph, they won't know why we seek Estrada. I'm not sure what they've gained by it."

There was a brief pause, and I assumed Archie was considering what was to be done next.

"All right," he said at last. "Sit tight, and I'll be back as soon as I can. Perhaps you'd better stick with Ramsey."

"I'll be all right," I said.

"I know it's less than ideal, Ellie, but I don't want you in danger. If someone broke into your room, they know who you are and, at the very least, that you've some connection with Suvari. And Suvari has been murdered."

That thought had occurred to me, but hearing it put into words brought a chill.

"If they meant to harm me, then they could have done so last night," I said. I hoped it was true—that they hadn't meant to harm me.

"Don't let your prejudices compromise your safety," Archie replied. It was a very Uncle Mick sort of thing to say.

"I'll be careful."

"I'll be back this afternoon, but if you'll at least let Ramsey know what's happened, I'll feel much better in the meantime."

In all fairness, Ramsey did need to know about this. If I examined things impartially, I recognized that, were it any other ally, there would be no question of not informing him. I sighed. "I'll let him know."

"Good girl."

We said our goodbyes, and I set the receiver down with another heavy sigh. No doubt Ramsey would still be in the dining room. It would take only a moment to let him know that the photo was gone.

I left my room and reached the lift just as it opened. Ramsey stepped out and almost directly into me.

"I beg your pardon," he said, his hand lifting instinctively to steady me and then dropping without touching me.

"I was just coming to speak to you," I told him. "The photograph is gone."

"Then someone was in your room, after all."

"It appears so."

"I'd better make a search," he said.

I didn't particularly want him in my room. "There's nothing to see," I said lightly. "They didn't take anything else."

"They may have left something," he said. I knew then what he meant. My room might have been bugged. I wondered if I had just made a mistake in talking to Archie on the phone.

"All right," I said, turning back toward my room.

We reached the door, and he looked down at the lock. The scratches on the brass strike plate were obvious. "Not professionals," he observed, as I had.

"No. Not at lockpicking, at least."

I entered the room, and he followed, closing the door behind him.

The room felt smaller with him in it. It wasn't just because he was a big man, tall and broad-shouldered and solid. It was because both my anger at him and my unrequited love for him seemed to suck up a good deal of the air.

I stood aside as he made a quick but thorough search of the room. I supposed he was looking for hidden recording equipment and things of that sort, but he came up empty.

"Nothing here," he said, turning to me. "It seems they were only after the photograph. Under the circumstances, I think you must be very careful. Do you still intend to go out this morning?"

"No, not now. Archie phoned. He said for me to remain here until he gets back."

I saw the annoyance cross his face, though I'm sure he didn't mean to show it. It seemed he didn't like that I was obeying Archie when he'd sacked me for not following commands. Well, he ought to be pleased I'd learned my lesson.

"I doubt they'll come back here," he said. "But I should be working in my room most of the morning. I've brought along several cases from London that need my attention. If anything happens, you've only to tap on the adjoining door and I'll come immediately."

I nodded. "Thank you."

He left, and I locked the door behind him.

Archie arrived that afternoon. I'd had another pot of tea and some toast in my room and perused my mythology book, still looking for clues within the notes written in the margins. So far, I'd found nothing out of the ordinary, though I'd lost myself for long moments in the retelling of some of my favorite myths.

When Archie rang up and asked if I would meet him downstairs, I hurried to leave my room before I would be forced to share an uneasy ride in the lift with Ramsey.

He was waiting for me in the lobby. Ramsey was with him.

"Hello, Ellie," Archie said when I reached them. "Everything has been all right today?"

"Yes, it's all been rather uneventful," I replied. "I've been reading."

"Have you had lunch?"

"I had something sent up."

He nodded. "Ramsey tells me nothing else was missing from your room. Do you suppose there's any way the photo might have fallen out on our way back from the café?"

"I thought of that," I said. "But I doubt it. They're rather deep pockets, and I've frequently carried things in them without losing them."

No use telling them it was a jumper I'd worn on burglaries in the past, and that it had carried tools as well as the fruits of our illicit labors without ever misplacing a thing.

"Well, then, we'll have to assume that someone was, indeed, in your room. I wonder if we should look for somewhere to move you."

"I don't think it's necessary," I said. "Presumably, they got what they wanted and won't be back."

"I'm right to hand now, should anything go amiss," Ramsey said. We both turned to look at him. Rather rudely on my part, I'd given him only a short glance in acknowledgment of his presence when I'd arrived, and Archie and I had been talking as though he weren't there at all.

"Yes, that's true," Archie said. "I suppose she'll be safe enough with you next door. Perhaps you might keep the adjoining door unlocked, in case of an emergency."

I glanced at Ramsey then, but he wasn't looking at me.

"Let's go sit down there," Archie said, nodding toward a small cluster of chairs to one side of the lobby. "We can go over what I've learned and what might be the best next course of action."

It was, I realized, thoughtful of Archie to have asked us down to the lobby to discuss matters rather than doing it in one of our rooms, which might have felt too personal.

"Do you suppose we're being watched?" I asked when we were seated, the thought occurring to me suddenly. This was, after all, rather out in the open.

Archie shrugged. "It's entirely possible. In addition to whoever was in your room, there are usually agents from the various intelligence agencies that come through the hotel at different times of day, just to get the lay of the land."

"Not to mention the man who was watching me from across the street," I put in.

"Have you seen any more of him?" Archie asked, even as I felt Ramsey's eyes on me.

"No, but I haven't been out on the balcony since."

"Well, anyway, I don't anticipate anyone would be eager to try anything here in the lobby. It's such a public place."

"They killed Suvari in a public place," Ramsey said, his tone cool.

"Yes," Archie agreed. "But Suvari had a great deal of information that we do not. He was a merchant of information, one might say. He sold only enough to keep people coming back for more."

"He seemed such a vital sort of man," I said. "It was tragic, what happened to him."

Archie nodded. "And I'm sorry you had to see it, Ellie." He reached out briefly and patted my hands, which were folded in my lap.

"You said you learned something in Porto?" Ramsey's tone was clipped, as it became when he grew impatient.

"Yes," Archie said. "I have a source there who, while not often venturing to Lisbon, gets a great deal of information from this quarter. He was able to give me an address where he thinks Fernando Estrada is staying."

"Oh, good," I said. "Then we might be able to find him before whoever took his name and photograph from my pocket does."

"That's the hope," Archie said. "My plan is this. Ellie and I will go to the address I've been given and try to make contact with Fernando Estrada."

Ramsey said nothing, though he had clearly been pushed out of pursuing our biggest lead.

He outranked Archie, but this was Archie's mission, and Archie was the one making the decisions. Archie did, however, contrive to keep the deference in his tone as he said, "Major, I know you are pursuing your own lines of inquiry, but if you are free this afternoon, I thought perhaps you might go and speak to a man called Velo. I saw him at the door of the café where Ellie went to speak to Suvari. It was the reason I didn't go in with her. I didn't want to tip him off that Suvari was a contact."

I didn't miss the little flash in Ramsey's eyes at Archie's words. He apparently hadn't known that Archie had sent me in to speak to Suvari alone. It was the sort of thing he had always given me trouble about. Archie had trusted me to do it. Ramsey would have protested.

"I would still rather Velo not know that I was there," Archie said. "But if you could go and speak with him, it will leave me clear of it. I don't know where he lives, but he's often at a certain café in the afternoons."

"Certainly, I'll speak with him," Ramsey said.

"Excellent," Archie said. "Then we've all got our jobs to do. Perhaps we can reconvene for dinner and share what we've learned."

"I look forward to it," Ramsey said. Something in his tone gave me the impression he was being less than sincere, but I didn't look at him to be certain.

"Do you have your lockpicking kit handy, Ellie?" Archie asked. "Just in case we need it."

I patted my pocket. "Of course." I carried it everywhere with me, a habit instilled in me by Uncle Mick. It had come in handy more times than I could count.

"Then let's be on our way."

CHAPTER TEN

Archie and I left the hotel. Major Ramsey did not walk out with us, nor did he say much as he wished us farewell.

Archie looked at me after we had walked a few blocks from the hotel. "He wasn't best pleased to be left out of the main event."

"No," I agreed.

"I don't mean to pry," he said after a moment. "But there's clearly been some sort of fallout between you and Ramsey."

"Yes," I said, my tone neutral. "He dismissed me. He told you that?" I knew he had, for he'd told me himself that Archie had gone over his head to his superiors to get me on this job.

Archie paused, obviously trying to decide how much to say. "He did indicate you would no longer be working for him," he admitted at last. "But he gave me no details."

"I'm too much of a loose cannon," I said as lightly as I could. No sense sugarcoating it.

Archie said nothing, and I looked over at him. "I suppose he warned you about that, too."

"I find loose cannons can be highly effective if aimed in the right direction," he said, smoothly avoiding an answer.

"You don't have to worry," I assured him. "I don't tend to run amok in a city I don't know."

He smiled. "I'm not concerned."

We walked on for a few moments, but it seemed Archie was not quite done with the topic.

"Your, er, incompatible methodologies may be why you're no longer working with Ramsey . . . but that wasn't exactly what I meant when I said there'd been a fallout. You shared more than just a professional relationship—I don't think I imagined that."

I didn't look at him and spoke with what I hoped sounded like carelessness. "There was a mutual attraction, but, in the end, it wasn't going to work. Our 'incompatible methodologies,' as you so delicately put it. So nothing came of it. No harm done."

That wasn't quite true. Even now I felt the sting of the cold, officious way Ramsey had dismissed me as if I'd been an employee caught stealing money from the till. Yes, I had gone behind his back and done two jobs—two technically illegal jobs—without telling him. Yes, a condition of my employment was no illegal activity. When one looked at it in black and white, his decision couldn't be argued with.

But it wasn't black-and-white. Two nights before he had dismissed me, he had kissed me breathless in the moonlight. He had told me we would discuss our future.

I had thought, for one shining, happy moment, that we might be able to make it work. That the differences between us could be overcome. But I realized now that kisses in a moonlit garden were not the foundation on which lasting romance could be built. That was the stuff of fairy tales, and I was too old for fairy tales.

"I'm not trying to delve into your personal life," Archie said when the silence stretched. "It's just that I'm wondering how things will go now that Ramsey is here."

"Professionally," I said. "Things will go professionally."

He didn't look convinced, but he let the matter drop.

I had the impression that Archie wanted to draw me out where Ramsey was concerned, to get me to express my feelings about the major. But, while I liked Archie a great deal and trusted him, I did not intend to unburden myself to him. I had shared too much about my personal feelings as it was already.

Once again, Archie took a very circuitous route, looking frequently behind us, to be certain that we were not being followed. Once he was certain there was no one tailing us, he flagged a cab.

"Do you think we'll find Estrada?"

"I don't know," he admitted. "It's possible our enemies have reached him first."

I felt a chill at the words, and Archie must have seen the horror of the idea on my face.

"Of course, just having a name and a photograph doesn't mean that it will be easy for them to find him. It took quite an effort for me to get his information."

"Yes," I said, though I knew he was being optimistic for my sake. "Let's hope you're right."

We exited the cab before we reached Estrada's address, as Archie didn't wish to draw any additional attention to our movements.

Though I was anxious about our visit to Estrada, I couldn't help but enjoy the scenery as we began walking through what Archie told me was Alfama, a neighborhood of the city dating back to the Romans and built up by the Moors. It was so different in appearance from London.

The buildings were constructed on a slope, close together, with narrow, steep streets opening onto winding staircases and intimate little courtyards. It might have felt labyrinth-like without Archie's capable navigation, but it was immensely charming.

In the distance, towering above us, I could make out a castle-like building. "Castelo de São Jorge," Archie told me. "St. George's Castle. It was a Moorish citadel. It was restored a few years ago. Perhaps I'll take you there one day. The views from the ramparts are some of the best in the city."

"I'd like that," I said, taking a deep breath at the top of yet another staircase. "Though I hope I can manage the stairs."

Archie laughed. "There's a tram."

"Well, thank heavens for that."

We passed little cafés and shops and sleepy-looking taverns. We saw mothers with babies, old men smoking and playing cards, children kicking a football back and forth, and women hanging clean laundry in the sun. It was a beautiful and homey area. I thought I could happily spend days just wandering Alfama.

After walking unhurriedly through the neighborhood for perhaps half an hour, as though we were on no particularly important errand, we reached our destination.

The building in which Estrada lived was in a block of colorful, close-built houses with clay-tiled roofs. Archie opened the front door, and we entered and walked up three flights of stairs, as though I hadn't walked enough stairs in the past thirty minutes.

There was the sound of a radio playing behind one of the doors, the sound of children laughing drifting up from the streets below. More than one person was preparing dinner, it seemed, for there was a mixture of delicious scents in the air.

We reached the flat in question, and Archie motioned for me to stand back. Men were forever being chivalrous, and I usually found it annoying. Nevertheless, I stepped back a bit, and Archie knocked on the door.

We waited. No one came to the door, and there was no sound from within.

We looked at each other. Archie knocked again, a bit harder this time.

Just then a woman came out of one of the other flats along the corridor. She was wearing a dark floral dress over which she wore an apron that had not quite managed to catch all of the flour she had clearly been baking with. An absolutely mouthwatering smell was drifting from the open door behind her.

"*Boa tarde, senhora,*" Archie said, flashing her his friendliest smile. He then began speaking to her in Portuguese. She wiped her hand on her apron as she listened and then answered.

Archie turned to me. "She says that she hasn't seen Estrada in several days. She was used to seeing him almost every day, as she would take him loaves of the bread that she makes. But the past few days he hasn't answered her knocking, and none of the neighbors seem to have seen him either."

"Then he was gone before whoever it was took the photo from my pocket."

"Yes."

"Odd that he didn't tell anyone he was going away," I said. "Unless, of course, he had to get away in a hurry." I didn't voice aloud the other option: that he had been murdered even before Mr. Suvari had told me about him.

Archie turned back to the woman, a smile on his face, and began to speak to her again. He was, I assumed, asking her about her baking, from the way that her face lit up and she began to point behind her into her flat. Then she motioned inside and invited us forward. Or perhaps just Archie, I wasn't sure. She seemed to have taken to him.

That left me free to find my way into Estrada's flat.

I was, I'll admit, a bit afraid of what I might find. The last time I had entered a room in a situation like this, Ramsey and I had come across the very bloody body of a dead woman.

There was no smell of death in the hallway, however. I took that as a promising sign. If he had been dead for several days, surely someone would have begun to notice by now. Even the smell of baking bread wouldn't hide that odor.

I could hear Archie and the woman still talking inside the flat as I pulled my lockpicking kit from my pocket. Removing my pick, I crouched before the door. There were other pick marks here, I noticed. Someone had been here before me. Someone less skilled than I was. Perhaps the same person or persons who had broken into my hotel room.

I paused for just a moment, wondering if I should wait to let Archie know. What if someone was in the flat even now? But that seemed unlikely. The scratch marks didn't look especially fresh, and, putting my ear against the door, I could hear no sound of movement from inside.

Inserting the pick into the lock, I worked to disengage it. It would not have taken more than a few moments normally, but I thought that whoever had broken in previously had damaged the mechanism a bit with their lack of finesse.

At last, the lock clicked, and, with a glance behind me toward the apartment where Archie and the woman were still engaged in conversation—*"Delicioso!"* Archie said with gusto, more than once—I pushed the door open and stepped inside.

I stood still, listening, for a long moment and took in my surroundings. The door opened into a big room, large and bright, with pale lace curtains over the windows and the sun shining through onto the wooden floors.

It had been ransacked. There were things strewn everywhere. The red fabric of the sofa had been shredded, the stuffing trailing out like spilled intestines. Paintings were askew on the walls, books pulled from the shelves and lying, pages crumpled, on the floor.

I was surprised that the neighbor hadn't heard this happening, but I realized that there wasn't much broken glass. Most of what had been done would not have resulted in loud crashing. The searchers might have been inexpert lockpickers, but they were certainly thorough searchers.

Moving past the living area, I poked my head into the bedroom. It looked much the same. At least, I reflected, as I looked cautiously around, there didn't seem to be any signs of violence. Estrada had apparently left before the searchers had come. Or perhaps he had come home to this mess and realized it would behoove him to take a holiday for a while.

The bathroom had met the same fate, though there was less to look at, I supposed. The cupboard was open, the contents rifled through, and the rug had been pushed aside to be certain that the floor wasn't concealing any sort of hidden compartments. The bathroom would be an odd place for such a thing, I reflected, but I supposed one never knew.

I had just stepped out of the bathroom when the door opened quietly, and Archie stepped inside. He cast his eyes over the room and looked to me with his brows raised.

"Someone's beaten us here," I said.

"I had hoped you hadn't managed all of this in ten minutes."

I laughed. "My searches are much more subtle."

"I have complete faith in your methods, whatever they may be."

"I tip my hat to yours, as well," I said. "You certainly did a wonderful job of distracting the neighbor."

"I know it's usually the job of the beautiful woman to serve as the distraction, but I strive to do my part." He gave me one of the winning smiles that had so charmed Estrada's neighbor. "Find anything?"

"Not yet. But perhaps you'll see something I didn't."

"I doubt it," he said. But he began to move around the room.

I left the sitting room and went into the kitchen, the final place I had yet to search. This room had been gone through, too, items dumped out of boxes and cartons, rice and other grains scattered across the counters and on the floor.

There was, I noticed suddenly, a nearly clear footprint in the flour on the floor. I crouched down to look at it. It was clearly a man's print, a large boot or shoe with something of a crisscross pattern across the sole. It was an unusual print, and I thought it might potentially prove a useful clue.

I had a notebook in my pocket, and I took it out and made

a sketch of the print so I could remember it. Though I doubted I would mistake it if I saw it again.

There was nothing else of interest that I could detect in the kitchen, so I went back out into the sitting room where Archie was still doing a methodical search.

He looked up as I came into the room. "Anything?"

"There's a footprint in the flour on the floor," I said. "Nothing else that I could find."

"Nothing here either," Archie said. "There may be fingerprints, but I assume these people wore gloves."

I nodded. "I would assume so. They knew what they were doing." Except, of course, that footprint. That had been rather careless.

"We might as well go . . ." Archie said, and then his gaze was caught by something on the floor to my left. I turned to see what he was looking at. It was a framed photograph of a woman.

He went to pick it up. "I know this woman."

I looked at it over his shoulder. It was a glamorous photo, a black-haired beauty with an off-the-shoulder gown looking at the camera, dark eyes smoldering. She had the Hollywood glamour of Hedy Lamarr.

"Who is she?"

"She's another player in the intelligence community in this city. She's a . . . Well, she . . . works at a local—and very exclusive—brothel."

"Were she and Estrada . . . involved?" I asked. I looked again at the photo.

For Fernando. All my love, Aline was scrawled in the corner.

"It seems so," Archie said.

"Well, perhaps she knows where Estrada is. Can you get in touch with her?"

"Yes, I think so."

I looked down at the photograph again. "Do you think whoever came here before us would recognize her?"

"Not likely. There's no reason why they should. It's not even clear if she knows anything about Estrada's work, but . . ."

"But she might," I said.

"She might. It would be a bit of a coincidence, otherwise."

Then at least we had garnered two clues from our little escapade into breaking and entering. We had a footprint with a unique appearance, which would likely prove helpful if we ever came upon the prints again. And we had another person who might know where our missing friend was.

"Now we have only to make our escape from this flat without the neighbor noticing," I said. "I should hate for her to ring the police about us, especially after you've just gotten chummy."

"I wouldn't think it possible of my friend Senhora Benedita," he said. "But let's try to get out quietly, nonetheless."

Archie and I made our way out of the building without encountering anyone. He took my arm, and we began to walk away.

"There's a public square not too far from here," he said. "We should be able to find a taxi there."

"I love walking," I said. "I'm always walking in London."

"The terrain here is a bit different," he said as we reached the top of yet another long stone stairway.

"Yes, I've noticed that."

We descended the staircase and walked along in companionable silence for some time, with Archie occasionally pointing out things he thought might be of interest. He was an excellent tour guide.

My mind, however, was still going over what little information we had gleaned from Estrada's flat.

"When are you going to find this Aline?" I asked at last.

"I'll send someone to her place of employment this evening," Archie said. "Someone who will be able to blend in a bit better than you or me."

"I suppose we do stick out a bit," I admitted.

Archie smiled. "This coppery hair of mine is one reason I chose the diplomatic rather than intelligence service."

"Now you find yourself embroiled in both."

"That's one thing about war," he said. "There's never a dull moment."

"No," I agreed, my smile fading ever so slightly. "There certainly isn't."

CHAPTER ELEVEN

Archie dropped me back at the hotel. I suspected I might find the afternoon long, but, when I lay down on the bed to rest for a few moments, I dropped off to sleep, awaking just in time to bathe and dress for dinner.

I had just spritzed on a bit of French perfume Felix had given me when there was a tap at my door. I had been expecting Archie to ring me up from the lobby as he had this morning, so I became instantly wary of someone at my door.

I went to the door, opening it a crack, my foot parallel to the bottom so no one could push their way in. But it was not an intruder. It was Major Ramsey.

"Good evening," he said. "Blandings suggested I escort you downstairs."

"Oh," I said. "Yes. One moment. Just let me get my things."

I left the door ajar, went to collect my handbag, and draped my secondhand fur wrap over one arm. I had decided to forego my coat for the evening, as the fur over my shoulders would keep me warm enough. With one final glance in the mirror, I returned to the door and stepped out to join Ramsey in the hallway.

I saw his eyes sweep over me as I pulled the door closed behind me. I was wearing one of the new evening gowns I had purchased. It was long-sleeved and floor-length in a dark green velvet, and I knew it suited my coloring extremely well and matched the color of my eyes.

He didn't comment on my appearance, of course. Instead, we walked silently down the hall together.

"Did you have a successful day?" Ramsey asked as we entered the lift.

"Not to speak of," I said. "Though Archie thinks we might have a lead. What about you?"

"The same," he replied.

We were spared thinking of something else to say as the lift stopped on the floor below ours and a loud, boisterous group entered. They were talking to one another in excited French and didn't seem to notice when two of them jostled me.

I was pressed into Ramsey's side, his hand moving automatically to my back to steady me. I felt myself stiffen involuntarily, and he removed his hand. Though I tried to shift away from him, there was not much room to do so, and I was uncomfortably aware of his nearness, of the subtle scent of his aftershave, for what seemed like a very long trip down to the ground floor.

Archie met us where we'd sat that morning. He leaned to grind out his cigarette and rose to his feet as we approached.

"Good evening. You're looking lovely, Ellie," he said as he took my wrap from me and settled it over my shoulders.

"Thank you."

"I thought we'd go to one of my favorite night spots. I think you'll both enjoy it."

"I leave myself in your capable hands," I said.

"Just where I like you," Archie said with a wink.

I laughed, though I was a bit surprised at this open flirtation. While our relationship was easy, I had expected him to exhibit a bit more formality in front of Ramsey. Not that it mattered to me.

I glanced at Ramsey, and our eyes caught for just an instant. Then he looked away, his jaw tight.

We took a cab, and, though I'd hoped to contrive to sit at the window, I ended up between the two men. I found myself leaning slightly into Archie to avoid touching Ramsey.

Archie gamely did most of the work of keeping up the conversation during the drive through the vivid city streets. It wasn't that I was trying to make things uncomfortable. It was just that I was so achingly aware of Ramsey that I couldn't seem to muster the nonchalance the situation called for. The major was also less than chatty, though this was not unusual for him.

We got out at the end of a busy street, and I again thought how strange it was for the city to be so bright, like London before the blackouts. Everywhere were streetlights and neon signs and the unshuttered lights of automobiles. The city was almost painfully alive, and I felt a sort of hollowness as I remembered how dark it was at home. I tried to push the feeling aside and do my best to enjoy the evening.

Archie had indeed picked a popular nightspot, for there were people flowing in and out of the building, and we were lucky to have a spot at a small table along one wall, an unused chair from an adjoining table pulled up to make a table for two suitable for three.

The waiter gave us our menus and then disappeared into the haze of conversation and cigarette smoke.

I looked around the crowded room; I could feel it pulsing with energy. Just as I had observed in most other places I'd visited in Lisbon thus far, the restaurant was filled with people from diverse backgrounds. I heard snippets of French, Spanish, and a few other languages in addition to Portuguese.

I also noticed there were several shifty-looking characters, eyes darting watchfully around the room.

"Are there other intelligence operatives here?" I asked in a low voice.

Archie nodded. "There are the usual information scavengers. And then there are the official operatives. Two tables to your left is a PVDE man. The men three tables behind Major Ramsey are Abwehr."

I looked at the men behind the major. They weren't among the people who had drawn my attention. In my head the Germans had taken on the persona of monsters, but these intelligence officers were two perfectly ordinary-looking men. Of course, good spies didn't go about looking sinister. I'd had ample proof of that in my work already.

"Are we safe talking here?" I asked.

"Oh, yes," Archie said. "The music is much too loud for us to be overheard. That's why you see so many different agents meeting in places like this. Busy cafés and restaurants with loud conversation or music are ideal for private conversations."

The waiter returned, and Archie ordered for himself and chose something for me. Major Ramsey, to my surprise, made his own selection in what sounded like very good Portuguese.

"Your Portuguese has improved, Major," Archie said with a smile.

"I've been brushing up on it," Ramsey said. "It's not as good as I'd like, but it's passable."

"Major Ramsey is something of a linguist, Ellie. Did you know?" Archie asked.

"I know he speaks French and German," I said. He had used them both on previous missions.

"He also picked up Arabic in Egypt as though he'd been born to it," Archie said. "His Spanish is excellent, and now it seems it won't be long before he's fluent in Portuguese, too."

"That's impressive," I said. I was sincere, but the words, as they were wont to do when I addressed Ramsey, sounded strained and artificial.

The conversation dropped off then, though at least we all had the pretext of listening to the music to cover the silence.

"Well, Major," Archie said when the waiter had brought our

drinks and left again, "I hope you have had more success today than Ellie and I did. We found Estrada's flat empty, though it was clear we were not the first ones to have been there. It had been quite thoroughly searched."

"Did you find anything?" Ramsey asked with a glance at me.

"There was a footprint in some spilled flour in the kitchen," I said. "I assume it belonged to whoever was there searching before us. Other than that, nothing telling. Except, perhaps—" I looked at Archie, to give him his cue to talk about the photograph of the woman.

"It could be, of course, that he simply enjoys a . . . liaison with her," Archie said when he'd caught Ramsey up to speed. "But you know as well as I do that there are few coincidences in this business."

Ramsey nodded. "It's a lead worth looking into, certainly."

"I made a few contacts when we returned this afternoon," Archie said. "I'm hoping I will hear something else. And what about you, sir? Did you have any luck with Velo?"

"No," Ramsey said. "He wasn't at the café you mentioned. I did speak to a young woman, a waitress there, who told me the best place to find him would likely be the Feira da Ladra tomorrow."

Archie nodded. "It's a flea market with origins in the thirteenth century. Velo is often there. I believe he collects a good deal of information from both the vendors and the customers. It's a good place to pass along information, as it is always incredibly busy and difficult to keep track of anyone for long."

"Then I suppose I may as well try there tomorrow," Ramsey said. "Do you happen to have a photograph of him?"

"No, but Ellie has seen him," Archie replied. "I pointed him out to her when we were at the café to meet Suvari."

Both the gentlemen looked at me.

"Yes, I would recognize him," I said. I had a good eye for faces. It came mostly, I thought, from all the years of thieving, of watching our marks and searching passersby for suspicious glances.

"Then you and Ellie should go to the market," Archie said. "I've got an appointment I'm hoping will lead to more information about Estrada."

"Very well," I said neutrally.

I waited for Ramsey to object, but he said nothing. How could he? He wouldn't recognize Velo without me.

Our dinner came, and, despite how delicious it all was, I found myself able to eat only small amounts of it. I moved the food around on my plate a good deal to try to conceal the fact I wasn't consuming much.

We had finished the meal when Archie excused himself to make a phone call to his office.

I fought down the sense of dismay when he left me alone with Ramsey. I was going to have to grow accustomed to this. We were going to be alone together for a good portion of the day tomorrow, it seemed. I had to learn to get my emotions under control.

I looked up at him and smiled. "The food is very good, isn't it?"

"You haven't eaten much of it."

I was spared having to answer by a burst of applause as a woman stepped into the room. She was wearing a black ruffled dress with a black fringed shawl draped over her shoulders and a red flower in her black hair.

Two men accompanied her to the stage, one of them with a guitar and one of them with an instrument similar to the guitar but of a rounder shape. I felt an excited expectation in the air.

The men sat and began to play, their fingers moving nimbly over the strings in a quick and complex yet mellow melody. Then the woman began to sing, and the gooseflesh rose on my arms at the sound of her voice, at the expressively sorrowful power of it.

She sang, her tone rich with emotion, and the music began to swell through the air, haunting and melancholy. It felt as though the entire audience were frozen in time, under the spell of the singer.

I didn't understand the words, but the song spoke to me all the same. It was entrancing—the resonance of the guitars and the rich, plaintive voice that seemed to dance through and around the instruments' music. The song touched the deepest parts of me, dredging up the emotions I had tried to suppress these past weeks, the feelings of sadness and longing and uncertainty.

I didn't fight the tears that came to my eyes. Indeed, I didn't even notice them until the song was over and I felt the wetness on my face.

As the final notes faded away, I drew in a deep breath as though I had been holding it a long time. I felt suddenly as though the spell had been broken. I blinked. It was then I realized I had been crying.

I wiped at my face, glancing over at Ramsey. "That was beautiful."

His eyes were on mine, his expression unreadable. "Yes."

"What was she singing about?" I asked, my words coming out in a strained whisper.

There was a noticeable hesitation before he said, "Lost love."

I nodded slightly, my gaze sliding away from him and back to the singer, who was still making her bows.

Suddenly, he reached out and wiped away a stray tear from my cheek with his thumb, the barest brush of his fingers sending a little electric pulse through me.

I looked back at him, and something in his expression made me still. Our eyes caught and held for a long moment.

And then Archie was back at the table. "Did you enjoy the fado?"

I looked up at him, my eyelashes still wet with tears. "It was breathtaking."

"Amália Rodrigues is one of the most popular *fadistas* in the city. I'm glad you got to see her perform."

"So am I."

I noticed he had not taken his seat, and his next words told me why. "I'm afraid I've been called away. Will you mind escorting Ellie back to the hotel, Major?"

I felt a little pang of apprehension bordering on panic at the thought of being alone with him after that moment of intimacy, but there was nothing to be done. *Get yourself under control, Ellie McDonnell,* I told myself sternly.

"Of course," Ramsey said.

"Thank you. I've taken care of the bill already. I may be gone most of the day tomorrow, but perhaps we might have dinner together again and you can tell me if you have success finding Velo."

I met Archie's gaze as he prepared to take his leave, and he winked at me. I took it as a gesture of encouragement.

He bid us farewell, and Ramsey turned to me. "Do you want to stay and listen to the music?"

"I'm ready to go back when you are," I said. I was suddenly unutterably weary, and I was not sure I could listen to any more of this heartbreakingly beautiful music without going to pieces.

"All right. Then we'll go back now."

Ramsey politely pulled back my chair as I rose and then reached to settle my fur wrap over my shoulders as Archie had done at the hotel. I picked up my handbag and made my way through the maze of tables, Ramsey close behind me.

The streets were still bright and lively as we exited the restaurant, though it was getting fairly late. We'd had blackouts in London for only a little more than a year, but now it seemed as though it was the only way of life I remembered. There was some part of my brain that kept warning me that bombs might be dropped from the sky at any moment.

He hailed a cab, and we rode back to the hotel with the silence broken only by occasional observations about the city.

We made our way into the hotel amongst other groups coming in and going out, everyone laughing and talking as though they hadn't a care in the world. I knew most of them did have cares; they just hid them better than I seemed capable of at the moment.

"What time would you like to go to the market?" Ramsey asked when we were in the lift.

"Whatever time you think is best. Did the woman you spoke to mention when she thought Velo might be there?"

"No. I had the impression he hung about the market for most of the day."

"We should probably start earlier. It will give us more time to search. Perhaps nine o'clock?" I suggested.

He nodded as the lift doors opened on our floor. "Yes, that sounds good."

"I'll meet you in the lobby, if you are going to breakfast first," I said as we walked toward our rooms. "You needn't come back up for me."

"You don't intend to eat breakfast?"

"I usually have something sent up to my room," I lied.

"You're welcome to join me if you'd like to," he said. "Perhaps at eight?"

"Thank you," I said, noncommittally.

We reached my room, and I put the key into the lock. I was very aware of him standing close rather than moving to his own door.

"Would you let me search it before you go in?" he asked as I prepared to turn the knob.

I looked up at him. It wasn't necessary, but there was no sense in arguing. I turned the knob and pushed the door open, making a gesture for him to go in.

He switched on the light, and I waited in the doorway as he did a quick sweep. He gave me a nod. "All right."

I entered my room, pulling off my fur and tossing it over the chair.

"Thank you," I said.

He moved to the door that led to the hallway, but, his hand on the knob, he paused, then turned back to me.

"Electra."

I looked up at him, caught off guard as I always was by his use of my full given name. No one ever called me Electra but him, and before things had grown romantic between us, he had preferred "Miss McDonnell."

Now I supposed he was caught between the two: we were well past the point of formality, but calling me by my given name felt dangerously personal. I had noticed he hadn't directly addressed me by name since he'd arrived.

"Blandings thinks my being here for this mission is important," he said. "But it is, no doubt, uncomfortable for you. Are you willing to work with me?"

I met his gaze coolly. "I'll do whatever I need to do to find Toby."

He nodded. The silence stretched out.

When he spoke again, his tone had softened ever so slightly. "I know that what happened in London—your dismissal—was not an easy thing—"

"We needn't rehash it," I said, rudely cutting him off. And then, feeling a bit remorseful at the rashness of my reply, I said in a perfectly neutral tone, "There were reasons for what I did, but I understand you had reasons of your own for your decision. So I suppose we must leave it at that."

It was as far as I could go toward an apology. I was sorry I had let him down by keeping secrets from him, but my motivations had been pure, and I had done what I felt was necessary. Given the option, I would make the same choice again.

He looked at me for a long moment. Perhaps it was just wishful thinking, but I thought he might say something else, something about the personal relationship we had lost.

But he only gave a short nod and pulled open the door. "I'll see you in the morning, then."

"Yes."

He left, closing the door behind him.

I went to lock it. Closing my eyes, I leaned my head against the cool wood and prayed we would find Toby quickly so this mission could be over.

CHAPTER TWELVE

After the challenge of sorts that Ramsey had issued, I could not very well refuse to meet him for breakfast.

So I dressed in a white blouse, a pale blue wool skirt, a handbag with a long strap I could wear over my shoulder, and shoes that would be comfortable for walking, put my navy jacket over my arm, and was downstairs by eight o'clock.

The conversation at the breakfast table was a bit stilted, but, in a way, it was easier now that he had addressed the strain that existed between us. It was out in the open; we had only to work around it.

My appetite was no better this morning, but I ate a piece of toast with some jam and drank two cups of tea.

Then the major helped me into my jacket, and we were on our way.

Archie had given us directions to the Feira da Ladra. We took a cab to São Vicente and then walked. We passed an enormous white, red-roofed building, and I looked up at the towering walls.

"The Monastery of São Vicente de Fora," Ramsey said.

"It's beautiful." It was all beautiful. I loved this city, even having been here only a few days.

The sun was bright and warm, and I couldn't resist turning my face up to it for a moment as we walked down a cobbled side street. There was the faintest floral scent in the air that mingled with the saltiness of the sea, and I could hear the cry of gulls as a backdrop to the city noises. There was something comforting about it all, about feeling the world rush on around me.

I think most people instinctively dislike feeling small, but sometimes it is immeasurably soothing to feel that there are so many bigger things than one's problems.

I opened my eyes and saw that Ramsey was looking down at me. I had the impression I'd missed something he said.

"I'm sorry," I said, refusing to be embarrassed that he'd caught me daydreaming. "I was just enjoying the sun. It's felt so far away in England these past few months."

"Yes," he said, his eyes still on my face.

I pushed a curl the breeze had dislodged behind my ear. "Did you say something?"

"The market should be a few blocks ahead," he said. "I thought we should perhaps discuss strategy."

"Of course," I said. "What do you have in mind?"

"I think it would be better if we separate. I will follow you un- obtrusively, and, if you see our quarry, you can give me the signal."

"And what is this clandestine signal?" I asked, feeling amuse- ment pulling at the corners of my mouth. When he spoke like this, I felt very much as though I'd slipped into the pages of a spy novel.

His eyes swept over me. "Perhaps you can take your jacket off and drape it over one arm, as though you've grown warm."

I nodded. "And then what?" I was determined to follow his instructions, determined not to act recklessly. He would have no cause to admonish me for deviating from the plan. I would follow orders without question and do only what was asked of me. I would not give any further cause for complaint.

"I think you should approach him first," Ramsey said, surprising me. Usually, he always wanted to charge into danger first, leaving me behind.

"Why?" I asked, before I could think better of it.

"For one thing, you're more likely to get close to him without drawing notice." That was a fair point. I was of average appearance and dark-haired. Ramsey was a head taller than most people and fair-haired to boot.

"Yes, that makes sense."

"Once you approach him, engage him in conversation, try not to let him get away. Stick with him if you can, and I'll make my way to you."

I nodded. It was a sound plan.

Ramsey and I walked to the outskirts of the market together. I wouldn't say that things had become easy between us, but at least I no longer felt as though I were suffocating when I was with him. We had a mutual objective, and that was the main thing. We could focus on our mission without awkwardness.

"If we don't see him within, say, two hours, let's make our way back here and discuss next moves."

"All right. Synchronize our watches," I said, looking down at my wrist.

Ramsey did not play along but moved off, leaving me alone to start making my way through the stalls.

I moved along through the market, and, despite our objective, I found myself enjoying browsing the wares and discovering what various stalls had to offer. There was so much to see, so many sights and sounds and smells to take in.

I saw fresh produce, homemade sweets, handmade furniture, jewelry, flowers, dishware, clothes, and antiques. One vendor sold some sort of tantalizing sugary pastries.

The more I saw, the more I was tempted to buy souvenirs. I refrained, however, because I had only a small handbag and thought it was probably better if my movements were unobstructed. Maybe

Archie would bring me back here one day so I could buy a few things for Uncle Mick and Nacy.

I had been browsing for perhaps an hour, keeping a close eye out for Velo, when I stopped short before a stall. The tables were covered with old locks and keys, and I felt my throat constrict with longing for my family.

I'd been gone less than a week, but it suddenly felt much longer. As much as I had been enjoying Lisbon, I was homesick for Uncle Mick's sage advice and Nacy's warm meals and warmer embraces.

Moving toward the stall, I looked down at the paraphernalia of the trade, running my fingers over a few of the ancient skeleton keys.

The man came over and said something to me in Portuguese.

"I'm so sorry," I said. "I only speak English."

He nodded. "See something you like?"

"My uncle is a locksmith," I said. "Your stall reminds me of him."

He smiled. I thought his English was probably limited, but I felt the shared sense of camaraderie.

"He would like this," he said, turning to another table and picking up an object. He came back to me and opened his hand. In it was what looked to be an ancient silver key. Instead of a bow to turn it with, there was the carved image of some sort of bird. A hawk, perhaps.

"Roman," he said. "I found at the seashore."

I took the key from him, looking at the delicate engraving that someone had done thousands of years before. It was worn from the water and the passage of time, but it had endured. Something about it, about holding this piece of history in my hands, spoke to me.

"How much?" I asked.

He gave me the price, and, as it was within the range of what I could pay, I purchased it for Uncle Mick. There were few things he would like more than to add this key to his collection.

"Thank you," I said, slipping it into my handbag.

Though I made my way past several more stalls, I didn't make any additional purchases. This market was fantastic, and at any other time I would have greatly enjoyed myself, perusing the stalls, examining the wares in great detail, and losing track of time. But now it was time to focus, I reminded myself. I hoped I hadn't missed Velo while I had been shopping, though I knew that I had been attuned to searching for him even as I browsed.

I glanced casually around again as I had been doing every few minutes. Still no sign of him, nor did I see Ramsey. I was confident that he was somewhere nearby; he wouldn't have let me out of his sight. Despite this, I hadn't caught more than a glimpse or two of him in the past hour.

The market had become busier as the day went on, and I had not quite anticipated how crowded it would be. I hoped that I could find Velo in the throng.

I noticed that, in addition to the stalls and tables and blankets displaying wares, there were also several individuals moving about, showing objects to shoppers in an apparent attempt to get them to purchase whatever it was.

I passed one, and I realized they were selling jewelry. Good stuff, by the look of it. Refugees, I realized. They had escaped from their home countries with few possessions and were now trying to sell them so they could afford to live or to get someplace safer for themselves and their families. I felt a pang of sadness and reminded myself to count my own blessings.

Suddenly, I caught sight of a familiar-looking face talking to one of the refugees who was selling jewelry. I saw them conferring in low tones, and then Velo handed the man what looked to be money. Rather than jewelry, however, the refugee took a piece of paper from his pocket and handed it to Velo. They had been exchanging information, then.

I looked around for Ramsey, but, once again, there was no sign of him. Nonchalantly, I took off my jacket and draped it over one arm to give Ramsey the signal. I had to believe he was watching from close enough to see it.

Then I moved toward Velo.

The refugee had moved off, and Velo had just purchased a bottle of beer and was taking a long drink from it. Excellent. His guard was down.

I knew better than to move too quickly or draw attention to myself. So I stopped at a few of the tables along the way to examine the wares. I kept a watch on Velo out of the corner of my eye as he moved, also unhurriedly, through the stalls.

I had the impression that he was also looking for someone, though I wouldn't have picked him out as suspicious if I hadn't been watching him. It seemed he, too, must be well-versed in the art of keeping a low profile.

He stopped to converse with a second wanderer, and I watched again the careful exchange of money and some sort of paper.

The closer we got to midday, the busier the market seemed, and I nearly lost Velo once or twice amidst the growing crowds. I still hadn't caught sight of Ramsey, but I decided it was better that I approach the man before I lost him.

I saw him stop beside a stall of handmade jewelry and made my way over to stand beside him.

"Beautiful, aren't they?" I said.

The man turned. He took me in with a quick glance, and I saw the wariness cross his features at my use of English. I would need to tread carefully.

"Yes."

I didn't glance around me, but I knew Ramsey was likely not far off. He would reach my side quickly if the man looked as though he was going to flee.

Velo didn't seem to be inclined to small talk, so perhaps I would need to be direct.

"I don't mean to bother you," I said in my friendliest tone. "But I was hoping I might speak to you for a moment. I believe you were at the café when . . ."

I didn't have time to finish the words before he shoved me. Hard. I had good balance, but I hadn't been expecting this, and I stumbled backward, landing hard against the table with the jewelry displayed on it. I caught myself before I fell to the ground, but pieces of jewelry scattered everywhere, several bracelets and rings falling to the ground and rolling.

The woman whose jewelry I had just scattered cried out, but it was at the retreating man she directed her invectives.

"I'm so sorry," I told her. It was against all of Nacy's training that I left her to clean up the mess and ran after Velo in hot pursuit.

He had taken off at a sprint, and, given the time it had taken me to regain my balance, I was a good way behind him. The only thing working in my favor was that, given the crowded nature of the street, he wasn't able to get up to full speed. Then again, there was also the danger I might lose him in the crowds. I had to weave through the shoppers, trying to keep up with him and keep my eyes on him.

Velo was faster than me, but he seemed to be less agile, because he kept knocking into people, which slowed him down. Meanwhile, I was able to zip around the bystanders, thanks in large part to my days of playing rugby with Colm, Toby, and the neighborhood boys. It had taught me I needed to move fast if I didn't want to be flattened.

I saw him look over his shoulder more than once. He knew I was still on him.

I couldn't lose him, not if I could help it.

It was then I caught sight of Ramsey, the flash of blond hair gleaming in the sun. He was moving parallel to me, along the next row of vendors. We were reaching the end of the market, and there was a building coming up, the road splitting on either side of it. He signaled that he would go behind while I continued in front.

Ramsey was tall and fast. If we were lucky, he would be able to cut off the man and I wouldn't have to tackle him myself. Then again, I wouldn't mind being the one to stop him after the way he'd shoved me.

And, in all honesty, I rather suspected Velo would prefer me to get to him before Ramsey did. Ramsey kept his temper on a tight lead, but there were times when it escaped, and, however Ramsey felt about me, he didn't hold with the rough treatment of women.

I gave an extra burst of speed and found myself gaining on him. Velo glanced over his shoulder then, and our eyes met. He saw I was close.

We reached the building and, as we were now outside of the market, there was more space to move. He took off at a full run, and I was forced to put on more speed. My shoes were terrible for running, and I took a few seconds to pull them off so I could pursue the man in my stocking feet, shoes in hand. I was going to ruin these stockings on the rough cobbles, but that was the price that must be paid.

People were looking at me as I chased after Velo, but there wasn't much comment made. I was sure the people of Lisbon had seen stranger things than this throughout the course of the war.

We reached the end of the block, and I saw Velo dart around a corner into the alleyway between two buildings. I knew that chasing a man into a deserted alleyway wasn't ideal, so I hoped that Ramsey was somewhere on the other side and would catch him if I didn't.

I turned the corner at full speed. I barely had time to register the dark shape there and the flash of movement that I raised my arm to deflect before I felt a tremendous pain in my forehead accompanied by a bright burst of light, and then everything went black.

CHAPTER THIRTEEN

I woke up on the ground a few seconds later, my head pounding, as a small crowd began to gather around me, talking excitedly. For a split second, I was worried because I couldn't understand what they were saying, and then I remembered I was in Portugal.

I sat up automatically, and my vision swam as I felt the warm flow of blood down the side of my face.

Bracing myself against the ground with one hand, I lifted the other to my forehead. It came away slick with blood. I swore beneath my breath.

The boys and I had taken enough tumbles over the years that I wasn't exactly alarmed by the amount of blood flowing from my head; I knew head wounds tended to bleed profusely. All the same, it was a nuisance. And, worse than that, I'd lost our quarry.

A gentleman knelt at my side, said something in Portuguese, and then offered me a clean white handkerchief from his breast pocket. I took it with thanks and an apologetic expression and pressed it to my forehead. The source of the pain—and the blood—was clearly high on my head, near the hairline.

I winced at the sting of the cut as I pressed the handkerchief to it. Behind that sharp pain was a throbbing ache in my head. Whatever

I'd been walloped with had packed a punch. My ears were still ringing from the blow.

There was a murmur around me as people looked down at me, and I debated getting onto my feet, but my head was still swimming a bit, and I was sure I looked a sight with my blood-smeared face and hand. I could feel it on my neck where it had run down in rivulets, and my white blouse was dotted with it.

The jacket I'd had draped over my arm and the shoes I'd taken off were both lying a short distance from me, where I'd no doubt flung them as I fell. My handbag was still strung across my body.

I pulled the handkerchief away from my head to survey the damage and wasn't best pleased to see a large area of the fabric was soggy with blood. It had seeped through the handkerchief and between my fingers. What a mess.

"Electra."

I looked up at the sound of my name to see the crowd parting for Ramsey as if he were a veritable Moses. His face was a mask of cold fury, though his eyes on me held a different, gentler emotion I couldn't quite interpret.

"I'm all right," I said. I made a move to start to rise, but his curt command stopped me.

"Don't get up."

A moment later, he was crouched at my side. He said something to the crowd, and they began to disperse as he leaned over me, his hands on my head as he surveyed the damage. I winced as his fingers pressed the area near the wound, no doubt trying to gauge how deep it was.

"Did you catch him?" I demanded.

"No," he said. "What did he hit you with?"

"I assume it was that," I said, pointing to a broken glass bottle I had just noticed on the ground not too far away. I remembered that Velo had been drinking a beer before I'd approached him. Apparently, he'd held on to it. It had indeed been a hard blow, for the bottle had cracked.

"Nacy always said I have a hard head," I said. "Turns out, that's a lucky thing."

"This cut is going to need stitching," Ramsey said. I wasn't surprised. The warm trickle of blood continued down the side of my face as he examined the wound. A bit of it rolled over my eyebrow and threatened to get in my eyes before I swiped it away. It was a good thing I wasn't squeamish.

"Hold this tight," Ramsey said, lifting my hand with the handkerchief to press it back against the wound.

I ground my teeth against the pain of it. What a bother this was going to be.

"Did you lose consciousness?" Ramsey asked. His hand had dropped to my shoulder, supporting me as though he suspected I might faint again at any moment.

"For a few seconds, I think. Basically, just on my way to the ground." My right hip and shoulder throbbed, so I assumed I'd hit on that side first.

"Did you hurt anything when you fell?" he asked, looking me over as though he could x-ray through my clothing. An alarming thought.

"I don't think so." I, too, looked down at myself and then said ruefully, "Just my stockings." There were long ladders in both of them.

Ramsey seemed to think this was of no concern, for he ignored it.

"Look at me," he said, tilting my chin up with his hand.

His eyes met mine, checking the reaction of my pupils to light, I assumed. It occurred to me that this was the closest we had been since he'd arrived in Lisbon, but I was feeling too sick at the moment to be affected by his nearness. I was dizzy enough as it was.

"Follow my finger with your eyes."

I did so.

"Are you seeing double?"

"No."

"Do you feel as though you're going to vomit?"

"No."

I answered his tedious questions until it seemed he was satisfied that I was not in imminent danger of dropping dead.

"Stay here," he said, rising and moving out of the alley and back toward the street.

I considered trying to tidy myself up but decided it was a lost cause. Instead, I continued to sit on the ground in my stockinged feet, covered in blood, until Ramsey returned.

He reached down and slid his arm around my waist and pulled me up. "I'm going to carry you to the taxi."

"Don't you dare."

"Electra—"

"I don't want to be carried," I said firmly. "I'm perfectly capable of walking." To prove it, I began moving out of the alley on my own two feet. The last thing I wanted was to be swept up like a helpless damsel. It was just a little cut, not worth a lot of fuss.

He relented, but his arm remained around my waist, shepherding me toward the waiting taxi.

"I'm going to get blood on your clothes," I protested. He ignored me.

We reached the taxi, and he opened the door, easing me into the backseat. He was about to close the door when something else occurred to me.

"Will you get my jacket and shoes?" I asked. "They were lying near where I was sitting."

He glanced down at my stockinged feet and then, without comment, returned to the alley. He came back with my discarded items and then went around to get in the car.

He set the shoes on the floor before me, and I slipped my feet into them. I was glad he didn't try to assist.

I leaned my head back against the seat and closed my eyes, fighting off another wave of dizziness.

"Don't go to sleep," Ramsey said. "You need to stay conscious for a while to make sure there isn't any lasting damage."

"I've been knocked in the head before this," I said, though I opened my eyes. "I'll survive."

He didn't reply. I couldn't quite get a gauge on his mood, for, though his tone was calm and even, his posture was stiff. I had to imagine he was processing what our next move would be, now that we had lost Velo.

At the moment, I didn't feel much inclined to think about it. My head was beginning to throb in earnest, from both the cut and the blow I'd sustained. I kept my eyes open to appease Ramsey, but I squinted against the brightness of the day as a thunderstorm went on inside my skull.

We reached the hotel, and, Ramsey, despite my protests that I could manage on my own, helped me from the car.

There were several curious glances at us as he led me through the lobby. Though I was steady enough on my feet, he insisted on keeping his arm around me. He didn't even break stride as he told the man at the front desk something in brusque Portuguese. I assumed he told him to ring for a doctor.

We took the lift, and, when we arrived at my room, he reached for my handbag. "May I?"

I acceded gladly, for I was still holding the handkerchief to my brow, and bending my head to look for the key in the bag made it pound. I hadn't taken into account the fact that the strap was still across my body, and, as he lifted the handbag, it tugged me closer to his side.

He quickly located the key amidst the loose coins, lipstick, mirror, cigarettes, and other detritus that gathers in handbags and opened the door.

"Sit down," he said when we were inside.

"I want to see how bad it is," I said, moving toward the standing mirror near the armoire.

The initial glance I got of myself was not encouraging. As I'd assumed, I looked an absolute fright. My clothes were mussed and splattered with blood, my hair was a mass of unruly curls, and the left side of my face was covered in blood. Beneath the carnage, my face was pale as linen.

I removed the blood-soaked handkerchief and surveyed the actual damage. There was an ugly gash, a little more than an inch across, just at the hairline on the left side of my head. It had stopped bleeding, thankfully, but it still looked ghastly.

"I'm going to have a scar," I said. I wasn't thrilled about it, but there wasn't much I could do and there was no use crying over it. At least it wasn't my face. My hair would cover it easily enough.

"Come sit down," Ramsey said, coming up behind me, his hand closing around my arm as his eyes met mine in the mirror. There was a gentle support in it, but also a command. He wasn't going to leave me alone until he had thoroughly assessed the situation.

"I'm all right," I said for perhaps the dozenth time, though I allowed him to guide me to a chair. The sight of blood had never bothered me, but after Ramsey's brush with death in Sunderland, seeing so much of it on myself in the mirror had left me feeling just the teeniest bit woozy.

"We'll let the doctor decide that," he said.

Once I was seated, he went to the bathroom. I heard the sink, and a moment later he came back with a wet cloth.

Taking my chin in his hand, he began gently wiping the blood from my face.

My head, though still pounding with pain, had cleared a bit, enough for me to be discomfited by his continued nearness. His eyes, in the bright light shining through the window, looked that vivid periwinkle color that had caught me off guard when I'd first noticed it.

He was leaning close as he wiped my face, and I could smell

his shaving soap and the warm, sunshiny scent of someone who'd been outdoors for hours.

I shifted slightly. "I can go to the bathroom and do this."

"You need to be still," he said. It was more of an order than a suggestion, and my mouth tensed as it usually did at being bossed. The movement pulled at my gash, and I winced.

"You'll have to stop frowning at me for the foreseeable future," he said. His tone was flat, but he was teasing me, so I took that as a good sign. I knew he was likely irritated that we had failed to catch our quarry.

"I was so close to catching him," I said.

"We'll catch him. It's only a matter of time." He spoke calmly, but I knew him well enough now to catch the undertone of steel in the words.

He moved the rag down to my jawline and then my neck, scrubbing off the blood that had begun to dry on my skin. He was working quickly and professionally, so I couldn't tell what he was thinking. His hands, as always, were perfectly steady, his fingers warm and gentle as they turned my head to better reach the creases in my neck.

"What are we going to do now?" I asked, because I was becoming too aware of the intimacy of the moment.

"I'm going to confer with Blandings about how we should proceed."

Normally, I would have argued with him about being excluded, but I didn't feel much up to arguing at the moment. Perhaps the blow to the head had affected me more than I thought.

There was a rap on the door.

Ramsey went to open it, and he admitted the doctor.

Doutor Ferreiro, as he introduced himself to Ramsey, was a tall, distinguished-looking man with a gray mustache and sharp brown eyes. His English was only lightly accented, and I surmised the desk clerk had summoned the doctor who usually tended to English-speaking guests.

"What have we here?" he asked, moving into the room. "Taken a nasty fall, have you?"

I didn't reply, and he didn't seem to expect one. He examined the wound and then announced, as Ramsey had, that I was going to need stitching.

"Get me a hairpin from that table near the bed, will you?" I asked Ramsey. A lock of my hair, matted with blood, kept falling into my face, and I wanted it out of the way. I'd neglected my unruly hair since the start of the war, and it had grown unfashionably long—well past my shoulders now. There was always a pile of hairpins on my bedside table at home; it was no different here in Lisbon.

Ramsey did as I asked, and I twisted the tangled curl back from my face and pinned it into place, glad the wound had not been a little higher where the doctor might have recommended shaving the hair away so he could stitch the scalp.

Doutor Ferreiro had turned to rummage in his black bag. "I'll give you a shot in the area to numb the pain before I do the stitching."

"All right." I looked up at Ramsey. His eyes were on my face. I gave him a faint smile. Of reassurance, I realized. I was letting him know that I was all right—because he was concerned.

He hadn't said as much, of course, but his behavior had been kind and caring, and there was still a certain set to his jaw that let me know he was not quite as relaxed as he appeared.

These thoughts were driven quite forcibly from my mind as the doctor inserted the needle into the wound.

It hurt like the devil. I clenched my teeth against the pain, my eyes watering, my hands holding the arms of the chair in a death grip. The injection took only a moment, and soon the numbing agent took effect. I let out a relieved breath that the worst of it was over.

It was not over.

The injection had dulled the pain, but it had not numbed the area entirely, and I could feel the thorough cleaning the doctor gave the wound, followed by each stitch. He worked slowly and steadily, and I focused on thinking about what we would do next, now that we knew Velo was clearly a person of interest. Innocent people did not flee or bash their pursuers over the head with glass bottles.

I wished I could have caught him, or at least that Ramsey had. It would have made being injured much more palatable had it happened in a successful pursuit.

"There," the doctor said after what seemed like ages, stepping back slightly to review his handiwork. "Keep it clean and don't pull the stitches, and it should heal nicely."

"Thank you."

The wound tended to, the doctor gave me a brief examination much as Ramsey had and seemed to come to the conclusion that there was no lasting damage. My faculties were still in order. He gave me some tablets to help with the pain and recommended that I get some rest.

At last, he took his leave, and the major and I were alone together again.

"You needn't have stayed," I said as Ramsey closed the door behind the doctor. "I thank you for all your help, but I hate that I took up so much of your time."

"Nonsense," he said. "I needed to make sure you were all right."

"I told you I have a hard head," I said. I smiled, but I could feel it was a wan one. My head was pounding furiously now, to say nothing of the sharper pain of my forehead where the doctor had stitched me up. The numbing agent was beginning to wear off.

Ramsey went to the little carafe of water on the table and poured a glass. He brought it to me. "You had better take the tablets."

"Thank you." Unlike Ramsey when he had been suffering from his bullet wounds, I did not take convincing to medicate myself. I took the tablets gladly. The pain was enough to make my eyes water, and I didn't want Ramsey to think I was crying over a minor injury.

"He did a good job," Ramsey said, looking down at the stitches. "It should heal nicely. I doubt the scar will be very noticeable at all."

I shrugged. "It doesn't really matter. My hair is usually curling about my face anyway."

"Yes." His eyes came to mine and held for just a moment. And then he stepped back. "You were a very brave patient. I've seen soldiers make more fuss about stitching."

I smiled, both absurdly pleased at the compliment and fairly certain he was humoring me. "It wasn't my first set of stitches," I said. The boys and I had played rough as children, and I had the scars to show for it.

"You're certain you don't feel sick or disoriented?"

I was about to shake my head but caught myself in time. "No. Aside from a screaming headache, I'm fine."

"All right. Then I'll leave you to get some rest. You've only to tap on my door if you need anything."

"Thank you," I said. I was itching, quite literally, to be out of my bloody clothes.

I looked up at him and saw his eyes were on my face again. "I'm sorry you got hurt today. That was my fault."

I stared at him, surprised. "It wasn't your fault."

"It was," he said. "I told you to approach him first and not to let him get away from you."

"I would have chased him anyway," I said. "You know that."

"All the same, I feel responsible . . ."

I had yet to see Ramsey contrite, and I wasn't certain how to react to this new emotion from him. "I've had worse than this from a day climbing trees with Colm and Toby," I said. "You needn't fret."

He looked as if he wanted to say something else, but he gave only a brief nod instead. "I'll come back to check on you in a few hours."

"All right. Thank you."

He left through the adjoining door to his room, and I let out a breath. I went into the bathroom and once again surveyed the damage. As Ramsey had said, the stitches were tight and neat. At least the black thread would blend with my hair.

I stripped off the bloody blouse, stained skirt, and ruined hose and left them in a pile on the bathroom floor. I knew Nacy would recommend treating the stains as soon as possible, but I supposed even she would forgive my negligence in this instance.

I considered a bath, but I didn't feel up to it. Instead, I washed the places the major had missed, namely the skin of my chest and my shoulder where blood had seeped through my blouse and the clump of hair where blood had matted. I would have to wash my hair thoroughly, but not now.

My brassiere was stained, too, and I added it to the pile. Then I went and crawled into the cool sheets of my bed wearing only my knickers.

The pain tablets had begun to take effect by then, and I sank into a welcomed hazy slumber.

CHAPTER FOURTEEN

It was dark in my room when I woke up. There had been a noise. Was it footsteps, or had that been a dream?

I sat up in bed and then had to orient myself as the blood pulsed in noisy waves through my head. Remembering I wore only my drawers, I mentally chided myself for not putting on some clothes before I'd fallen asleep and pulled the blankets up to my chest. I waited, listening, my heart and my head both hammering away.

Suddenly, the light switched on, and I saw Ramsey standing beside my bed.

I stifled a gasp at this sudden appearance and blinked up at him, the light sending a searing pain through my head and splotches across my vision, even as I pulled the covers up higher on my chest.

"What the blazes are you doing?" I demanded.

"I wanted to be certain you were all right. You didn't answer my knock."

"I didn't hear it," I said irritably. "I was asleep until I heard you creeping about."

We looked at each other. He was, it seemed to me, making a concerted effort not to look at the bare skin of my shoulders above the sheet. As he was standing beside the bed, he probably had a good side view of my back, as well.

"Well, I'm sorry to have disturbed you," he said. "I'm going to order some dinner sent up for you. Is there anything else you need?"

"I don't think so." Suddenly I remembered that we had an appointment this evening. "What time is it? We're supposed to have dinner with Archie . . ."

"I've been in contact with Blandings. I've told him you won't be able to see him tonight."

I felt both relief that I wouldn't have to get up and leave the room and a bit of irritation that he had peremptorily canceled my plans. Ramsey was not in charge of this operation or of my activities. I was not, however, up to an argument just now.

"You'll let me know what he says when you see him?" I asked.

He frowned. "I'm not going to see him either. I'm going to stay here with you while you eat and then remain next door. Head injuries are not to be toyed with."

"I'm fine," I said. "I feel much better after getting a bit of sleep."

Truth to tell, my head still ached, my body was sore from falling, I was groggy from the pain tablets, and my mouth felt as dry as the desert. The last time I'd felt this wretched was when I'd had a bout of influenza.

As if reading my mind, Ramsey moved to pour me a glass of water from the carafe. It was empty, and so he went to the bathroom to refill it. With a pang of embarrassment, I remembered the pile of discarded clothes on the floor.

He came back with the water and handed it to me.

"Thank you."

I took several grateful drinks of it before giving the glass back to him so he could set it on the table.

"Your shoulder is bruised," he said, though he was still avoiding looking at it.

"I landed hard," I said. "It's nothing."

"You ought to have told the doctor you'd been injured in the fall."

I sighed. "I appreciate your concern, Major. Really, I do. But I don't need to be wrapped in cotton wool because of a little bump to the head and a few bruises."

"That 'bump to the head' might have killed you, Electra," Ramsey said. "That man might have killed you. If he'd had a gun . . ."

I was surprised that there was still a note of disquiet in his voice. I wondered if this afternoon he had remembered too well how it felt to be covered in blood.

"'Ifs are the stuff of dreams and nightmares, but life is made when we're awake,' Uncle Mick always says," I told him.

His eyes met mine. "All the same, it was a bad business. You were bleeding more than you realized, I think."

"No real harm done," I said. It felt a bit silly to be having this argument with the blankets pulled up to my collarbone as he stood beside my bed.

"Nevertheless, I'll keep you company during your dinner," he said. "I want to make sure you eat something."

He was coddling me, but I found that some part of me appreciated it. Nacy had always done the same thing when I'd been injured, clucking worriedly over me and bullying me into staying hydrated and nourished.

Ramsey was not exactly Nacy, of course, and that fact was brought back to me by the remembrance of my close-to-nude state.

"Do you . . . suppose I might get dressed first?" I asked, one brow arching slightly and sending a pang to the area beneath my stitches.

His eyes did flicker to my shoulders then, and I knew it must be perfectly obvious that I was not wearing much of anything beneath the blankets.

There was an awkward pause as his eyes came back up to mine. And then he gave a brief nod.

"Certainly," he said, his tone neutral. "I beg your pardon. I'll come back in half an hour, shall I?"

"That will be fine," I said, with great dignity.

He left again, closing the adjoining door behind him, and I threw back the covers and rose slowly from the bed. My head had cleared a bit, and the ache seemed more localized to the spot where my skin had been stitched.

I went to the wardrobe and pulled out a comfortable black dress over which I pulled a red jumper. I found my slippers under the edge of the bed and slipped them on.

It was a rather informal ensemble, but all things considered, it was a good deal more formal than what he'd just seen me in.

There was a knock at the door perhaps twenty minutes later. Expecting the dinner Ramsey had ordered, I went and opened it. I was surprised to see Archie standing there, a bright bouquet of flowers in his hand.

"Hello," he said, his eyes moving over my face and quickly landing on the stitches on my forehead. "Major Ramsey told me you were hurt. I've come to check on you."

"Thank you," I said, taking the flowers from his outstretched hand. "They're beautiful. I'm feeling much better this evening, but Ramsey has insisted I stay in tonight. Dinner's being brought up. He'll be back soon to discuss the case. Would you like to join us?"

Aside from the fact that we were to have met with Archie this evening anyway, I thought it would make things easier if he were a buffer between Ramsey and me. A third person would help to ease the awkwardness.

"You're certain you're up to it?" he asked.

"Yes, I'm sure." I stepped back, pulling the door open, and he entered.

"I'm glad it wasn't worse, but I'm sorry it happened all the same. Does it hurt very dreadfully?"

"Not really. It pays to be hardheaded," I said lightly. The empty vase I'd prepared to bash Ramsey over the head with did nicely for the flowers.

I was still arranging them when there was another knock at the door. "I'll get it," Archie said.

He moved to open the door, and a moment later a waiter was entering with the cart, on which rested an assortment of dinnerware, a dish covered with a serviette, a silver covered tureen, two small silver pots, and two cups with saucers.

Just after the waiter left, Ramsey tapped on the adjoining door.

"Come in," I called from my seat on the sofa, still looking down at the abundance of food on the cart in front of me.

Ramsey opened the door. It seemed to me that he paused ever so slightly upon seeing Archie seated comfortably in one of the armchairs.

"You're just in time," I said. "Dinner has just arrived."

"I only ordered for you," Ramsey said.

"There's coffee here," I said, pointing to a silver pot beside the teapot. Ramsey knew better than to order coffee for me.

"I believe that's hot chocolate. I thought you might enjoy something sweet after your dinner."

I had a sweet tooth, and the major always remembered it. He really was coddling me after my injury.

"That was thoughtful. Thank you."

"I've already eaten," Archie said. "You needn't worry about me."

Ramsey came and, as Archie had the chair, sat beside me on the sofa.

"I'm going to feel rather a glutton eating all this while you two just sit here," I said.

"Nonsense," Archie said.

"I'm really not very hungry," I protested.

"You should eat, all the same," Ramsey said. "You've barely eaten anything today."

I felt a tinge of annoyance, but I knew he was right. I'd had toast for breakfast and then slept the afternoon away after a rather strenuous run. I needed to eat to keep up my strength.

I took the lid off of the silver tureen and the most delicious scent rose with steam from the dish. My stomach rumbled to life at the smell of it.

"What kind of soup is this?" I asked.

"Caldo verde," Ramsey said.

"It's a traditional Portuguese soup," Archie offered. "A sort of cabbage and potato soup, with sausage."

"It smells wonderful." Despite the audience, I couldn't resist picking up the spoon and taking a taste of the soup. It was just as delicious as it smelled, warm, soothing, and rich. The green of the cabbage—different from English cabbage, I thought—paired wonderfully with the potato and the smoky, slightly spicy sausage. I would have to see if I could get a recipe to bring back to Nacy.

I lifted the serviette and saw there was a basket of bread beneath it. I took a piece of the dark, rustic bread on the tray and was delighted with the flavor of it. Ramsey had certainly chosen the perfect meal. It was comforting and, though native to the area, familiar in the sense that Nacy often made soup with fresh bread for dinner.

The appetite that had been elusive, at best, for weeks made an appearance for this simple and delicious fare. The men made polite small talk for a few minutes while I ate, but I felt Ramsey's eyes on me frequently as he made sure I wasn't shamming at taking nourishment.

At last, Archie shifted the topic to the events of the day.

"It isn't likely we'll be able to get hold of Velo now that he knows we're onto him," Archie said. "If I had to guess, I'd say he's in Spain by now."

I gave him a rueful look across the table. "I was so close to catching him."

"Too close," Archie said with a smile. "We'll have to try another tack."

"Why do you think he was so desperate to get away?" I asked.

"I didn't get a chance to say much before he ran. There must be some reason he was so . . . skittish."

"Yes," Archie said slowly. Something in the way he said it made me wary.

I looked over at Ramsey. He was watching Archie, too.

"I'm beginning to think it might have been Velo who broke into your room."

"But how?" I asked. "He didn't follow us back here. We were so careful."

"That's just it," Archie said. "Velo knows me. He has worked with me before. He knows that we have rooms reserved here. It's entirely possible he came here directly without needing to follow us."

"You think he saw Suvari pass me that note and knew to come back to the hotel and look for it."

"It seems the likeliest scenario."

"But I'm fairly certain he was no longer at the café when I left. Do you think he killed Suvari?"

Archie shook his head. "I don't think so. Despite the violence he so regrettably showed toward you today, he isn't the sort of man I'd thought a murderer."

"No," I agreed. "He might have done more harm than he did to me."

"He might have done a good deal less," Ramsey said tersely.

"We won't find him now, in any event," Archie said. "Something had him spooked enough to do what he did today, and, as I said, I imagine he's long gone from the city by now. We'll have to explore other avenues."

"Like the mysterious Aline?" I asked.

"Yes, about Aline. The man I sent couldn't get into the establishment, so I've made a date with her myself for later tonight. Cost me a pretty penny, too—and for only half an hour!"

I raised my eyebrows.

He looked suddenly chagrined. "I beg your pardon, Ellie, but you did know that she's a . . . er, lady of the evening."

"Then I suppose evening is the best time to find her," I allowed with a grin.

Ramsey looked between the two of us. "I assume you're speaking of the woman in the photograph in Estrada's flat?" There was the faintest note of irritation in his voice.

"Yes," Archie said. "Her name is Aline Baros."

I'd been so caught up in the situation that I hadn't realized I'd finished the entire bowl of soup. Ramsey, without comment, moved it away and placed a cup in front of me, pouring out the hot chocolate.

I took a sip of it and closed my eyes in appreciation. It was hot and rich and decadent. Once again, Ramsey had known just what would make me forget my lack of appetite.

"You've chocolate on your lip," Archie said, leaning forward to wipe it away with his thumb.

Beside me, I felt Ramsey tense slightly. I looked over at him, and our eyes caught. I saw the displeasure in them. He hadn't liked Archie's familiarity, then. I felt an immediate jolt of elation at the thought but ruthlessly suppressed it.

Acknowledging jealousy on his part would only give me false hope. Just because he felt a certain sort of territorial desire for me meant nothing. In fact, the more Archie nettled Ramsey, the better, as far as I was concerned. Let Ramsey regret what he had thrown away.

"Your color is better," Ramsey said, breaking the silence.

"I feel marvelous," I replied, a bit too brightly.

"I doubt that," Ramsey answered. "We should probably leave you to get some rest."

He rose from his seat then, but Archie didn't. "I'll stay a few more minutes."

Ramsey, who had already risen, could not gracefully reseat himself. I wondered what game Archie was playing. He wasn't interested in me romantically; I was certain of that. There was nothing in his friendly, easy manner to indicate he had any such designs. But he had read the displeasure in Ramsey's face as easily as I did, I had no doubt, and he was deliberately playing on it.

"Let me look at your stitches," Archie said, moving to take Ramsey's vacated place beside me on the sofa. He took my face in his hands, pushing back the hair from my face and leaning in to look closely at the stitching.

"He did a neat job, but it must have hurt. Poor Ellie." His hands dropped to my shoulders and squeezed them. "What you need is a good, strong drink."

"That's inadvisable." Ramsey was still standing there.

"Is that what the doctor said?" Archie asked the major.

"It's common sense," Ramsey said tightly.

"I don't need a drink," I said, reaching out to pat Archie's arm. "But thank you."

He covered my hand on his arm with his. I saw the muscle in Ramsey's jaw jump.

I looked up at him with a pleasant expression. "I thank you so much for your assistance today, Major Ramsey. You were very kind."

It was a dismissal, and he knew it. "I'll wish you good night, then. You've only to let me know if you need anything else." His expression flickered to Archie. "Blandings."

"Good night, sir."

Ramsey went into his room then and closed the door behind him.

"What was that all about?" I asked Archie, halfway between amusement and exasperation.

He gave me an innocent expression. "To what do you refer?"

I frowned at him, pulling my stitches. "You're being overly familiar with me to irritate him."

"If he has parted ways with you, there's no reason I can't step into the gap, is there?" he said mischievously. "Make him realize what he's missing."

"You don't mean to tell me you're a romantic, Captain Blandings," I said. "Well, you may as well save yourself the effort."

"It's no effort at all to spend time with you, Ellie."

"Major Ramsey is not going to change his mind, however much you flirt with me. And he's right; we are not suited to each other."

"You're much too smart to believe that," he said kindly.

"On that note of gallantry, I think you'd better go," I told him dryly. "My head is beginning to ache."

He grinned as he rose from his chair. "My apologies. We'll continue this discussion later, shall we?"

"No, we shall not," I said as I walked with him to the door. "It's a closed issue. But please do let me know as soon as there is something else I can do . . . and please stop provoking the major."

He grinned. "Very well. But you must acknowledge that while Ramsey is a capital fellow, he needs the starch taken out of him occasionally."

"Good night, Archie," I said, and pushed him, laughing, out the door.

CHAPTER FIFTEEN

I spent most of the next day in bed, due mainly to the imperious nature of Ramsey, who checked in at regular intervals to be sure I was hydrated, fed, and medicated. It was very much like having an overbearing nurse.

Archie didn't ring about his meeting with Aline, but I assumed he would contact me when he had more information. As there was nothing else to do, I gave in to Ramsey's bossing and took the tablets for my aches and pains. Consequently, I spent most of the day in a hazy half sleep, plagued by vague yet unsettling dreams. I awoke more than once with a gasp and had to recall where I was and that I was safe.

Ramsey sent up trays for breakfast, lunch, and dinner. He was being none too subtle about pushing food on me. As it reminded me of Nacy, I decided to take it with good humor and ate as much as I could between drug-induced slumbers.

When the tablet I'd taken after dinner had worn off, it was dark. I got out of bed, drank two glasses of water and the cold tea left in my dinner teapot, and felt my head clear a bit.

After being abed all day, I wasn't the least bit sleepy, and I couldn't bear the thought of another tablet.

I remembered there was a pack of cigarettes in my handbag,

and I went to fetch them. I didn't smoke very often, but I was feeling restless and on edge and thought perhaps a cigarette in the fresh air would do me good. I pulled on a robe, then opened the French doors and went out onto the balcony. Lighting the cigarette, I inhaled deeply and blew the smoke out into the chill night air.

I looked out at the city. As ever, the nightlife continued unabated by a world at war. On the streets below, the traffic rumbled and horns blew, hundreds of headlights shining brightly. I thought again how strange it was to see the city aglow. As far as the eye could see, lights dotted the buildings, glittering like stars.

"How are you feeling tonight?"

I turned as Ramsey appeared in the doorway to his room. I hadn't realized our rooms shared this balcony, and I'd been so lost in thought I hadn't even heard the door.

He was dressed casually, for him. He wore no jacket or necktie, and his sleeves were rolled up to the elbows, his collar unbuttoned. He still managed to look elegant.

I, meanwhile, was wearing my oldest (and therefore most comfortable) pajamas beneath a rather tatty blue robe, and my hair hadn't seen a brush all day. I hadn't bothered with slippers, and my feet were bare. But he'd no doubt seen me looking worse.

"Like I had to escape my room," I said.

"I don't suppose the fresh air will hurt you."

"I don't suppose I'm in much danger of being hurt, Major," I said patiently. "I'm not a china doll, and I haven't been shattered by a blow to the head."

"No. A china doll is the last thing to which I should compare you."

I resisted the unkind urge to point out it was exactly how he had been treating me.

Instead, I changed the subject. "It's a beautiful city."

"Yes." He stepped out onto the balcony then, though he stayed on his side of it. "All the light seems strange compared to London at the moment, doesn't it?"

I nodded, my eyes on the skyline. "A few months of blackouts have changed how I view the world. I hope I will be able to adjust to lights in London again when the war is over."

"You will. Humans are, by and large, very adaptable creatures, and you, perhaps, more than most."

"Yes, I suppose I am rather adaptable," I agreed. "Adapting is a thief's greatest skill, after all."

He looked over at me. I knew he hadn't missed the edge to my words, but he didn't comment on it.

We contemplated the city in silence for a few moments while I smoked.

"You're up late," I said at last, for something to say.

"I've been attending to some paperwork for my London cases."

"It was less than convenient, I suppose, for you to pick up and come to Lisbon."

I could feel him mentally weighing his response. He'd been ordered, more or less, to assist in this matter, but he no doubt thought it rude to point that out.

"What we're doing here is important," he said, avoiding a direct answer. "Besides, I didn't mind seeing Lisbon again."

"You've been here before, then."

"Several times, but not since the war has begun." He looked over at me. "I remember you said in Sunderland that you wanted to see more of the world. I hope this taste of travel is living up to your expectations."

It was the sort of polite remark he probably made at society dinners, but I felt a little pang at the memory of our Sunderland trip.

"Yes," I said, releasing the word in a puff of smoke. "Head injury aside, I've enjoyed being here very much."

"But we can't put the head injury aside, can we?"

I looked over at him, caught by something in his tone. Was he still blaming himself for what had happened with Velo? "I told you yesterday, I would have chased him whether you told me to or not."

"You've already been under a great deal of strain—"

"We're all under strain," I said impatiently.

"Yes, of course. But the sort of work you've been doing, the things you've seen, it takes an emotional toll, and now you've been physically injured—again."

I shrugged. "A minor battle scar."

"It was not minor. You're lucky you're not in hospital."

"You were shot full of holes only four months ago," I pointed out. "By rights, you should still be convalescing, and yet here you stand."

"We're not talking about me."

I scoffed. "Fine. But there's no sense in talking about me either. A few wounds along the way to victory are the least of my worries. In the grand scheme of things, it doesn't matter at all."

"It does matter. Because I brought you into all of this, and I have an obligation to protect you, whatever you might think."

I turned to look at him. He was watching me, his face in shadow, so I couldn't see his expression.

There was an intimacy to this moment, the two of us alone here in the midst of a city teeming with people.

I thought suddenly of the last time we'd stood together in the shadows, of the way he'd held me close and kissed me until my head swam. I felt the hollow ache of emptiness in the place of what might have been. The ugly weight of the word *obligation*.

If that was all I was to him now, I'd rather be nothing at all.

"That's gallant of you," I said with a tight smile. "But as we established back in London, I'm not your responsibility anymore. Consider yourself relieved of the obligation."

"Electra . . ."

I ground out my cigarette in the ashtray on the small iron table. "I'd better go back to bed," I said. "Good night."

I heard him curse in the darkness as I stepped back into my room and closed the door behind me.

Archie rang up and asked to meet with Ramsey and me the following morning, and I insisted that we go somewhere other than my room. I was sick to death of looking at the same four walls.

And so, an hour later, we found ourselves seated at a table in a warm café, custard tarts and drinks before us.

"Ellie, you look much better today," Archie said. "As lovely as ever."

I'd put on a bit of rouge this morning, as I was still pale, but, naturally, I wasn't going to admit to this. "Thank you."

I'd worn my hair down today, letting the curly waves at the front of my face cover the stitches. As I'd assumed, very little had to be done to hide the wound, as my hair naturally waved over that place.

I saw Ramsey's eyes stray to the area more than once, however, and I suspected he wanted to check up on how I was healing but was too polite to ask.

"You never told me," I said to Archie. "How was your appointment with Aline?"

He looked over at the door. "She told me the, er, establishment in which she worked was not a safe place to talk. She's going to meet us here."

I was glad I would have a chance to hear what she had to say firsthand.

He looked over at the door and lifted a hand. "Here she is now."

I turned to see the woman in the doorway. She was even more beautiful in the flesh than she had been in the photograph in Estrada's flat. Her dark hair gleamed blue-black in the halo of light from behind her.

She came to us in a mist of some expensive, spicy perfume,

the gold bracelets on her wrists jangling. She was dressed in a chic chocolate-brown silk dress.

The gentlemen rose, and Archie pulled out a chair for her to sit.

"Ellie, Major, this is Aline Baros. Aline, allow me to introduce you to Ellie McDonnell and Major Ramsey."

"How do you do?" Ramsey said.

"Hello," I said with a smile.

"I'm glad to meet you," Aline replied. Her voice was low and lightly accented.

"May I order you something?" Archie asked.

She looked up at him. "Perhaps some coffee."

Archie tended to this, and then we got down to business. "Thank you for meeting with us, Aline."

"I'm sorry I was not able to tell you more when you came to see me," she told Archie, her dark eyes on his face. "But, as I said, it was not safe to talk."

Archie waved away the apology. "As I said, we are trying to contact Senhor Estrada. Do you know where he is?"

She shook her head. "No. I do not know what's become of Fernando. He hasn't contacted me."

"Do you know where he might have gone?" Archie questioned.

She shrugged an elegant shoulder. "We do not have . . . that sort of relationship. If I had to guess, I imagine his work had been discovered, and he thought it prudent to leave the country."

"What work is that?" Ramsey asked.

"He has been helping escapees from the occupied countries—prisoners of war, refugees, political dissidents. It is dangerous. If he has escaped alive, I am happy for him."

Archie nodded thoughtfully. "But who will continue the work now?"

"Fernando was not the only one doing this." She took a sip of her coffee. "I know of another man who may be able to give you the information you seek, but getting it from him without detection may be difficult."

"How so?" Archie asked.

She looked at him. "Do you know a man called Max Hager?"

Archie looked surprised. "Max Hager is an Abwehr agent."

"Yes," she agreed. "He is also one of my . . . clients."

We waited.

"He is rather indiscreet. Braggadocio is not a good quality in a spy. But he is quite efficient, I think. A godlike quality for Germans. He mentioned to me that he has this man under surveillance."

"And who is the man?" Ramsey asked.

"His name is Adriano Carrico Santos. He is a registrar at the Conservatória do Registo Civil. The Civil Registry Office, I think you would call it. Unfortunately, as Max Hager tells it, Santos helped one too many loose-lipped people in the early days of the war, and now he's watched day and night."

That certainly didn't sound good. But surely he wasn't unapproachable. "There must be some way we can get in touch with him," I said.

Aline shrugged. "According to Max, his phones are tapped, and his office is bugged. Max keeps Santos's secretary on his payroll and in his bed. They take his mail and sift through it before he sees it. I don't know how you might get in touch with him without giving him, or yourselves, away."

"We are already being watched," I said. "Does it matter if we speak with him?"

"Yes," Archie said reflectively. "Because if the Germans are working this hard, it means they have nothing to tie him definitely to the work he is doing. At this point, it is only suspicion. If you meet with him, it will be, in some sense, proof of what he is doing. And that could bring all the work he's doing to an end."

Aline nodded. "The networks have tightened considerably

since the beginning of the war. Speaking too freely has cost more than one life. It is, I am sure, why Fernando left."

"But Portugal is a neutral country," I said.

"Indeed it is," Archie agreed. "But that does not stop enemy agents from acting here. You saw what happened to Suvari. And he isn't the first."

I felt myself pale beneath the rouge. "You think they would murder him out of hand?"

Archie gave me a grim smile. "My dear, the Nazis will indiscriminately murder anyone who gets in their way."

I felt a chill, but my chin tipped up with determination in the next minute. We weren't accustomed to being thwarted in my family.

"Well, I shan't give up until I think of something," I said. If there were some way to pass off paper between myself and the registrar in some other context, he might be able to tell us what we needed to know. I felt even more responsible since I was the one who had let our quarry get away.

Aline's eyes came to me. "If you want to create a distraction, Max would like you," she said. "He's partial to black-haired women. Not very Aryan of him."

"No," Ramsey said flatly.

"I don't think we ought to put Ellie into Hager's path if we can help it," Archie agreed.

Aline shrugged. "Well, you have a bit of time to decide how to approach Santos. Max mentioned to me last night that his wife has just given birth to their first child, and he won't be back to the registry office until next week."

A new father. Yes, we needed to be sure this man was protected. He was risking so much for this work.

Archie seemed to read my thoughts. "We'll work something out that will keep him safe. Leave it to me."

"Be careful," Aline warned. "Max Hager is a dangerous man."

CHAPTER SIXTEEN

And so we were left with nothing to do but pass the time until Santos returned to work and we could think of some way in which to make contact with him.

A wait that might have been excruciating was alleviated by Archie's willingness to play tour guide. When he was able to get away from his work, he took me sightseeing. We visited the Mosteiro dos Jerónimos in Belém with its soaring vaulted ceilings and stained glass windows; walked through the Praça do Comércio, the lovely and bustling square that opened onto the Tagus; and took the Elevador de Santa Justa, an iron lift, up to the viewing deck and gazed out at the breathtaking city views. I tried an endless array of delicious Portuguese dishes and purchased souvenirs for my family and Felix.

In the evenings, we went to various popular nightspots, enjoying music and dancing until late into the night.

As on edge as I was about the stagnation of our mission and Toby's whereabouts, I took great enjoyment in touring the city. I didn't know when or if I would be able to leave London again, and I soaked up every bit of history and culture I could.

Doutor Ferreiro came back and took out my stitches. The wound had healed nicely, and there was no puckering of the skin around the thin pink scar. I thought that, in time, it would fade until it was probably quite unnoticeable.

We didn't see much of Ramsey during those days, and I found myself both disappointed and relieved. I missed him when I wasn't with him, but it was much easier not to have to pretend I was indifferent to him. He had dinner with us on two occasions but otherwise was fully engaged with, I assumed, whatever work he had brought with him from London.

There was one other occasion when we saw him, however.

Archie and I were coming in one night from an evening of dinner and dancing when we encountered Ramsey in the hallway outside my room. Archie was accompanying me to my door, and we were talking and laughing as usual when Ramsey stepped out of his room and into the hallway. I didn't miss the way his eyes swept briefly over me, taking in my evening dress and the way my arm was linked through Archie's.

The quick friendship and easy rapport between Archie and me had solidified over our sightseeing adventures, perhaps because, in some way, he reminded me a bit of my cousins.

All the same, Ramsey didn't need to know that. It did me no credit to admit that I hoped that he was jealous. He had been so solicitous when I'd been injured and then had virtually ignored me since our conversation on the balcony. It was petty of me, but my pride wanted him to regret it. And so I didn't release Archie's arm or let my smile falter as Ramsey approached us.

"Good evening, Major," Archie said.

"It's one o'clock in the morning," Ramsey said.

"So it is," Archie answered mildly. "I didn't realize it was quite so late. Did you, Ellie?"

"I thought it was later," I admitted. "We were out until nearly two last night, I think."

"Were we really? You're making a shocking reveler out of me."

I laughed, turning my eyes back to Ramsey. "Did you need something, Major?"

"No," he said. His tone was curt. "I was simply concerned, given the dangers posed by the current situation and my lack of knowledge of your whereabouts."

There was a definite reprimand in the words. We should not be enjoying ourselves at a time like this. Well, I didn't intend to sit glumly in my room waiting for something to happen when I might never have a chance to explore a foreign city again.

"Archie takes good care of me," I said lightly.

Ramsey's eyes flashed. I didn't miss it, and neither did Archie.

"If you like, sir, I can leave you the names of the places we intend to go in the evening in the event you need to reach us."

"Is it necessary to stay out until all hours?" he asked, his tone mild though his posture was stiff. "I think, with whoever killed Suvari still on the loose, it might be wiser to return Miss McDonnell here after dinner rather than risking unsecured nightspots, don't you?"

He wasn't looking at me. He was looking at Archie, and I knew that, without saying so, he was pulling rank. It both irritated and gratified me that he was concerned about my safety. I might have argued with him, but a hotel hallway at one o'clock in the morning was neither the time nor the place.

"We'll consider that when we go out tomorrow night," I said breezily. Then, before Ramsey could reply, I wished them both good night and slipped into my room.

The major's opinion didn't much matter in the long run because it was only the next day that things began to go vastly awry.

It was quite early the next morning when Archie rang up to my room and asked me to meet him downstairs.

A glance at the clock confirmed I'd barely had six hours of sleep and Archie no doubt even less, so I assumed there must be news. I dressed quickly and went down to meet him.

"Breakfast?" he asked me as I met him in the lobby.

"I could do with some strong tea."

When we were settled in the dining room, I noticed that Archie seemed a bit uneasy. I wondered if there was bad news.

"Something's happened, hasn't it?" I asked. It was better to get it out in the open, I knew, though my hands had gone cold at the idea that Archie might have heard something of Toby's whereabouts.

"No, no," Archie said quickly, realizing my assumption. "That is, I don't know anything new. But I've received word that Santos is to return to work tomorrow, and we're no closer to finding a way to contact him."

"I've been thinking about it, too," I admitted. "But Aline made it sound like it will be impossible not to draw notice."

"I've turned the matter over in my head all night, and I might have come up with an idea."

"Oh?"

"It's . . . rather outlandish, but it just might work."

Something in his manner set off alarm bells, though I couldn't be sure why. Perhaps it was just that Archie, who was always so very relaxed, looked distinctly uncomfortable.

"What is it?" I asked.

He drew in a breath and then he came out with it. "Would you have any objection to marrying me?"

CHAPTER SEVENTEEN

I stared at him, wondering if I had heard him right. But I knew I had. Was I mistaken about his impression of our relationship? I had been certain there was nothing romantic in his attentions. Could I have been so very wrong? I didn't think so . . . but then why this strange proposal?

Because I could think of very little to say, I managed a startled smile and the customary phrase. "Why, Captain Blandings, this is so sudden."

He grinned at my use of the cliché. "Yes, I know. But I've been racking my brains over the best way to get to Santos without drawing attention to ourselves or to him, and I think this might be it. Civil marriage ceremonies are performed at the Conservatória do Registo Civil, and Santos is one of the registrars who performs them."

My mind was whirling as I tried to take in what he was saying. He was right. It was an outlandish idea. All the same, if there was no way to speak to the man without drawing attention to ourselves, this did seem like the perfect solution. But it was absurd.

"It's rather a drastic plan . . ." I said.

He laughed, and I blushed.

"No offense to you, of course, Archie. But I'm certain that

being saddled with a wife you barely know was not your intention when you embarked on this mission."

"If you're worried that my intentions are less than honorable, I assure you the marriage will be in name only," he said. "And I'm reasonably certain we can get an annulment when things are done. If not, a divorce. If you haven't any . . . moral objections to such a thing."

"Not particularly," I replied honestly. I'd said all along that I was willing to do whatever I could to get Toby home. And this marriage wouldn't count, not really. After all, we would both know it wasn't real from the outset. "But won't that take a long time?"

"It may take a few months to be undone," he agreed. "If there is some obstacle . . ."

I shook my head, perhaps a bit too emphatically. *The lady doth protest too much, methinks.* "No. No, I only meant it would . . . tie you up for the foreseeable future."

"I'm unattached at the moment. It won't be any inconvenience for me, if that's what worries you."

I said nothing, my mind in a whirl.

He had very quickly and systematically done away with the biggest potential obstacles to my saying yes.

What, then, was the problem?

You know what it is, I told myself. The problem was that I was terribly in love with another man.

Well, what of it? I had acknowledged that I was in love with him, but there was nothing else to be done about it. He didn't want me, and that was that.

I wasn't going to die over it, and I didn't intend to stop living over it either.

"Thank you, Captain Blandings," I said with grave formality. "I would be honored to marry you."

He grinned. "I think perhaps you'd better keep calling me Archie. It usually takes a few weeks for the paperwork to come through, but I think I can expedite matters. We should, I think, be able to do the thing within a week."

"All right," I agreed, feeling a bit numb.

The matter settled, Archie set upon his breakfast with gusto. I drank my tea, trying not to think too hard about what I'd just agreed to.

It wasn't as though it would be a binding agreement. Marriage was a frightening-sounding word, but this would be part of a job like anything else, a disguise I slipped into. Nothing to it.

"I heard from Aline again, as well," Archie said. "She told me that Max Hager will be at Casino Estoril tonight. I thought we might do a two-pronged offensive. In addition to the marriage, we might go to the casino and contrive to give him the impression our interests lie outside of Lisbon."

"Won't that just call undue attention to our movements?" I asked.

"I believe our movements are likely being observed anyway. We may as well play into it."

"Yes, perhaps you're right." In truth, I liked the idea of counter-espionage at a casino. It sounded like an exciting way to end what had already been an exciting day.

As we left the dining room, Archie turned to me. "In order to make this story believable, we may need to start being a bit more . . . demonstrative. In case we are being watched, you understand."

I raised my brows at him. "What do you have in mind?"

"Perhaps I might hold your hand?" he said, reaching for it. I slipped my hand into his, and he gave it a little squeeze.

"I might also need to kiss you occasionally," he said with great casualness.

We had arrived back at the lifts, and I could hear one making its way down. It would open soon, releasing guests on their way to breakfast.

Archie looked down at me. He gave me a mischievous smile. "Shall we give it a go now? Someone is coming down. It's our chance to perform for an audience."

I laughed. "All right."

He stepped closer and put his arms around me, drawing me toward him. Then he kissed me.

This was not the first time I had faked a romantic embrace for an audience. Ramsey and I had done it once before, early in our acquaintance. I tried not to think too much about that as I rested my hands on Archie's chest.

It was a light, pleasant kiss, and he was polite about it. Closed lips and none of the trimmings.

The lift dinged as it reached the ground floor, and I heard the doors open. Then Archie pulled back, and I felt a sinking feeling as he focused on the open lift doors.

"Oh. Good morning, Major," Archie said, confirming my fears.

I turned to see Ramsey standing there looking at us. His expression was impassive, but his eyes glittered in a way I could describe only as dangerous.

Immediately, I felt heat rise to my face. I was blushing to the roots of my hair, I was quite sure. What must he think?

What does it matter? I asked myself.

Archie smiled, completely unruffled, and turned toward the major, one arm still draped around my waist. "Ellie and I were just practicing our role."

"And what role is that?"

I didn't meet Ramsey's gaze as he asked the question in a quiet voice. Archie's arm continued to rest around me in a way that felt friendly but no doubt looked more than that.

"You may wish to be the first to congratulate us, sir. Ellie has graciously consented to be my wife."

I still didn't look at Ramsey. Perhaps I was afraid I would see indifference. I did see his head turn from Archie to me from the corner of my eye, but I couldn't bring myself to look up.

Ramsey said nothing for a long moment, and when he did, his tone was measured. "Let's go somewhere a bit more private to continue this conversation."

As there were several people beginning to queue up to use the lift, I thought this was an excellent suggestion.

Archie led us to a small, wood-paneled lounge off the lobby, and we sat. This was a warm, elegant room I hadn't been in before, and it was currently unoccupied.

I finally ventured a look at Ramsey. His face was set, and he wasn't looking at me.

"Now," he said to Archie. "Why don't you tell me what is going on."

Archie explained the plan as he had to me, more succinctly now that I had agreed to it. He did not seem at all worried about Ramsey's less than enthusiastic reaction.

"If you believe you are being watched, you can't falsify the marriage documents for this," Ramsey said when Archie had finished summing up the scheme. "If Max Hager has contacts in the registry office, he'll be onto this farce immediately."

"No, it'll have to be a real marriage," Archie said. "Legal, that is. The paperwork will need to be in order for it to be convincing."

"And then . . . ?" Ramsey asked.

"Well, we can get it annulled once the thing is over."

"Once the war is over, do you mean? You'll not want to compromise Santos and his work before then."

"No," Archie agreed. He looked over at me. "That is a good point. We may need to take several months—even a year—before we can dissolve the marriage without drawing attention."

"I don't see why that should be a problem," I said.

I felt Ramsey's eyes on me again. I expected him to ask me

at any moment what my thoughts on the matter were, and I was prepared to be as breezily nonchalant as Archie was about our imminent nuptials.

"Give us a moment, Blandings," Ramsey said instead. I hadn't expected him to dismiss Archie, and I felt both alarmed and oddly . . . hopeful, for some reason I couldn't name.

"Of course," Archie said, glancing at his wristwatch. "I have a meeting this morning anyway. I'll just go and break the news to my lovely secretary that I shall be off the market. We'll go to the casino tonight. I'll pick you up at seven, Ellie?"

I nodded.

"Very good. Until this evening, my love," he said with a wink. "Major."

Major Ramsey did not reply, nor did his eyes shift from me as Archie took his leave.

Once we were alone, I decided to go on the offensive, beat Ramsey to the punch.

"Archie didn't coerce me into this," I said quickly, almost achieving the nonchalance I had hoped for. "I told you before I'm willing to do whatever needs to be done to help Toby, and I meant it."

"Blandings comes up with a great many harebrained schemes, but I'll admit I didn't expect this one." His voice and his expression were unreadable.

I smiled tightly. "It will work for our purposes. And it's only temporary."

There was a silence that seemed to stretch to excruciating length. At last, Ramsey said, "Temporary is a relative term. As I noted, it may be some time before you can secure a divorce. Are you certain you want to make that commitment?"

"It doesn't matter," I said. "If there's no other way to contact Santos without drawing attention to his activities, then so be it."

There was a long silence. A part of me wished he would say

that he didn't want me to do it. That he couldn't bear the thought of my marrying another man. But he wouldn't say it, of course.

"Then let me be the first to congratulate you," he said instead, in that horribly formal way of his.

Our eyes met. His eyes had taken on that reflective silvery shade that revealed nothing, but I thought, for just an instant, that I saw the flicker of some suppressed emotion in their depths. Then it was gone.

I managed a polite smile.

"Thank you, Major Ramsey. I'm sure we'll be very happy."

CHAPTER EIGHTEEN

I cried when I got back to my room.

I'd never been a woman much given to tears, but I'd shed more than my fair share over the past few months. I soon enough dried my eyes, however. This was a time for clear thinking. Not wallowing in self-pity.

Was I really going to do this? Was I going to marry a man I barely knew just to give us the opportunity for a few moments of conversation with Santos? But I already knew the answer, had told it to Ramsey. I would do whatever was necessary to find Toby.

I wouldn't be able to tell Nacy and Uncle Mick, at least not for a long time. Nacy would be sad that her romantic dreams for me had been in vain, and Uncle Mick was perhaps still Catholic enough to object to my cavalier treatment of the matrimonial state.

But perhaps when the war was over and done with, the boys safely home, I could reveal this strange facet of my adventure.

"Mrs. Ellie Blandings," I said to myself in the mirror. I could live with that.

Since we were to go to the casino where, according to Archie, many of the crème de la crème of society were to be seen, I chose the most daring of my new dresses. This one was bloodred satin, the bodice tightly fitted with thin straps and the rest clinging to every curve. I had a filmy red lace wrap that draped about my shoulders. It wasn't warm, by any means, but I did look rather glamorous.

I pulled my hair into an elegant chignon with soft waves at the front of my face, covering the scar, and did a heavy-handed application of makeup.

Tonight I would blend in by standing out. Every woman wanted to look her best in such social situations.

Archie tapped at my door right on time. I opened it, and his eyes swept over me, brows rising appreciatively. "You look marvelous, Ellie."

"Thank you. You look rather dashing yourself." He was wearing a white dinner jacket with black trousers and bow tie.

"No coat?" he asked, as I stepped toward the door.

"No. Just this ineffectual wrap, I think."

"The pains of fashion. Well, rest assured: I shall be the envy of every man in the place."

"You're turning into a flatterer, Captain Blandings."

He smiled. "I believe it's customary to flatter one's fiancée. Besides, it's not flattery if it's true."

I returned his smile, though there was still a knot in my stomach when I thought about marrying him, charming and amiable though he might be.

We took a car to Casino Estoril. Simon Woods was our driver. I was surprised when he congratulated me on our engagement.

"It is, I think, about time Captain Blandings settled down," he said with a grin.

"It just took the right woman," Archie said, picking up my hand and kissing it. It seemed he was telling few people that our engagement was a ploy; that was probably for the best.

As we drove, Archie and I discussed tonight's plan. I would, if possible, talk to Max Hager and indicate that Archie, my fiancé, had been taking trips to the south of Portugal, meeting escapees there. If we could focus Hager's attention in the wrong direction, it would add a layer of protection around Santos.

Archie had apparently discussed the details with Ramsey at some point during the day, and he told me that Ramsey would meet us there to help facilitate the plan. I was simply relieved he wasn't riding with us.

We went over the script, as it were, and I committed it to memory. I was rather looking forward to playing my part.

At last, Casino Estoril came into view. There were rather a lot of cars leading up to the entrance. Expensive cars.

I was glad I had taken care with my appearance, for I saw the glamorous women who were entering the casino on the arms of gentlemen in sleek evening dress.

My arm through Archie's, we walked inside. This was the nicest casino I had ever been in. Granted, I hadn't been to any big gambling cities before, and the underground gambling dens in London were nothing to speak of, especially in polite company.

The décor here was sleek and modern, and the place smelled like money. Money mingled with expensive perfume and cologne and cigarette and cigar smoke.

The gaming tables were full this evening. There was the murmur of conversation and laughter and the clatter of the roulette wheel and the shuffling of cards. Most people had a drink in their hand.

There was the dazzling gaiety of society nightlife—laughter and the hum of conversation—but beneath it all I sensed a sort of desperation, a frantic energy that was staving off pain and despair. For the most part, everyone in this room was escaping something. The joviality was fragile. All that glitters is not gold, as they say.

There was, however, plenty of gold, too. A bit of the old Ellie, the one with nefarious intentions, couldn't help but look around at all the easy money to be made. Not just at the gaming tables.

Casting a practiced eye around the room, I could see several unattended handbags, the bulge of wallets in the loose pockets of drink-loosened gentlemen, and jewelry that could be easily unclasped by deft fingers. I had to imagine that there were any number of thieves in the place at this moment. The pickings were too good for no one to be taking advantage of it.

I was pulled from this reverie by Archie's hand on my waist. He slid an arm easily around me and pulled me a bit closer.

"Your target is there playing baccarat," he said, leaning in to speak in my ear with all the appearance of intimacy.

Max Hager was a tall, well-built man with fair hair, perhaps in his early forties. He was wearing spotless evening clothes and carried himself with the languid appearance of a man-about-town. However, practiced eyes—eyes like mine—would notice that there was a hint of military erectness in his posture that he hadn't quite managed to suppress and a watchfulness in his cold blue gaze.

I smiled up at Archie. "Yes, I see him."

"You're certain you want to go through with this?"

"Of course."

"Be careful." And he dropped his head to brush a kiss across my bare shoulder. A nice bit of acting, that.

It was then, as fate would have it, Archie's lips on my skin, that my eyes met Ramsey's across the room.

He was dressed in a black dinner jacket and tie. I seldom saw him in black, and it gave him a somewhat menacing look that only served to make him more attractive. He was terribly handsome in uniform, but I could grow used to dinner jackets.

Our eyes slid away from each other, making no acknowledgment, but I saw that his eyes looked a stormy gray at this distance.

I was relieved to have a task to take my mind off him. There was no sense enjoying his jealousy when I was going to marry Archie in the next few days and, in all likelihood, never see Ramsey again once this mission was complete. The circles in which we traveled were so vastly different that I need never worry about bumping into him in London.

"You'd better get me a drink," I said. "Club soda, I think."

"Certainly."

Archie went to fetch the drink for me, and I drank it rather quickly before setting the glass in his hand. With something of an irritated expression, he went and got me another. If anyone was watching, they would notice that I was drinking too quickly and that there was trouble in paradise.

Over the next half hour, I wandered away from Archie more than once, smiling at other gentlemen. Each time, he came to find me, a tight smile on his face. I thought we were doing a good job of letting the story unfold.

As all of this went on, I kept an eye on Hager. He, too, was giving every appearance of enjoying himself. So far as I could see, however, he drank and gambled sparingly. Instead, he cultivated the impression of high living while keeping a clear head and interacted with a great many people. No wonder he was a successful spy.

"I think now is the part where we'd better start disagreeing," I said, looking up at Archie with a slight frown between my brows.

His own shot up. "Do you? Well, I think you've had enough to drink." This second part was said in a loud whisper.

His hand reached out to take my arm, but I jerked it away from him. The sharp movement drew the notice of several people around us, though they were trying not to show it.

"I don't think that's any of your business," I said, stepping back from him, just the slightest bit unsteady on my feet.

"It most certainly is."

"It's not. I'll drink whatever I want."

"Fine. But I'm not going to carry you back to your hotel like I did last night," he said.

I had to fight the urge to laugh at those words. What an excellent line.

"Don't you dare talk to me like that," I said, my voice rising.

"I'll talk to you however I please," Archie said, doing a bang-up job of acting like a rotter.

"Then I hope you don't talk to me ever again!" I shot back, loudly enough to be overheard by those making an effort to listen.

I slammed my empty glass down and stalked away from Archie, and he, throwing up his hands, went off in the other direction.

Doing my best to look in a high dudgeon, I began to make my way slowly around the perimeter of the room. There was no need to hurry my meeting with Hager; our quarry wasn't likely to leave until late into the night, not if he wanted to keep gathering information.

As I moved around the room, I realized I was enjoying myself. There was something rather exciting about being in this glamorous setting in a glamorous gown. I liked the challenge of fitting in; I liked an objective to achieve; I liked the risk, to be honest.

Besides, the casino was exciting in and of itself. I was half tempted to try my hand at roulette. It had been awhile since I'd done any gambling. Uncle Mick, despite his criminal history, was short on personal vices, and he'd never overindulged in any of them. Friendly games for small stakes were one thing, but he'd always warned the boys and me against getting in over our heads.

"Can I buy you a fresh drink, beautiful?" a man asked, stepping into my path. I ran an eye over him. Tall, distinguished, dark-haired. In short, not Max Hager.

I smiled up at him. "I don't need a drink just now, but thank you."

"Are you certain? You looked rather hot a moment ago. I thought you might be thirsty." He didn't move out of my way. My tiff with Archie had had its effect, then. Unfortunately, this man was not my mark, and he was wasting both our time.

"Oh, that," I said, feigning embarrassment tinged with lingering resentment. "That was nothing."

"But perhaps you could use a listening ear?"

"No. Thank you."

"If you change your mind, you have only to let me know."

I needed to escape this fellow, and soon. I had seen Ramsey move away from the wall and take a step in our direction. The last thing we needed was his drawing more attention.

"I'll keep that in mind," I replied, giving the man's arm a friendly pat and then pushing him—ever so lightly. A hint that he was to move out of my way. To his credit, he took it.

I looked up and caught Ramsey's eye, shaking my head subtly. He relaxed, and I moved, once again, toward our quarry.

Hager was at the roulette table now, and I thought it would be beneficial for me to blend in. It was a good thing, then, that I had nicked a few chips from the pushy man's pocket.

I moved to the table across from Hager and leaned to place my chip on black, giving him a good view of my décolletage as I did so. This seemed to do the trick, for I saw his eyes linger there for a moment before they came up to my face. I gave him a minute to look and then raised my eyes, pretended as though I hadn't noticed his ogling, and gave him a slight smile across the table.

"No more bets," the croupier said, tossing the ball into the wheel. There was a rattle as it danced across the numbers. I watched the ball as it landed on black. A win for me.

I collected my chips and settled into playing. Now that I had Hager's attention, I didn't think he would wander away.

Though I was concentrating on the game, I noticed as he began edging his way around the table. By the time I'd collected a small pile of chips, he was at my side.

He said something in French, and I shook my head with a little flutter of lashes. "I'm sorry . . ."

"You're lucky tonight," he said in flawless English. His accent was nearly as polished as Ramsey's. I would never have guessed that he was German.

I looked up at him, a faint smile on my lips. "I am, aren't I? Perhaps it's as they say: lucky at cards, unlucky at love. Of course, these aren't cards."

"Are you?" he asked, his pale eyes on my face. "Unlucky in love? It seems, if you'll forgive my saying so, rather difficult to believe."

He was a fast worker, this one. Well, all the better for our purposes.

"I seem to be. But perhaps my luck will change," I said with what was, I fancied, the perfect blend of sweetness and coquetry.

"I hope so," he answered with a smile.

"No more bets!" said the croupier, ending my chance at playing this game.

"My name is Max," the man said, holding out a hand, though he was already standing quite close. "Max Hager."

CHAPTER NINETEEN

"Ellie McDonnell," I said, slipping my hand into his. He gripped it gently. His skin was soft and warm.

"Would you like a drink, Ellie McDonnell?"

"I've already had a drink or two tonight," I said, with the appearance of reluctance. "But . . . I suppose one more wouldn't hurt."

I gathered up my winnings, dropping them into the small beaded handbag I carried, and we walked toward the bar. He kept a hand on the small of my back on the pretext of guiding me through the crowds, but I noticed it slipped a bit lower once or twice.

"Did you come here alone?" he asked. I knew he knew I hadn't.

"No," I said. "My fiancé is here somewhere, but I'm cross with him."

He smiled. "That is why you are unlucky in love? And what did he do to make you cross?"

"Oh, it's a long story," I said. "And I'd rather not talk about him now."

"I am happy to oblige you in that, though you will allow me to say that I think the young man exceedingly foolish."

I laughed, gave another flutter of lashes. "You're very kind, Monsieur Hager."

"Please, call me Max."

"Then you must call me Ellie."

This informality established, Max ordered our drinks, and we went to sit on a little settee near a potted palm that secluded us, at least partially, from the view of the rest of the room.

"What brings you to Portugal, Ellie?" he asked, taking a cigarette case from his pocket. He offered me one, but I declined.

"My fiancé," I answered flatly.

"Ah, then we will not discuss it," he said, putting a cigarette between his own lips and lighting it with a gold lighter from his pocket. "But what do you think of Lisbon so far?"

"I love it," I replied. "It's marvelous."

I took a sip of my drink. As I had suspected it would be, it was terribly strong. Nevertheless, I swished a bit of it around in my mouth so, if he got any closer, he would smell it on my breath and not know I'd been lying about drinking earlier.

He leaned slightly toward me, and I found myself in the focus of those cool blue eyes. "What have you seen so far?"

I went into a lengthy description of the sights Archie and I had toured. If, perchance, anyone had been following me and Hager knew about it, my story would ring true.

I continued to pretend to sip my drink. Then, at one point, when his gaze had wandered for a moment, I poured most of it into the palm.

"I'm glad to hear you're enjoying Lisbon so much," he said at last.

"I was having so much fun until tonight," I confided miserably.

"I'm sorry to hear that." His arm had slid along the back of the settee.

"It's just that my fiancé is terribly jealous," I confided, with a light slur in my voice. I had begun leaning into Max ever so slightly. "That's why we argued. He always thinks I'm too . . . free with other men."

"Does he?" Max tsked.

I nodded sadly, my lips pouting, and ran a hand along the satin lapel of his jacket. "I can't help it that I'm . . . a friendly person."

"Certainly not," he agreed. "Can I get you another drink?"

"I really shouldn't," I said, looking down at my nearly empty glass. "But maybe just one more."

"I won't be a moment," he said, patting my hand before rising and going back to the bar. What an utter cad. He'd taken only one or two sips of his own drink. He was keeping a clear head while plying me with liquor, though he thought I was half-tiddly already.

I pulled a curl loose from my chignon and twirled my finger in it absently and then shifted so that one strap of my gown fell off my shoulder. Then I dipped a finger in my glass and dabbed a little of the liquor on my wrists and neck like I would perfume. It would all serve to give me a bit of a dissipated air.

I had no fear that I would be required to carry things much further with Max. Archie would come to my rescue before then, I was certain, feigning indignation that I was talking with another man.

But I needed to plant this information as subtly as I could before that happened. The trick was going to be confiding enough to tell Hager what we wanted him to know without making him suspicious.

He came back with the drink a moment later. Another tiny sip confirmed it was stronger than the last. I spit it surreptitiously back into the glass.

"Thank you," I said. "You're very kind."

"Not at all, my dear. I'm always happy to help a beautiful woman."

I smiled at him. "I wish Archie would say things like that to me instead of being such a . . . a bully."

"Perhaps he doesn't appreciate you."

"He doesn't. He . . . he only cares about his work."

"Oh?" he asked with apparent disinterest. He was clearly good at this job. If I *were* a sad, neglected fiancée, I would have no in-kling that he was eager to get information from me. No doubt he'd had past success in plying women with drinks—and not just to get information from them.

"He's been going so often to Faro, lately," I said, beginning to lay out the script Archie and I had prepared. "He's always gone. And then he gets angry if I spend time with friends. I got him to bring me here tonight, but then he started an argument the very first thing."

His arm had made its way around me now, and he was pulling me slightly closer. Aline had not been wrong about his proclivity for seducing black-haired women.

I sniffled, wiping at imaginary tears, and allowed myself to lean into him. I tried not to think about the fact that I was this close to a German agent. In my mind, the enemy was always a shadowy fig-ure radiating menace, not a suave gentleman in evening wear whose scent of mingled cologne and cigarettes reminded me of Felix.

"I don't even know why he goes to Faro so often," I said. "He won't tell me anything about his work."

"Perhaps it's of a confidential nature?" Max suggested, his hand lightly rubbing my back.

"I don't know. I think he just enjoys keeping secrets. I . . . I have wondered if there's another woman."

"Surely not," he said, his hand on my back sliding down and around to my hip. "Not when he has a beautiful woman like you at home."

"I followed him once," I said, appearing to take notice of nei-ther his roaming hand nor the way his mouth was getting closer to mine.

"Oh?" he asked, his breath warm against my ear. I suppressed a shudder. He was not, on the surface, an unattractive man, but, if Aline and Archie were right, he was a cold-blooded killer.

"Yes. I went to Faro and waited for him to arrive. Then I fol-

lowed him. He went to a café and met with two men. One of them
was very gaunt and haggard-looking, as though he hadn't had anything to eat in ages. I don't know why Archie would be talking to
a man like that."

"A Portuguese man?" he asked, his lips lightly brushing my jaw.

I let out an unsteady breath, as though I were succumbing to
his seduction. "N . . . no. They spoke English."

"And what did they say?"

"I couldn't hear them clearly. I was across the street."

If he wasn't getting the impression that Archie was meeting
escaped POWs in Faro, he wasn't half as good a spy as I thought
he was.

"I don't know why he'd prefer their company to yours," Hager
said. He took my chin in his hand, turning my face to his, and
leaned to kiss me then. I was glad I had taken at least one sip of the
liquor because he'd definitely have noticed the lack of it now.

I was just wondering how I could comfortably extricate myself
from his clutches when there was a loud clearing of the throat.
"Miss McDonnell."

I pulled away from Hager and looked up to see Ramsey looking down at us.

"Oh . . ." I said, only half feigning my dismay. First Archie
and then Hager. Ramsey was constantly walking in on me kissing
men today. It was only when I realized his expression held open
censure that I understood he was playing into the plan.

"I hate to interrupt," he said in a cool voice. "But Blandings
is looking for you. I said I'd bring you back to him if I . . . came
across you."

I sighed. "All right."

Hager had unobtrusively removed his arm from around me,
and he stood as I did. He didn't speak to Ramsey, and Ramsey
never looked at him. He simply watched me with undisguised dis-
approval.

"Thank you for the drinks, Monsieur Hager," I said.

He gave a stiff bow that was distinctly Germanic. "It was my pleasure."

I stepped toward Ramsey then and wobbled to appear unsteady on my feet.

Ramsey acted instantly, his arm sliding around my waist. I smiled up at him. "You're so sweet." Then I gave him a worried frown. "You won't tell Archie that I . . . ?"

With his other hand, he took the glass from my hand and set it down pointedly on the table.

"My apologies," Ramsey told Hager stiffly.

"Apologies for what?" I demanded. I let my head loll a bit to the side, and Ramsey's grip on me tightened.

"Come along," he said, trying to guide me away.

"I don't need your help," I slurred, leaning woozily into him. "But you won't tell Archie, will you?"

He led me away from Hager without further remark, and Hager made no attempt to stop him. I had, by all appearances, reached the stage where I could provide him with no more information or amusement.

"How much *have* you had to drink?" Ramsey whispered as he led me across the casino floor. "You smell like pure antiseptic."

"Charming observation," I answered, throwing in a stumble that he instantly steadied. "I poured my drink in the potted palm, but I also put a little on myself for effect."

"I hope you weren't observed pouring out your drinks."

"I wasn't," I said.

"Are you certain? Your act wasn't exactly subtle. Every man in the room was looking at you. With that many eyes on you, it's easier to be observed."

No one knew better than Ramsey how to make a compliment sound like an insult. I tamped down my anger. "Did *you* see me?" I challenged.

He didn't reply, and I knew that was answer enough.

Ramsey led me into a small lounge. I still leaned against him, though I let up a bit on the drunken act now that we were out of Hager's sight.

Gentlemen and a few ladies were sitting at the tables drinking, smoking, and engaged in conversation. There was an atmosphere of intrigue about the place, intrigue with an undercurrent of danger. Deals were being made here, information exchanged, people's fates decided.

Ramsey led me over to a table along one wall near the back of the room.

"Let me get you some coffee," he said. "As though I'm sobering you up."

"No. You know I hate the stuff."

He sighed and deposited me in a chair and then took the one across from me.

"Tell me everything you said and how he responded."

I slouched in my chair and related the whole of it. "It was easily done," I said when I had finished.

"Yes, almost too easily. I wasn't certain you'd had time to talk before he began pawing you."

I lifted an eyebrow. "Are you critiquing my technique, Major?"

"I can't argue with results," he replied, though his tone held an edge.

"You can, and you have," I said. "But I relayed the information. I did exactly as Archie asked."

"Yes. You seem to be good at doing what Blandings asks."

I looked up at him, feeling the flare in my eyes. "You sacked me for disobeying orders. Maybe I've learned my lesson."

"Or perhaps you just find taking orders from him more palatable." I couldn't read his tone, but I understood it was an accusation.

"Or perhaps he appreciates my abilities better than you did," I retorted.

His jaw tightened. My chin tipped up. Battle lines were drawn without words.

"Are you really going to marry him?" he asked at last.

The question caught me off guard. I swallowed down the ache in my chest to answer. "Of course I am."

"Just like that? No thought for the consequences?"

"There are no consequences," I said, my throat tight.

"You think not? And what do you suppose Lacey will say when you arrive back in London with a husband?"

I was surprised he brought up Felix. It was the only time he had ever allied himself with Felix's opinion.

"Felix asked me to marry him before I left England," I said. I wasn't sure why I told him this. No, that's not true. I told him because I wanted to see if he would react. I wasn't disappointed. He kept his face in check, of course, but I saw the flash of some emotion in his silvery-blue eyes.

"Then I imagine he won't be pleased to find you 'Mrs. Blandings' upon your return."

"I value Felix too much as a friend to complicate things with marriage," I said as lightly as I could manage. "Anyway, no one in London will know I'm married, and Archie will contrive to get it quickly annulled, I'm sure."

"I still think it's a drastic and unnecessary step—"

"Do you have a better plan?" I asked, my tone sharper than I intended.

"No, but—"

"Then I don't see we have a choice." I had control of my voice now. It was composed, almost cold. "Besides, it has nothing to do with you. If I don't mind, I don't see why you should."

He leaned forward across the table, eyes alight with anger and some other emotion I couldn't decipher.

"What do you want from me, Electra?" he demanded harshly.

"I don't want anything from you, Major Ramsey."

Our eyes met, a thousand unspoken words blazing there in the air between us.

And then Archie walked up to our table, glass in hand. "I've brought you another soda water, Ellie."

He stopped when he saw us leaning toward each other, the clear tension in our postures, but it was too late. The moment was gone.

"Thank you," I said, turning to take it from him with a hand that wasn't quite steady.

"Miss McDonnell has accomplished her objective, Blandings," Ramsey said, rising from his seat. "You'd better take her back to the hotel."

He walked out of the lounge without looking back.

CHAPTER TWENTY

I had to meet Archie and Ramsey for breakfast the next morning. I expected it to be an excruciating experience, but it ended up being even worse than I imagined.

I went downstairs thinking that at least Archie should have most of the details about when the wedding would be settled. The sooner we got it over with, the better.

He hadn't broached the tension between Ramsey and me when he'd accompanied me back to the hotel last night, and for that I was grateful.

Ramsey gave me one cool nod when I reached the breakfast table, and I responded in kind.

It had been another nearly sleepless night. I'd seen the results of it in the mirror this morning, in my pallor that emphasized the darkness beneath my eyes. I'd replayed our conversation over and over, what I might have said differently, how things might have ended some other way.

But the truth of it was that I didn't want anything from him, not if he was unwilling to give it. He had made the decision to end things between us, and there was no reason I should be forced to continually rehash those emotions.

There was silence at the table for several long minutes after the waiter brought our orders. Archie was buttering his toast and enjoying his breakfast. I sipped my tea, and Ramsey drank black coffee.

It wasn't until he had finished eating that Archie blithely dropped his bombshell.

"Well, according to my sources, several of Hager's men were on their way to Faro early this morning. My congratulations on your success, Ellie."

"I'm glad it worked. Perhaps it will distract him long enough for us to contact Santos without his notice."

"Yes. There is, however, just one minor fly in the ointment," he said. From the way he said it, I knew that minor was the last thing it would be.

"What do you mean?" I asked warily.

"I was about to submit the paperwork for our marriage license, but I'd forgotten one detail."

"What detail?"

Archie gave me a chagrined look. "I am, technically, already married."

My mouth dropped open, my cup clattering into the saucer, and I heard Ramsey swear in an undertone.

"What do you mean *technically*?" I demanded.

Archie sighed. "It was an unfortunate decision made during my university days. When I began to get the paperwork in order with London, I was reminded that the matter is still officially un-resolved."

"You *forgot* you were married?" I demanded.

Archie ran a hand through his tousled hair. "It was eight years ago and lasted only a few months. I had put it out of my mind."

"Archie!" I said, exasperated.

"I know," he replied. "It puts rather a crimp in things."

I tried to think the matter out rationally. If I was honest, my first feeling was an overwhelming sense of relief. I hadn't wanted to marry him, despite the temporary nature of the connection. I wasn't an overly romantic girl, but I had always thought that if I were to get married, it would be to someone I loved. I had been willing to do it to help Toby, without hesitation. But now that the option was gone, I realized how much I had been dreading it.

"Then what do we do?" I asked.

"I haven't come up with any other good ideas," he said.

I considered. "A second marriage for you wouldn't count legally, but does that matter? Couldn't we go ahead and be married by the registrar anyway? That would do away with the need for an annulment."

He shook his head. "If anyone looks too closely, they'll notice it's a bigamous marriage, and it will likely draw unwanted attention. Besides, I don't relish the thought of getting myself into any sort of legal trouble. But there is one more option that occurs to me . . ." His eyes moved to Ramsey.

And I realized immediately what he meant. I felt the blood drain from my face and then rush back through it again.

"No," I said softly.

Archie was still looking at Ramsey. "Marriage, in name only. You can have it annulled when this is over, just as Ellie and I planned to."

"No, Archie," I said more firmly than before.

"It may be our last opportunity to get the information we need," Archie said. "Hager's focus will be back on Santos soon, and we'll have lost our chance."

"*Captain Blandings*," I said through my teeth. There was no way he could miss the warning in my tone.

Neither of the men looked at me, however. Finally, Ramsey said, "Give Electra and me a few minutes alone."

Archie nodded and stood, finally glancing in my direction. I shot daggers at him with my eyes, and I was fairly certain I saw amusement in his. "I'll be in the lobby."

He left the dining room, and Ramsey and I were alone with my colossal embarrassment. I finally ventured a look at him. As I might have known, his expression was impassive.

"I'm sorry," I said quickly. "Archie had no right to suggest this. Please forget he mentioned it."

"If there is no other way to get in touch with Adriano Carrico Santos, then Blandings is right. I don't see what choice we have."

Surely, he wasn't agreeing to the proposition? He couldn't be.

I shook my head, wanting to be out of this situation and out of this room as quickly as possible. My face was aflame. "We'll think of something else. Please, just forget it."

I began to rise from my seat, but Ramsey's hand reached out and closed gently over my wrist. "Wait a moment."

I sank back into the chair, hoping he would remove his hand before he could notice the frantic beating of my pulse.

"It's the only solution within our time constraints," he said calmly, releasing my wrist. "It's not a difficult decision. We're out of time and out of options."

I tried to keep my tone calm. "I appreciate your . . . willingness to help, but I can't allow you to do this."

His eyes met mine. "You were going to allow Blandings to do it."

"He . . . I . . ." I might as well be honest. "Marriage doesn't mean much to Archie. Obviously. He wouldn't mind it. You would."

He was, after all, the nephew of an earl. He would be expected to marry well, to do things properly.

"You saved my life in Sunderland," he said. "It's no great hardship for me to do this to help you and to get the information we need to secure the escape line."

I shook my head again. "I don't want repayment for what I did in Sunderland."

"There's no sense in arguing about it," he said brusquely. "We're going to do it."

My chin tipped up. "No. We are not. Nothing could induce me to agree to this plan."

There was a challenge in his gaze. "Not even saving your cousin's life?"

I felt my stubbornness lose purchase on the slippery slope of my emotions. I couldn't say anything to that. Because I would do almost anything for Toby.

But this? I couldn't possibly.

The silence stretched on.

"Will you do it for Toby?" Ramsey pressed.

What else could I do?

"I hate you," I said tiredly.

"I'll take that as an acceptance of my proposal." He rose. "I'll have Blandings draw up the paperwork."

CHAPTER TWENTY-ONE

Archie came back into the dining room after Ramsey left.

I was still sitting at the table trying to get my head together. I could not believe that this had just happened.

He sat down across from me.

"My felicitations," he said.

"This isn't funny," I retorted.

He had the good grace to stop smiling, but his eyes still held amusement. "I'm sorry, Ellie. But there isn't any other way, not if we want to get this done quickly."

I sighed, toying with my spoon on the table. Never once had I considered things might turn out this way, and I still didn't see how we could possibly pull it off.

"I . . . we . . . Ramsey and I won't be remotely believable as a couple," I said.

Archie shot me a look. "I think we both know that isn't true. The tension between you is so thick I could cut it with a knife."

I glared at him.

"That being the case, my dear former fiancée," he went on, "I think we're going to have to part ways for now. It won't do for me to blithely accept your throwing me over for another man."

I looked up at him as he rose, and I didn't have to feign my anger. "That's fine with me. I'm furious with you."

His mouth twitched at the corner. "I'll get the license ready for you and Ramsey. And I'll be in touch again after you've spoken to Santos. I think, with Hager diverted, we should be able to find the escaped POWs before they do."

I nodded. It was the one bright spot in this jumble.

"Until then," he said, giving me a grave nod. Anyone else in the room might think we were solemnly parting, but I could see the twinkle in Archie's eyes.

He rose from the table and paused. "I hope you'll be very happy with him," he said.

"Get out of my sight, Archie Blandings."

Ramsey was still in the lobby when I left the dining room.

He came up to me and leaned in, his hand on my arm. "Will you accompany me on a walk?"

Though I still hadn't had time to get all my emotions in check, I knew we needed to talk. And the sooner the better. "All right."

We left the hotel and began walking down the crowded street in silence. I let Ramsey decide where we were going, and he seemed to have a destination in mind, for before long we were on a much-less-crowded street. He kept walking, but he slowed our pace.

"Blandings mentioned that it will be better for him not to contact you for the near future?"

"Yes."

"He will, of course, be in contact about the proper documentation."

"Yes," I said again. I could not seem to come up with an original comment to save my life.

He stopped walking and turned to face me. I forced myself to look up at him, my expression neutral.

"I know things are not, perhaps, as easy between us as they

once were," he said. "But we're going to have to appear comfort-able with each other."

I knew what he meant. We were meant to be in love, after all. So in love that I had broken off my engagement with another man.

"Of course," I replied evenly.

"Then you have no objection to my . . . being affectionate with you when we're in public."

I sighed. "No, Major."

"You'd better call me Gabriel."

"I will."

"No. I mean it will need to be natural. You'd better use it in private, too, to accustom yourself to it."

"Very well. No, Gabriel. I have no objection to your feigning affection for me in public. I certainly won't misconstrue it to mean anything it doesn't, if that's what you're worried about."

His eyes met mine, and I saw the flash of irritation in them. "Electra . . ."

"What's the next step?" I asked, cutting him off.

He hesitated for just a moment, as though deciding whether he wanted to pursue the previous course of conversation. In the end, he decided against it.

"Blandings thinks he can rush things through for us. We can likely get married tomorrow."

Tomorrow. That was sooner than I'd expected. But that was good. It meant we were that much closer to finding Toby.

"All right," I said.

"Do you . . . need anything?"

"What do you mean?"

"Anything in particular for the wedding."

I considered for a moment and then gave an awkward laugh. "Not that I know of. Perhaps we'd better scrape up a ring."

"Yes. I did think of that. I'll get it. Anything else? Do you . . . need a dress?"

It was sweet of him to think of it, and also it felt so very strange to be having this conversation. "I imagine I have something I can wear. I don't think a wedding gown is called for, under the circumstances."

"Well, if you think of anything you need, you have only to let me know."

"Thank you."

There was a moment of silence that felt strained.

Things had often been strained with Ramsey when he was my—for lack of a better term—commanding officer. There was a strange sort of formality between us that chafed. Now he was about to be my husband, and it seemed worse than before.

I was still trying to think of something to say when I caught sight of someone behind us in a shop window. I had seen a similar figure outside the hotel today—and on the day of my arrival. It looked like the man who had been watching me from across the street that first day.

I pretended to admire something in the window while I tried to get a better look at him. The angle of reflection wasn't ideal, but I was fairly certain it was the same person. What was more, he had paused now, too.

I was considering how I might alert Ramsey when he shocked me by putting his hands on my waist and pulling me close to him, leaning to brush a kiss across my jaw.

"We're being followed," he said into my ear.

"Yes, I just noticed," I replied, blushing up at him as though he really were my new fiancé whispering something scandalous to me on a busy street. "Tall fellow in a gray suit and hat."

"Do you recognize him?"

"No . . . that is, I think he may be the same man who was watching my room from across the street the day I arrived."

He leaned closer in a gesture that, from a distance, might give the impression he was nuzzling my neck. My traitorous body was fooled, too, for my heart began to pound in a manner that had nothing to do with potential danger. "We may as well establish our new relationship."

"Yes." I pressed closer to him, taking comfort in the solid warmth of his body. *It shouldn't be this easy to be near him,* my mind told me.

"In a moment, we'll go to the café down the street and sit for a while. Perhaps he'll grow bored with us."

I nodded.

At last, I pulled back and looked up at him, letting worry cross my features. "I do feel bad about Archie," I said, in a voice loud enough to be overheard if one was listening. After all, I had presented myself publicly as Archie's girl only last night. "But I can't help the way I feel about you."

"He doesn't treat you as you deserve," Ramsey said, one hand reaching up to hold my cheek. My heart gave a little stutter.

When I looked up at his face, he was smiling down at me. It caught me off guard, that smile and the hungry look in his eyes. It was part of the act—wasn't it?—but still I felt it all the way down to my toes.

Luckily, I'm sure we gave the impression of a pair of besotted fools. It was what we had hoped to convey.

Then the moment passed. I took his arm again, and we continued making our way down the street.

CHAPTER TWENTY-TWO

I awoke on my wedding day with butterflies in my stomach and a sinking feeling in my chest.

It was silly, really. I had never been an exceptionally romantic sort of girl. As a child, if I wanted to play with my cousins, there wasn't any chance that we would be cuddling dolls or having tea parties.

There were girls I had played with in the neighborhood, of course, but I didn't remember weddings ever being a part of our play. I had been to only two or three weddings in my entire life.

So there had been no grand dreams of what my wedding would look like one day. I had never imagined silk dresses and lace veils and trailing bouquets of flowers. Even romantic daydreams about fellows I had fancied had never gone as far as planning a wedding.

All this is to say that there should have been no reason I was feeling profoundly depressed at my lackluster wedding day.

"Chin up, old girl," I said into the mirror. "With any luck, this won't be your last wedding day." Then I laughed at my foolishness and felt a little better.

I wore the only suit I had brought with me: a cranberry-colored wool, which wasn't exactly glamorous, but at least it complimented my coloring. I wrangled my hair and put on a small amount of makeup.

There was a tap at my door, and I opened it, expecting Ramsey. Instead, it was Archie who stood there.

"May I come in?" he asked. "It wouldn't do for your former love to be seen lurking in the hallway."

"Yes, come in," I said ungraciously.

I was still angry with Archie. Had he planned this all along? I wondered suddenly. He must have. He certainly could not have forgotten that he was already married. One didn't just forget that sort of thing.

It was, no doubt, some scheme on his part to push Ramsey and me together. He had made no attempts to hide his efforts thus far.

I shot a cold glance at him, but he looked back at me with an expression so guileless I began to wonder if perhaps I was mistaken.

"I've brought you an early wedding present," he said, holding out a box wrapped with a pink bow.

"Thank you," I said, taking the box.

"Silk stockings," he said. "I visited a local shop and told them that I needed a gift for a bride."

"And they suggested you give me stockings?" I said, my brows rising. "Rather a cheeky gift from a young man who is not the groom."

Archie grinned. "Well, the proprietress is French, and I didn't mention I wasn't the groom. I simply said I needed a gift for the loveliest bride in Lisbon."

"You are incorrigible, Archie Blandings."

"I wish I could be at the wedding," he said. "But I am meant to be still nursing a broken heart."

I almost wished he would come with us, but I supposed the trip to the Civil Registry Office would be even more excruciating with Archie making his typically irreverent comments.

He left, and I opened the box. I gasped when I saw that, in addition to the silk stockings, there was a cream-colored satin nightdress edged with exquisite lace. It was beautiful, and it would have done any bride justice on her wedding night. Any bride but me, that was.

I had just finished pulling on the stockings when there was another knock at the door. I shoved the nightgown back into the box and into the wardrobe before I moved to open the door.

Ramsey was standing there, looking handsome in a dark gray suit. I felt nervous and momentarily tongue-tied, like a silly girl on her first date. Only this wasn't a first date. It was much, much more daunting than that.

"Good morning," I said, brazening it out. "I'm nearly ready. If you will come in for a moment . . . ?"

He came inside and closed the door behind us.

"I've brought you a corsage," he said. I hadn't noticed the box in his hand.

"Oh," I said. "Thank you."

"May I pin it on for you?"

"Oh . . . yes."

I moved back to stand before him as he took the corsage from its box. He was being so formal that I wondered if, impossibly, he might also be a bit nervous about our wedding day. But his hands were perfectly steady as he pinned the flowers onto the lapel of my jacket.

As much as I wanted to retreat, I looked up at him. "Thank you. That was thoughtful of you."

"It's the least I could do."

"Are you certain that you . . . that you are willing to do this?" I asked. My voice sounded breathless to my own ears. Perhaps because I could barely breathe.

His gaze was steady. "Yes. I'm sure."

I nodded. Then I went over to the mirror and put on the little hat that matched my suit, a jaunty thing with a bow. Though it wasn't my usual style, Nacy had insisted I bring it, and I was glad of it now. I collected my handbag and then turned back to him.

"Ready?" Ramsey asked.

"Yes."

"Electra." I looked up at him. "Try to remember this is a wedding and not a funeral."

The corner of my mouth tipped up. He was right. There was no reason to be so grim. It was all a part of our mission, and it was worth doing this and much more if it would help Toby.

As we walked out of the lift and into the lobby, I took his arm, looking up at him with a smile. We needed to look happy, after all. His hand rested on my back as he helped me into the taxi, and he moved close in the backseat.

We didn't talk much on the way there. I supposed we were both lost in our own thoughts about how different this marriage day was from any we might have imagined.

Ramsey had been all but engaged before, to a beautiful blond socialite. He'd even bought a ring before they'd called things off. I had to imagine he'd had some picture in his mind of a much more glamorous wedding day than this.

We got out of the taxi, and he leaned close to whisper in my ear. "Remember, this location is being watched, outside and in."

I smiled and reached up to touch his face, gazing intently into his eyes. "I remember," I said softly.

He gave a little nod. His expression might have been described as a mix of tender and smoldering. The look of a man who was both deeply in love and looking forward to his wedding night. I sometimes forgot what a good actor Ramsey could be.

That look did something strange to my stomach, so I was glad when he offered me his elbow. "Shall we go in?"

I took his arm and clung to it, leaning into his side, hoping to appear as eager as he did.

The building was bustling with activity, so it wasn't exactly difficult to take note of at least one of the watching spies, who sat on a bench in the hallway reading a newspaper as though he had nothing better to do.

As was his custom, Ramsey took charge, leading us to a desk and speaking in quick Portuguese to the person behind it. There was a few moments' wait, and then he spoke to someone else before we were finally ushered down another hall and pointed to a door at the end.

We stepped into the registrar's office, and suddenly the import of what we were about to do hit me. Oh, I knew it was temporary and didn't really mean anything. This was not a real wedding. Legal it might be, but it wasn't real. But it still felt like a rather solemn occasion.

Ramsey spoke in English, introducing us and handing over our marriage license. He handed the man something else, I realized—a piece of paper with a note written on it.

I knew what it would say, though I hadn't read it. We were looking for the man in charge of the Lisbon escape route. We were looking, in particular, for an escaped prisoner named Toby McDonnell.

The man read it and looked up at us, then over at his secretary— another of Max Hager's black-haired paramours—who was examining her nails, and shook his head quickly.

"Not safe," he mouthed, his eyes darting to her and then to the door. "We are being watched."

"I believe everything is in order," Ramsey said as he took the piece of paper over to the desk and picked up a pen. "Marry us legally," Ramsey wrote. Then he said aloud, "All the legalities have been properly observed."

Santos nodded, understanding in his gaze. Then he turned to look at me, as though trying to gauge my feelings on the matter. Perhaps he wondered if I had been coerced into it somehow.

I offered him what I hoped was an encouraging smile. He would realize, of course, why we were doing this. But perhaps he would assume we were a little in love, too. Well, he was half right.

I looked over at Ramsey and then back to Senhor Santos. His expression softened, and I thought he had probably seen the love in my eyes. I flushed, embarrassed to have been so transparent.

"The service will be conducted in Portuguese," he said. "Do you require a translator?"

Ramsey looked at me.

"I don't think so," I said with what I hoped was a radiant smile. "I think I should understand it in any language."

"Very good. My secretary will serve as the witness."

She looked up then, gave a short smile. She was bored with the whole thing, I realized. That was good. It meant that we had not raised any alarm bells.

"We will begin," Senhor Santos said, still in English. "Please, take your bride's hand."

Ramsey took my ice-cold hand in his warm one. His eyes met mine, and he gave me a reassuring nod. I nodded back.

The ceremony began.

I'm a bit ashamed to admit my mind wandered wildly during the particulars. I was thinking of Toby, of the moment I would bring him home to Uncle Mick and Nacy. That was the end goal, and this was one step closer.

Then Senhor Santos said something to me in Portuguese. I knew the gist of it: "Do you, Electra Niall McDonnell, take Gabriel Alexander Nicholas Bennett Ramsey to be your lawfully wedded husband?"

"*Sim*. Yes. I do," I said, as I realized how little I knew about Ramsey, including the fact that he had three middle names.

A repetition of the question to Ramsey. In essence: "Do you, Gabriel Alexander Nicholas Bennett Ramsey, take Electra Niall McDonnell to be your lawfully wedded wife?"

"I do." His eyes were on mine, but they were unreadable.

"*O anel, por favor*," Santos said. "The ring."

Ramsey took a ring from his pocket. A simple gold band. I

wondered where he had acquired it. He slipped it on my finger, and I was not surprised to find that it was a perfect fit.

The words blurred together again for a moment, and then I heard the final pronouncement.

No translation necessary. I understood the English equivalent well enough: "I pronounce you husband and wife."

We stared at each other.

"You may kiss your bride, senhor," Santos said in English.

I had avoided thinking about this moment because I'd had no idea how it would play out. Would he decline? But he couldn't even if he wanted to, not with the secretary observing.

I looked up at him for my cue, and he leaned down and pressed a kiss to my lips. It was gentle and brief, but it was enough. That zing of attraction still went through me.

I forced myself not to imagine what it would have been like if the circumstances had been different, if he had been marrying me because he loved me.

Then he smiled down at me and offered me his arm, and I took it.

"*Parabéns, Senhor e Senhora Ramsey,*" the minister said.

Mrs. Ramsey. My stomach dropped at the realization of what we'd done.

Just like that, we were married.

CHAPTER TWENTY-THREE

"*Obrigado*," Ramsey answered for both of us as the ceremony came to an end.

"If you'll come this way, you may sign the register."

I went through the rest of the motions in something of a daze. I couldn't believe we had actually gone through with this.

The man shook Ramsey's hand and then mine, and we were on our way. It was all very businesslike and rather less than romantic. If I had been a real bride, I would have been disappointed at the brevity of it all.

"That wasn't so bad, was it?" Ramsey said as we made our way down the corridor.

He wasn't one to jest on normal occasions, so I had to assume he was speaking lightly to put me at ease. Or perhaps to reiterate that all of this meant nothing and shouldn't be taken too seriously.

"No," I said, matching his tone. "Fairly simple, all things considered. Now I suppose we can be on our way."

We walked toward the front door, but his hand on my arm stopped me in the foyer. He leaned close, as though whispering something romantic in my ear. "Don't forget, we're likely to be watched when we leave here."

I nodded. "I haven't forgotten."

It would be easier for him to feign happiness, I thought uncharitably. I would be expected to be the glowing bride, but he never gave much vent to his emotions anyway. An expressionless face might mean he was perfectly content, and so he needn't put on a show.

I was surprised, then, that, as we exited the building into the bright morning sunlight and I turned to look at him, he looked down at me with a heart-stopping smile. I sometimes forgot how very lovely his smile was, those straight white teeth and the way it made his eyes seem warmer, the violet in the blue more prevalent.

It wasn't hard for me to smile back up at him.

Slipping an arm around my waist, he pulled me close and leaned to press a kiss into my cheek. "He slipped me a note when he shook my hand," Ramsey said.

Despite my interest, I was careful about the look that crossed my features. I had never thought about how difficult it was to play a part for any extended period of time. "What does it say?"

"I haven't opened it yet. I'll wait until we're somewhere I can guarantee not to be seen."

"Yes, of course."

"What would you like to do today?" he asked, leading me down the street.

"Oh, I don't know."

"We'll have to spend the day together, of course," he said.

"Of course. I'm happy to do whatever you like."

As his arm was still around me, I had slipped mine around him as well, and I found it awkward to be this close to him while having this formal conversation. I decided I would have to attempt to lighten the mood.

"Nicholas," I reflected.

He looked down at me inquiringly.

"Your second middle name. Another nod to your birthday?" I had recently learned that Ramsey and his twin sister, Noelle, had been born on Christmas. The connection to St. Nicholas seemed too obvious to have been unintentional.

He grimaced. "Initially, my mother wanted to name me Nicholas. My father, thankfully, talked her out of it."

"Oh, but 'Nicholas and Noelle' would have been darling."

"But, perhaps, a bit too on the nose."

I laughed. "And you should've hated to be called Nicky."

"Yes." Ramsey's aversion to nicknames was another of his quirks.

We talked easily then of his sister as we walked. He told me that he'd had a letter from her before we'd left London and related the latest antics of his twin nephews.

When we had walked down several streets in a leisurely and lovestruck fashion, it became clear that we weren't being followed. He let me go and took the note from his pocket. It seemed I wasn't the only one who could perform a bit of sleight of hand, for I had quick eyes and hadn't noticed the paper pass between the men.

"It's a name and address," he told me. "Carlos Motta."

"Should we go there now?" I asked. I knew he would likely prefer to go alone, but he couldn't very well abandon me on our wedding day. What would people think?

"Since it's fairly certain that we're not being followed, I think that would be wise. We shouldn't waste any time," he said.

Carlos Motta's address was a house at the end of a quiet street at the top of a hill. The climb up flights of winding stairs was rather strenuous, and I had the impression that, despite still recovering from bullet wounds, Ramsey slowed his pace for me more than once.

"Will you wait here until I've made sure all looks well?" Ramsey asked me when we were a few houses away.

"If you wish," I said, still catching my breath. There was no sense in irritating Ramsey now. Besides, it wasn't as though I disobeyed his orders for my own amusement.

Ramsey had expected me to argue, and I saw him search my face for sarcasm. Finding none, he gave a quick nod. "I'll signal to you."

"All right."

I moved to the shade of a small umbrella pine on the other side of the street, and Ramsey went to the front door. He knocked.

For some reason, I suddenly had an uneasy feeling in the pit of my stomach. My Irish intuition? I hoped not. More likely it was just because I was anxious at being so close to finding out where Toby was. I felt as though my cousin was just within reach, and I was frightened that he would somehow slip through my fingers.

There was no answer at the door.

That in itself was not unusual and certainly no cause for alarm. But I felt afraid nonetheless.

Ramsey knocked again, a bit more loudly this time. I couldn't help but think that this method lacked finesse. If Carlos Motta were at all nervous about being discovered assisting POWs through the escape line, a pounding at his door was not likely to put him at ease.

Another period of waiting followed by another bout of knocking. I stood where I was, clenching my teeth. I wanted nothing more than to hurry to Ramsey's side, but I had told him I would wait. And so wait I did.

A moment later, he looked over his shoulder at me. His brows rose ever so slightly, and I took this as signal enough.

"You have a rather officious knock," I said as I reached him, unable to keep the critique to myself.

Ramsey frowned at me.

"Perhaps he's worried you might be an enemy agent, come to question him," I said. "I wouldn't answer the door either, in that case."

"Foreign agents are not allowed to question him in neutral Portugal."

I rolled my eyes. "Since when has that stopped them from do-ing anything?"

Just on the off chance it might be open, I turned the door han-dle. It was locked.

Looking around, I saw the windows to the right of the door. From here I could see that the curtains were pulled back enough to look in. Moving past Ramsey, I went to the window. I went up on my toes and shielded my eyes from the glare of the light on the glass as I looked inside. It was all rather untidy. No, not untidy. It had been ransacked like Estrada's flat. Furniture was overturned, and . . .

"Electra—" Ramsey began.

But just then I took a quick step away from the glass, backing directly into him.

His hands on my shoulders steadied me. "What is it?"

I turned to look up at him. "There's . . . there's a body inside."

Ramsey swore beneath his breath. He cast a quick look around, but the neighborhood seemed quiet. From a distant street we could hear children shouting and, farther away, the honking of cars and boat horns.

On this street, nothing moved but the soft wind in the branches of the trees. There were, however, several houses with windows that faced in this direction. Any number of eyes might be observing us, even now.

"Can you get me in?" Ramsey asked in a low voice.

I nodded.

"Let's try the back of the house."

I made my way around the building, Ramsey close behind me, and I tried not to feel despair at another lead lost. More than that, another life lost. Carlos Motta, if it were he lying dead inside his house, was another name on the exponentially increasing list of casualties of this war.

There was no door at the back of the house. There were, how-ever, two windows, and one of them was opened halfway.

Ramsey put his hands against the glass and pushed up. The window didn't budge. He tried again, but it still didn't move. I could see the muscles of his arms bulging beneath his jacket, and if the window could withstand them, it was good and stuck.

"Stand back. I'll break it," he said.

"No," I said, grabbing his arm. "It'll be too loud. I can fit through. Lift me up."

"Electra."

I looked up at him.

"I'd rather you didn't go inside."

My lips parted to argue.

"You've seen enough," he said gently. "More than enough."

It was true that the last time we'd come across a dead body together had been rather hard on me. I felt that, no matter how long this war lasted, I could never accustom myself to it. I didn't know how men on the battlefield were able to do so, couldn't fathom what was required of them on a daily basis.

All this flashed through my mind in an instant, but I also knew that we didn't have many options. If I broke in through the front door, we might be seen by any number of people. There was nothing to say that whoever had killed Carlos Motta wasn't waiting in one of the nearby houses now.

"It doesn't matter," I said, shaking my head. "We need to get inside, and you're certainly not going to fit. Lift me up. Or . . . perhaps you'd better not, with your injuries. Perhaps I can—"

My words were cut off as his hands at my waist lifted me up toward the window. I gasped and grabbed the sill.

My balance regained, I slid my torso through the crack and then wiggled my hips and bottom through, which was a bit tighter of a squeeze. Ramsey's hands slid down my legs as he helped to hoist me, and I was glad of Archie's gift of new silk stockings.

This window was in the bathroom, and I landed in a heap on the tiled floor, narrowly missing banging my head on the edge of the bathtub and bumping my knee on one of its claw feet. I hurriedly checked my stocking and saw there was no harm done. I breathed a sigh of relief.

I stood up, smoothing out my skirt, and looked out the window at Ramsey. "I'll let you in the front door," I told him.

He nodded and turned to come back around the house.

I went out of the bathroom and down a narrow hallway toward the front room. I steeled myself as I walked past the prone body on the sitting room floor. I didn't look too closely at him, not yet.

I unlocked the front door, and Ramsey slipped quickly inside the house. He moved to the window through which I had first glimpsed the body and pulled the curtains all the way closed. Then he picked up a lamp, which had been knocked off a table, set it upright, and switched it on.

I felt the blood drain from my face as I looked down at the man on the floor. He had been beaten, his face bruised and bloody. Blood splattered the rug around him, and there was foam on his lips.

I pressed my own lips together, reining in my emotions.

"Will you search the house, Electra?" Ramsey asked. "Check the other rooms, see if you can find any hiding places that whoever already searched might have missed."

I nodded. I knew he was trying to get me out of the room, but I wasn't going to argue the point.

I turned and went back down the little hall. As I had done at Estrada's flat, I made a quick search of the rooms. They'd been thoroughly tossed. Still, I looked in the usual places: under the mattress, behind pictures on the walls, checking for hidden compartments in drawers. There was nothing.

Carlos Motta had, by all appearances, lived a simple and quiet life, and there were few possessions to look through. I didn't allow myself to think about the fact that the owner of these possessions was lying dead in the next room.

My search completed, I went back into the sitting room. Ramsey was crouched beside the body, apparently going through his pockets.

He looked up and rose when I entered. "Anything?"

I shook my head. "If there was anything here, they must have found it."

"Something tells me Motta was not the type of man who would have kept important information in the house. He was prepared for something of this kind to happen."

"What makes you think so?"

He nodded toward an overturned chair with ropes around it. "They were trying to tie him up, to continue their interrogation. But he slipped out of their grasp and was able to get to his cyanide capsules."

I'd seen the effects of cyanide capsules once before. The foam on Motta's lips was consistent with my experience of them.

I swallowed down the lump in my throat, averting my eyes. He'd been forced to choose death by poison to being interrogated and risking giving up the escapees and their route to the Nazis. At least it had been quick.

"Come on," Ramsey said, coming to my side and gently turning me toward the door. "Let's go."

It was near the door that I noticed it. A footprint in blood on the wooden floorboard. I stopped.

"That's the same footprint I saw at Estrada's flat," I said. "It was in flour there, but I'm certain it's the same."

Ramsey leaned down to get a better look. "Then it seems someone is on the same trail as we are. And right now, it looks like we're behind."

CHAPTER TWENTY-FOUR

We exited the house and walked away as quickly as we could without drawing notice.

Ramsey led me down several sets of stairs and through a shady courtyard and a series of narrow alleyways until we reached a public garden, where a good many people were out walking, enjoying the afternoon sunshine. Here, he slowed our pace, took my hand, and slid it back through his arm.

"Are you all right?" he asked.

"Yes," I answered automatically.

My head was still swimming.

Fortunately for Toby and others on the escape route, Motta, in an act of true heroism, had sacrificed himself before the information could be shared with the wrong people. Unfortunately for us, we were no closer to discovering Toby's possible location.

Not only that, but, though it might be of little importance in the greater scheme of things, I couldn't help thinking that Ramsey and I had been pushed into marriage for no reason. We'd gotten Motta's name, but all for nothing.

I was certain he must be thinking the same thing, and the idea mortified me, as though he might suspect I had done it on purpose.

I quickly refocused my thoughts to more immediate matters, but the uncomfortable sensation was there in the back of my mind.

"We need to go out tonight," Ramsey said after a long silence. "To keep up pretenses. I know you'd prefer not to, but it will be expected."

I nodded. "All right."

He drew me suddenly toward a bench, and I sat, glad to be off my wobbly legs. He slid an arm along the back of the bench, shifting slightly toward me, giving our conversation the appearance of intimacy to anyone who happened to pass.

"We'll find your cousin," he said.

I looked up at him. He was closer than I had expected. His eyes were clear and tinged with lavender in the bright afternoon light.

He reached over and covered my hands, which I hadn't realized were clenched together in my lap.

"Don't fly into a rage with me, Electra, but I must ask you something."

"Yes?"

"Do you need to go home?"

My lips parted, and I instinctively tried to pull my hands away, but his grip on them was firm.

"Listen to me for a moment," he said. "I know you want to help, and I know your skills are useful. But I also know this is taking a toll on you."

"It's taking a toll on all of us," I said sharply. "This is war. None of us will be the same once it's over."

"I know," he said. His voice was low and calm. The hand that had rested on the back of the bench was on my shoulder now. "But you have been through a lot in the past few months. You'll forgive me for saying so, but you're still losing weight, and, if I had to guess, you're not sleeping well either."

I couldn't deny it, but what did that matter when Toby was

somewhere between here and France, perhaps sleeping in the snow atop the Pyrenees with nothing to eat?

"Perhaps you're too close to this, Electra," he said. "If you need to go home, I will stay here and find your cousin."

"I'm not going home." I looked directly into his eyes. "You can't make me. I'm working for Archie, not for you."

His gaze, which had been open and warm a moment ago, was suddenly shuttered. Then he gave a short nod. "You're right. I can't make you."

I realized I had misstepped badly. He had been trying to be kind, to protect me. I opened my mouth to apologize, but it was too late.

He released me suddenly and rose to his feet, his features impassive. "We'd better start back."

We went back to the hotel to change for dinner.

Ramsey and I exchanged a few commonplaces on the way there, observations about the scenery, but there was a wall between us now. And I'd put it there.

I couldn't seem to find the words to apologize as he escorted me to the door of my room. Apologies had never come easy for me given how much I hated to be wrong.

"I'll have my things moved to your room while we're out to dinner," he told me in the hallway, loud enough that anyone listening in a nearby room might hear. Then he leaned to press a kiss against the corner of my mouth.

"I'll see you soon, darling," he murmured.

Then he went into his own room to change. I was relieved that we had bypassed the awkwardness of having to pretend to be entering the same room. That would come later, of course.

I took a cool bath and then went to the wardrobe and chose my prettiest gown. It was, after all, my wedding day. This one was secondhand, but Nacy had worked wonders on it. It was dark blue velvet with silver spangles. I'd even found a large silver barrette with faux diamonds to adorn my hair. I had just finished my makeup and spritzed myself with perfume when there was a tap at my door.

I opened it to find Ramsey standing there, resplendent in his black evening wear.

His eyes swept over me. "You look lovely," he said. I felt a momentary swell of pleasure and then saw a couple passing down the hallway behind him. So playacting was called for.

"Thank you," I said brightly. "I did my best to match the handsomest husband in Lisbon."

One of his brows rose. "Only in Lisbon?"

I laughed as he reached out to pull the door closed behind me. By necessity, I stepped forward and was pressed against him. I looked up into his face.

Then the lift dinged, the couple gone, and the flirtatious look on Ramsey's face vanished. He offered me his arm, but it was stiff beneath my hand.

We went to dinner at a popular nightclub. I did my best to eat, as I could feel Ramsey's eyes on me throughout the meal. It was clear from his comments today that he'd noticed my lack of appetite and the accompanying weight loss. He'd admitted he couldn't force me to go home, but I didn't want him to think I was weak or unable to stand up to the rigors of espionage.

Although, in the darkest part of my mind, I sometimes wondered if I was. I felt so very on edge. I was not certain I had truly relaxed in a month. At the moment, I felt perilously close to bursting into tears.

There was a band and a large dance floor at the center of the room, and couples at the tables all around us got up to dance.

"Will you dance with me?" he asked, when we had finished eating.

"Of course," I said, recognizing the now-familiar feeling of that bright, brittle smile on my lips.

He came to pull back my chair. Then he took my hand in his and led me to the dance floor.

We faced each other, his arm went around me, and I stepped closer to him as the music began.

As might be expected of newlyweds, he held me close, and I rested my head against his shoulder as we moved around the floor. As uncomfortable as it was, it was better than looking into his eyes.

I tried not to think of the solid warmth of his body pressed against me, of the smell of his soap and aftershave, the feel of his hand on my back. Some part of me wanted to enjoy these things, to savor this moment—even to ponder, perhaps, what it might have been like to really be his wife. But the wiser part of me knew it was better not to give in to those emotions. Nothing good would come of it.

"Let's call it an early night, shall we?" he said when the song had finished.

We went back to the hotel and up the lift in silence.

His arm moved around my waist, and we walked down the hallway together.

"I'll have to come into your room with you, of course," he said in a low voice.

"Of course," I replied.

I handed him the key, and he opened the door, ushering me inside with a hand low on my back.

The door clicked shut behind us, and we were alone in my bedroom. Man and wife.

As he'd requested, they'd moved his things into my room while we'd been out. It was best, he said, that everyone, from other guests to the maids, believe our ploy. I supposed he would also make his bed each morning before the maids arrived.

Annoyingly, I could feel myself flushing.

"I'll collect what I need to bring back to my room, if I may," he said.

"Of course."

He went into the bathroom, and I saw him pick up the small case that likely contained his toiletries. It rested near my makeup bag. I'd left things scattered across the counter, and I felt embarrassed about the mess.

I went over to the wardrobe and opened it. His things were neatly hung beside mine. It all felt so very intimate.

He came to the wardrobe and began to remove a few things, and I walked over to the balcony windows and looked out. The air felt heavy.

"I'm glad everything went well today," he said.

I turned to look at him, offered him a smile. "So am I."

He moved toward the door to his room then, but I stepped into his path. "Ramsey."

He stopped, looked down at me.

"I . . . I wanted to say . . ." I swallowed my nervousness. "I . . . want to thank you for . . . for what you said today. It was kind of you to consider my feelings, and, though I do want to stay, I . . . I didn't mean to . . . offend you." There. As inarticulate as it was, it was out, at least.

"I don't doubt your capability," he said. "Never that."

"I know."

His eyes met mine and held for what felt like a long time. Then, his personal effects in one hand, he held out the other hand toward me. I slipped mine into it, and he squeezed my fingers, which, I realized, had gone cold.

"Good night, Electra," he said.

"Good night, Ramsey."

He went into his room and closed the door behind him.

I let out a breath it felt like I'd been holding all day. I was glad that it was over, but there was also a strange feeling of disappointment.

I looked at the door between our rooms. It was strange to think of him on the other side of it, presumably preparing for bed. It would do no good to dwell on the thought.

I washed up and cleaned my teeth, then pulled on my comfortable pajamas and got into bed.

Switching off the lights, I lay listening to the sounds of the traffic on the street outside. Anyone watching my room from the street would assume that the newlyweds had retired early to bed.

I held up my hand. My wedding ring glinted in the dim light through the crack in the curtains.

Mrs. Electra Ramsey.

I remembered suddenly the first time I'd gone to meet Ramsey at a pub to prepare for a job. I'd wondered then, in my initial dislike of him, what kind of woman would willingly tie herself to such a man. Ah, the twists of fate.

I turned over, pulling the blankets tight around me, and fell asleep alone on my wedding night.

CHAPTER TWENTY-FIVE

Ramsey tapped on the adjoining door the next morning before I was dressed.

I quickly pulled on my robe and went to open it.

"Good morning," he said, his eyes making a quick sweep of me. "I'm sorry. I've clearly knocked too early."

"I slept later than I intended," I said. In truth, I'd slept very little, but there was no use telling him that.

"Well, no rush," he said, no doubt taking in the dark circles around my eyes. "Tap on my door when you're ready, and we can go out together."

I nodded.

Twenty minutes later, my face powdered, we exited my room together. A man was walking down the hallway as we came out, and I felt myself blush.

It was because I was not accustomed to leaving my room with a man, but if the stranger happened to be a spy, perhaps he would attribute my blush to being a result of my wedding night. The thought made my blush deepen.

I knew Ramsey would notice if I looked at him, so I kept my eyes trained on the end of the hallway as we walked toward the lift.

There were people on the lift when the doors opened, so Ramsey slipped an arm around me to usher me in. He didn't remove it as the lift began to move.

I knew that we had discussed appearing comfortable with each other in public, but having him constantly touching me in this way would take some getting used to. He was usually so reserved that these little displays of affection and husbandly possessiveness continued to catch me off guard.

We walked into the lobby, and I smiled up at him.

"What are we doing today?" I asked.

"A bit of sightseeing," he said. "If we spend the morning playing tourist, anyone following us will, hopefully, lose interest in our movements."

I felt both excited and dismayed at the idea of an entire day with nothing to do but play the blushing bride. At least I had the blushing part down.

We spent the day at the Museu Nacional de Arte Antiga, and I found I was able to lose myself in the art. Ramsey, too, seemed fairly relaxed. We ambled through the long galleries, talking easily about the paintings. In the afternoon, we walked through the beautiful gardens with a view of the river below. Lisbon was a fascinating city, and I thought I could spend a month here and not even brush the surface.

Ramsey was solicitous and attentive, though he didn't show much overt affection, for which I was grateful. By the time we went to dinner, I had found myself relaxing in his company once again. When he let his guard down a bit, he was very good company—intelligent, well-informed, and even funny on occasion.

We went back to the hotel after dinner. We were playing newlyweds, after all.

"You never heard from Archie today?" I asked when we were back in my room. I didn't see how he could have, as we hadn't been apart except for when we'd changed for dinner. But I wouldn't put it past Ramsey and Archie to communicate in some secret way.

"No," Ramsey said. "I believe he's letting us have our honeymoon."

It was just the sort of phrase to make me blush, and Ramsey knew it. I stubbornly met his gaze, even as I felt the flush creeping up.

"What can we do now that Carlos Motta is dead? There must be something besides just waiting and hoping that Toby finds his way to Lisbon. Even if he does make it here, how will we know?"

"Electra," Ramsey said.

There was something about the way he said my name that always drew my focus. Perhaps it was just that no one else called me Electra, but it felt like more than that. When he said my name, I felt as if all my attention were drawn to him, as if he caressed me with the word. I flushed again at this thought.

"Don't worry about it tonight," he said. "Blandings is working on it. And you know he's got a wily mind."

I did indeed. I was still not entirely certain he hadn't orchestrated this false marriage between Ramsey and me from the start.

I drew in a breath and nodded. "I know. I trust Archie. I'm sure he'll think of something."

We stood there for a long moment. And then Ramsey said, "I suppose I'll wish you good night, then."

I nodded again. The silence felt weighted suddenly.

He stood there for just a few seconds longer. Then he gave me a half smile and turned and went into his room. He closed the door behind him, and the atmosphere of unnamed tension went with him, leaving a strange emptiness in its place.

I rubbed a hand across my face. This was dreadful. I was so aware of him all the time; it was almost physically painful. If he was in the room, it was as if all of my senses focused on him, no matter what my brain told them to do. I would catch myself sitting tense, jaw clenched, stomach tight. If this was love, I might have been better off without it.

With a sigh, I went to take a bath and prepare for bed.

Standing in my towel sometime later, I realized belatedly that all my pajamas had been in the laundry I'd sent out today, and now I had nothing to wear to bed.

No, I realized suddenly. That wasn't quite accurate. I did have something.

I went to the wardrobe and pulled out the box I'd shoved into the back corner. It contained the part of Archie's wedding gift I had never intended to use: the satin-and-lace nightgown that had been meant for a bride. Well, there was no husband present to enjoy it, but it might as well be put to good use.

I returned the towel to the bathroom and slipped on the nightgown. Then I went back out into my room and surveyed myself in the large mirror.

If this were really my honeymoon, I would be very pleased with the result. It fit like a glove, the thin ivory satin clinging to my figure like I'd been doused in moonlight. The bodice was cut shockingly low, a sweep of lace along the edge of the neckline making only a half-hearted gesture toward modesty.

The cool satin slid against my legs as I made my way toward the bed. The nightgown was a bit too long, and I held up the hem with one hand so I wouldn't trip. All things considered, my flannel pajamas were much preferable.

I got into bed, not even bothering to pull the myriad pins from my hair. I was exhausted, and it felt like too much effort.

Switching off the light, I lay back against the pillows and stared at the ceiling, willing myself to drift off. I was tired all the time. Why was it, then, that it was so very difficult to sleep?

There was a clock in the room, and I listened to it ticking for perhaps half an hour before I finally acknowledged that it was useless.

With a sigh, I reached out and turned on the lamp. I wasn't going to fall asleep anytime soon, so I might as well get up and have another look through my mythology book.

As I got out of bed, one foot tangled in the long skirt of the nightgown, and I toppled forward. My free foot hit the floor with a thud and skidded forward, throwing me off-balance. Grasping for purchase, I reached out and caught the edge of the little table across from the bed. Unfortunately, this was the table that held the chinoiserie vase, and, rather than steadying me, it tilted as I grabbed it.

In slow motion, I watched the vase slide off the polished surface and hit the floor with a tremendous crash and the shattering of glass even as I landed ungracefully on one knee beside the toppled table. Blast this ridiculous nightgown.

It was then the door between my room and Ramsey's burst open, and he appeared in the doorway. The fact that he was shirtless distracted me for just a moment from noticing the gun in his hand.

Our eyes met, and we stared at each other for what felt like rather a long time.

"Just me being clumsy," I said as breezily as I could manage. "But thank you for coming to my rescue."

I expected him to return to his darkened bedroom and close the door behind him. Instead, he came wordlessly into the room, set the gun down on the coffee table, and moved to where I knelt picking up pieces of porcelain.

"Did you cut yourself?" he asked, crouching down to help me. "No."

In weighted silence, we finished picking up the broken chunks of vase and putting them atop the table for housekeeping to take away in the morning. I wondered just how much I would owe Archie to repay the hotel for this bit of vandalism.

Our task finished, Ramsey rose and offered a hand to help me up. I took it and stood. "Thank you for your help."

For the first time since he'd burst into the room, I allowed myself to look at his chest, at the scars from the bullets he'd taken in Sunderland what seemed like eons ago but had actually been only four months. Those jagged white marks on his otherwise flawless skin were a remnant of violence he would carry with him for the rest of his life.

He hadn't answered me, and I realized suddenly that his eyes were moving slowly over me, too, taking notice of the rather provocative satin nightgown.

With effort, it seemed, he pulled his eyes back up to mine. "Where did you get that?"

His tone was cool, and it set my back up. "Why?"

"It's . . . not the sort of thing you usually wear." He had, it was true, seen me in my tatty pajamas more than once, but it was impolite of him to notice.

I shrugged. "It's new."

I was fighting down the urge to turn and pull on a robe to cover myself. The nightgown left very little to the imagination, and Ramsey didn't seem to approve. But he had, after all, charged into *my* bedroom, and I could wear what I liked. Besides, he wasn't exactly covered to the neck himself.

"That's handmade French lace," he said. "You didn't get it in London. Not recently."

I failed to understand his preoccupation with the nightgown. "Archie gave it to me."

I realized as I said the words how it would sound, even as I understood what he had been getting at with his questions. I saw the conclusion he had jumped to cross his eyes in a flash of silver.

"French lingerie," he said tersely. "And what does he expect you to give him in return?"

I ought to have denied this baseless accusation, put a stop to this conversation, but I was getting angry, and that never boded well for doing the rational thing. My chin tipped up. "I don't see how that's any of your business."

I saw the anger cross his face but ignored it.

"Thank you for your assistance with the vase. Good night, Major."

I turned away from him, but he caught my arm and turned me back to face him.

"Look. We've got to have this out. Whatever is between us—"

I jerked my arm from his grasp. So he wanted to have this conversation, did he? Well, so be it.

"There is nothing between us," I said. "I'm merely an obligation. You said so yourself. You made your indifference very clear in London and ever since you've been here."

"Indifference?" His voice had gone tight, and his eyes blazed. I realized belatedly I had crossed some sort of line.

He stepped closer, and I felt that familiar sizzle of heat dance across the space between us. My skin prickled.

"The last thing I am is indifferent to you, Electra. As hard as I have tried to be, you make it impossible."

My lips parted, but I could think of nothing to say. I didn't even know if this was a compliment or an accusation.

"Do you know how difficult this has been for me? To watch Blandings dance attendance on you, touch you . . . kiss you?"

"No," I said, finding my voice. "I don't know. I only know that you dismissed me from your work and from your life without a second thought. So I don't see why it should make one bit of difference to you what I do with Archie or with anyone else!"

He swore savagely. "I told you then that you were a distraction to me, and it was true." His eyes moved over my face, lingered momentarily on my mouth, then came back up to mine. "It's still true. Sometimes I can barely think straight for wanting you."

The admission was like a grenade dropped in the space between us, a shattering blast followed by a moment of ringing silence. We stared at each other.

We were on a precipice. Whatever we did now would decide

things once and for all. I weighed the possible consequences, but only momentarily. I didn't want to fight my attraction to him anymore. And, anyway, his ring was on my finger. It was all proper. Legally, morally, emotionally. I had my bases covered, as the Yanks might say. And so I decided to push us over the edge.

"Then perhaps you'd better," I said.

A frown rippled across his handsome brow. "I'd better what?"

I met his gaze, but my voice came out in a whisper. "Have me."

He blinked, went completely still. Even his eyes were momentarily blank. In an unprecedented event, I'd thrown Major Gabriel Ramsey off-balance.

Then his jaw clenched and he drew in a slow breath, and I knew he was mustering his defenses.

"We're practically alone here in Lisbon," I said softly, forging ahead. "No one will know . . ."

"I . . . don't think . . ." he began. "That isn't . . ." But he was shifting ever so slightly closer, as though his body were moving of its own accord.

"No promises. No expectations. When we get back to London, you don't ever have to see me again." I closed the last gap so that I was pressed against him, the warmth of his skin seeping through my thin nightgown. I looked up to him, our mouths inches apart. "But we may as well have tonight."

His hands remained at his sides, not touching me.

"Electra . . ." His voice was rough, his body taut with tension. "My self-control is not limitless."

"I'm very glad to hear it." I went up on my toes, slid my arms around his neck, and pressed my mouth to his.

The kiss was like a match to kerosene. I expected one lingering moment of hesitation on his part, one final effort to resist me, but there was none. His arms went instantly around me, pulling me hard against him. I felt his resistance dissolve, literally felt the shift in his body as he decided he, too, was tired of fighting.

We'd shared kisses before, each of them passionate and exhilarating, but this one was in an entirely different class altogether. It was urgent, almost frantic, both of us giving vent to the pent-up desire and frustration we had felt over the past weeks.

His hands slid over the satin of my nightgown, caressing, grasping, pulling me closer. I clung to him, felt almost drugged with passion, my head dizzy with the intensity of my feelings for him.

He kissed my jaw, my neck, my shoulder. His fingers tangled in my curls, pulling out the pins. I heard the faint ping of each of them as they hit the floor.

"I've had dreams about your hair," he murmured against my neck.

I gave a little gasp, both at the thrill of the words and at the sensation of his warm breath on my sensitive skin.

The pins disposed of, he kissed me again, hands in my hair, a bit more gently this time but no less intensely. If it were possible for human beings to melt, I would have been a puddle on the floor.

Then, suddenly, he pulled back, took my face in his hands as he looked down at me, both of us gasping for breath. I was afraid he was going to tell me we must stop, until I saw the look on his face. He didn't want to stop this madness any more than I did—perhaps even less. But even in this, there was that last remnant of self-possession that held him in check.

His eyes, twilight blue in the dimness of the room, searched mine. "You're sure?"

I met his gaze, not an ounce of uncertainty in me. "Yes, Gabriel. I'm sure."

As he swept me up into his arms and carried me to the bed, I thought how immeasurably glad I was that I'd put on this satin nightgown rather than my ragged flannel pajamas.

After that, I did very little thinking at all.

CHAPTER TWENTY-SIX

I awoke slowly, just before dawn. The room was pale gray, the furniture cloaked in shadows. I had been in a deep sleep, and it was a moment before full consciousness came back to me.

And then I remembered that Ramsey was in the bed beside me.

I turned my head on the pillow to look at him. He was still asleep. He lay on his side, facing me, his posture and expression relaxed, peaceful.

I lay very still, trying not to wake him up. I wanted a few minutes to think things over.

If I had told myself six months ago that this would happen, I'd have thought myself barmy.

But here we were. We had consummated our pretend marriage. It was rather surreal.

The first emotion I searched for was regret, and I was both relieved and unsurprised to find that there was none. In fact, I was terribly glad it had happened. After all, I was in love with him. Even if we went our separate ways after this, at least I would have the wonderful memories of last night to comfort me.

I turned to look at him again and found that he was awake. Our eyes met, and I could feel the flush creep up my cheeks.

What was he thinking? I wondered. Was he regretting what had happened? I had to imagine he was. It was unlike him to succumb to temptation. However, I searched his gaze and could find nothing telling.

He reached out and twisted a lock of my hair around his finger. "You're very beautiful, Electra."

My flush deepened, but I was pleased at the compliment. "Thank you. You're not too shabby yourself."

The corner of his mouth tipped up, and I felt my heart flip as I realized this was a vast understatement. His always-smooth hair was mussed and his jaw had begun to bristle with stubble, and he had never looked so handsome.

He propped himself up on one elbow then and leaned to kiss me. It was disappointingly brief, and then he broke the romance of the moment by looking down at me and cutting straight to the point. "Would you like to discuss this now or later?"

I sighed, though I smiled a little at how typically Ramsey this was. "Perhaps . . . perhaps it might wait until we have some clothes on."

One of his brows flicked upward. "Probably the wisest course of action. I'll call down for some breakfast."

He got up from the bed and went into his room, taking the gun he'd set on the table last night with him. I rose quickly and shrugged into my robe, tying the belt around my waist.

I went over to the mirror and saw that my hair was in astounding disarray. I ran my fingers through it, calming the worst of the tangles, and left it hanging down around my shoulders.

Ramsey came back a few minutes later with his own robe on.

Our eyes met, and I felt my ridiculous blush creeping up again. This was all very awkward, but I hoped, when we discussed it, I could make it plain to him that I wasn't the least bit sorry it had happened, nor did I expect anything in the way of a lasting commitment from him.

"Tea with sugar, I know, but what do you want to eat?" he asked. "Sweet or savory? Never mind. I'll have some of each sent up."

I smiled. "All right." I was actually hungry this morning.

He moved toward the telephone, but it began to ring before he got to it.

We looked at each other. It could be the hotel calling for some reason, but it was most likely Archie. Ramsey could not answer my telephone at this time of morning.

I moved and picked up the telephone. "Hello?"

"Hello, Ellie. I'm sorry it's so early, but I was wondering . . . could I come up for a few minutes?"

I looked at Ramsey. "Well, I'm not . . . quite dressed, but if you give me a few minutes . . ."

Ramsey nodded, picked up his discarded trousers from the night before, and turned toward his own room.

"Yes, of course," Archie said. "I'm sorry. I know it's early, but it's rather urgent."

"Oh, yes, of course. Perhaps fifteen minutes?"

"Let's make it half an hour. Will that be enough time?"

"Yes. See you then."

He rang off, and Ramsey appeared back in the doorway.

"Half an hour," I said.

He nodded. Then his own telephone rang. No doubt Archie was calling him as well.

I turned, quickly grabbed clothes from the wardrobe, and went into the bathroom to bathe and change.

When Archie knocked on my door thirty minutes later, I was ready for him. The bed was made, my hairpins had been collected from the floor, and the door between my room and Ramsey's was closed. I assumed he would come over once he heard Archie's knock.

There was, of course, no real reason why we should hide what had happened from Archie, but it wasn't something I particularly wanted to advertise, especially not when I was still trying to parse through it all myself.

"Good morning," Archie said when I opened the door. "Again, I'm sorry to be here so early, but I've had some news."

I heard the hallway door to Ramsey's room open, and then he was there behind Archie.

"Good morning, Blandings," he said. "Electra."

"Good morning," I said, unable to meet his eyes. "Won't you both come in? Should I have some coffee sent up for you?"

"I took the liberty," Ramsey said.

"Then come and sit down." I led the way to the sitting area and sat on the sofa. Ramsey took the seat beside me, and Archie took the chair across from me.

Suddenly, I realized something was off. Archie's normally cheerful expression was muted, and there was something tense in his posture. I looked at Ramsey, whose face was expressionless.

My heart sank. "What is it?"

"Well, we may have . . . to change plans a bit," Archie said. "There has been a new development that may . . . alter things."

He was hiding something. That much was clear from this vague talk, which explained exactly nothing.

"There's something you aren't telling me," I said. "Something to do with Toby."

A look passed between the two men.

"I've had some intelligence," Archie said. The expression on his face made my stomach drop. It was the sort of look one uses to prepare someone for bad news, the signal that eases the hearer into something they don't want to hear.

"We intercepted a communiqué from some known Gestapo agents in Lisbon," he said. "There was a group of three men stopped by German agents as they reached the border. Two of them were captured and taken to a secondary location to be interrogated before being shipped to Germany."

"And the third?" I asked, my voice coming out in a strained whisper.

Archie's eyes met mine. I saw him draw in a breath, square his shoulders. "The third was killed. I'm so sorry, Ellie, but we have reason to believe it was your cousin."

My entire body went cold, like I had been doused suddenly in ice water.

I tried to make sense of what Archie was saying, but it was as though the thought were slippery and my mind could not find purchase.

Toby was dead? Sweet, funny Toby was gone, and this had all been for naught.

I felt lightheaded, and for just a moment my vision swam. I had told myself that I was prepared for his death—but that was before I had been given hope. Now it had been snatched away so suddenly, I felt as though the ground were shifting beneath me.

Ramsey was at my side, his hand on my arm.

I didn't look at him. I didn't feel as though I could move. I felt as if I were on the verge of shattering, like the china doll I had once accused him of treating me like.

"I'm so sorry, Ellie," Archie said again, from what seemed to be very far away.

I sat, trying to gather my thoughts. I couldn't seem to latch on to anything. The war had been terrible, terrifying in so many ways. But I understood now that I had not experienced real loss. That I had been woefully unprepared for it.

There was a knock on the door.

"That will be the tea," Ramsey said to Archie.

Archie went to answer the door, and I tried to pull myself together. Ramsey sat close beside me. I realized he was holding my hand.

The waiter pushed the tray into the room, but I barely heard his exchanges with Archie or the following exchange Archie had with Ramsey.

"Drink this," Ramsey said, handing me a little glass filled with amber liquid. This wasn't tea. It was brandy. They'd had a drink prepared to soften the blow.

"I don't want it," I said, trying to hand the glass back to him.

"Drink it, Electra," he said gently but firmly.

I took a sip, the liquid burning its way down my throat and making my eyes water. I gave a little cough.

Then Archie was setting a saucer and cup of steaming tea on the table in front of me. I watched the steam waft up for a long moment as the brandy continued burning its way into my blood.

It was wretched, especially at eight o'clock in the morning on an empty stomach. It did seem, however, to clear some of the fog away from my head.

How could it be that we had done all this work, come so far, only to lose Toby at the last minute? It just didn't seem possible.

"Are you certain?" I asked Archie. I could hear the pleading note in my voice as I asked him, and I felt sorry for him when I saw the look of sympathy cross his face.

"Fairly certain. I'm so sorry, Ellie."

"Where . . . where were the other men taken?" I asked. If we could find them, perhaps they could tell us something about Toby, at least. I could take home some news, other than this, to give Uncle Mick and Nacy.

"We don't know as of yet," Archie said. "I'm trying to find out, but the whole affair has been kept pretty dark. The Germans don't want it known in official circles that they're operating to this extent on Portuguese soil."

"We'll discuss that later," Ramsey said.

I looked down again at the cup of tea on the table. I thought of taking a sip to get the stringent taste of the brandy out of my mouth.

But I didn't want tea. I just wanted to be alone so I could grieve. If I was going to break into pieces, I wanted to do it privately.

"I'm going to take my leave, so you can have some time to . . .

be alone," Archie said, as if I had voiced my thoughts aloud. "If you need anything, you have only to ring me. Otherwise, I'll come back tomorrow. All right?"

I nodded. "Yes. Thank you, Archie."

He came to where I sat and placed a hand on my shoulder. Then he left.

Ramsey and I were alone. I couldn't believe the atmosphere felt so vastly different in the space of half an hour.

"I thought we would get him back," I said numbly. "I really believed it."

"I'm sorry, Electra," Ramsey said in a low voice. He was still sitting beside me, my hand clasped in his.

I had wanted to be alone, but I knew suddenly that I was drawing an immeasurable amount of strength from his warm, solid presence beside me.

"Drink a little tea," he said, reaching to lift the saucer from the table.

I took it from him and took a sip of the tea. It was hot and sweet. So familiar.

I didn't even know I was crying until my hands began to shake, and Ramsey took the cup and saucer from my hands and put them back on the table.

"I'm sorry," I whispered, wiping at my tears. I could feel myself on a steep decline into sorrow, and I didn't think I could stop it.

"It's all right," he said gently. "You don't always have to be strong."

Then he drew me into his arms and held me while I wept.

CHAPTER TWENTY-SEVEN

When I finished crying, I had a cup of tea and a piece of toast, at Ramsey's insistence, and then we went for a walk.

The sky was cloudy, and it looked like it might rain, which seemed appropriate. The beauty of the city felt shrouded in shadow now that Toby was gone. It was as though a lamp had been switched off somewhere inside of me. I thought I had known loss. I'd grown up without parents, after all.

But my parents were an old loss, a scar healed over. Losing Toby was a sharp pain, a gaping wound in my chest.

Ramsey held my hand as we walked. It played into the narrative of our being newlyweds, but I knew it was more than that.

After what had happened last night, we no longer had to pretend to each other that there wasn't something between us. I didn't know how deep his feelings went, but I knew it was more than just desire. He cared for me. Perhaps he wasn't in love with me, but at the moment it was enough to have him by my side.

I tried to keep my expression clear, to push down the grief I felt. Some part of me knew this wasn't over. We might have lost Toby, but that didn't mean our job here was done. I needed to pull myself together until we had completed the mission.

The winds grew progressively gustier, and I felt, in some way, as though the salty breezes were clearing my head. The grief was still there, a cold lump in my chest, but I had contained it now, rather than letting it overtake me. It was as though I had been able to pack it away until I had the leisure to open it again and experience it fully.

When we got back to the hotel, Ramsey stopped at the front desk. He said something in Portuguese to the desk clerk, and the man nodded.

"*Sim, senhor.* A package has arrived for you," he said. He handed Ramsey a thin envelope.

"Thank you," Ramsey said, tucking the envelope into his jacket pocket.

His arm around my waist, Ramsey led the way to the lift.

We went back into my room, and Ramsey took the envelope from his pocket.

"What is it?" I asked.

"I believe it's our marriage certificate," he said, looking closely at the envelope.

"Oh," I said, feeling incredibly awkward. Things had changed since we'd married, but, then again, the situation was much the same. We'd gone to bed together, but I'd told him "no promises" and I meant it. The marriage was still going to be temporary, and I wished I hadn't been with him when he received the reminder of the commitment I'd gotten him into.

He was looking at the envelope carefully.

"Is something wrong?" I asked.

He handed it over to me, and I looked down at it. The edge of the flap was slightly bumpy, as though the seal had dried and then been repasted down. "It's been steamed open and resealed," I said.

He nodded. "We knew they were watching Santos closely. It appears it was a good thing we did things officially."

"Yes," I said, not meeting his gaze.

"Open it," he said.

I slid my finger beneath the flap and opened the envelope. Then I removed the document inside and unfolded it. I read over it as best as I could, given that it was in Portuguese. I could see the pertinent information. Our names, the officiant, the date of the ceremony, and so on. "It . . . appears to be our marriage certificate, just as you said."

"Nothing else?"

I studied it again, looking for any sign of code, any hint that there might be some message, but there was nothing that I could see. Then I paused, brought the paper closer to my face. "There's the faint scent of lemons," I said. "Does that mean something?"

He moved over to the coffee table.

"Come here and lay it face down," he said.

I went and spread the certificate down on the table and took a seat on the sofa. Ramsey sat next to me. Then he took a lighter from his pocket and flicked it on. He held it close to the paper. I was—unaccountably—worried for a moment that he might catch this proof of our marriage on fire, but he held it only close enough for the heat to touch the paper.

And then I saw the surface was changing, letters becoming apparent on the back of the document.

"Invisible ink!" I exclaimed.

"Yes."

I'd heard of such things, but I hadn't really thought much about their existence outside of spy novels.

"There is a compound in lemon juice that reacts to heat," he said, moving the lighter over the surface. "It's fairly primitive as such things go, but perhaps that was the only thing he had at his disposal. He banked on whoever searches his documents making only a cursory search, and the gamble paid off."

Ramsey flicked off the lighter, and we looked down at the message Santos had left for us on the back of our marriage certificate:

*Motta is dead. POWs have been captured. Prisoners held
at the Castelo de Vento. They will be sent to Germany
within the week.*

A location! At last, we knew where the prisoners were. But that
wasn't the part of the message that seized me. *Within the week,* it
said. That meant we didn't have very much time. We had to break
the prisoners out before they were sent to Germany and tortured
for information.

I looked over at him. "We need to get in touch with Archie,
start planning."

"Yes," he said. "Perhaps he can get someone to break them out."

"Get someone?" I repeated incredulously. "We are the someone!"

"Electra—"

"We have a job to do," I said. "Just because I can't . . ." The
words caught in my throat, and I had to pause, take a deep breath.
"Just because I can't bring Toby home as I hoped doesn't mean that
I won't help the others."

It took everything within me to keep from crumbling at the
words, but I managed to keep my sorrow in its tight little bundle. I
would have the rest of my life to mourn Toby. Right now there was
a job that needed to be done, and I was, perhaps, the person best
suited to do it. "They can get back to their families, and we can
do that for them," I went on before Ramsey could respond. "And
they'll be able to tell us about the escape route so we can streamline
it for other escapees. We can still do what we came here to do."

"You are grieving," he said gently. "This is not the best time
for you to make this sort of decision."

"It's the only time we'll have, and there isn't much left." I looked
up at him. "Half the people in England have lost someone, and they
still get up every morning and do what has to be done. I can do this.
I *need* to do this. Please."

For a long moment we looked at each other. There was an

openness to his face that I had seldom seen there, and I could read tenderness and concern warring with understanding and approval.

At last, he let out a breath and nodded. "I'll ring Blandings."

We met with Archie in a café an hour later. The rainstorm that had been threatening all day had swept in from the sea, and the weather was wet, cold, and windy. This reminded me a bit more of London, and I felt oddly comforted.

I had a small pot of tea before me, while Archie and Ramsey drank coffee with the consistency of motor oil. Ramsey had related the message that had been written on the back of our marriage license.

"Castelo de Vento is an old castle perhaps thirty miles from the Spanish border. It was owned by a long line of Portuguese merchants but was purchased a year or so ago by an unknown buyer," Archie said. "It would be an ideal place to hold captives, honestly. It's secluded, and it would be easy enough for the Germans to ship them back into occupied territory from there."

"We should break them out," I said, watching the steam rise from my teacup.

Though I wasn't looking at either of them as I said it, I could feel the two men meeting eyes above my head.

I plunged ahead. "We must break them out. If the Germans get information about the escape line from them, they'll capture every escapee and everyone who's helped them."

"That's true," Archie said. "If they haven't got it out of them already."

The grim pronouncement hung in the air for a moment. It was indeed possible the men had been tortured for information already. But, perhaps not. And how were we to know unless we got them out?

"It's the least we can do," I went on. "They came so far. They . . . they're Toby's friends. We cannot leave them in German hands."

Archie considered for a moment. Then he said, "I've just thought of a piece of intercepted intelligence that may be related to this. Excuse me for a moment while I make a telephone call, will you?"

Ramsey's hand rested on the back of my chair, and, when Archie went to use the telephone, he leaned toward me and lowered his voice. "This is a big risk for possibly no reward."

"If we can save their lives, it will be reward enough."

I saw the expression on his face that always came when he was considering his words. "I don't want you to put yourself at risk if you're not . . . emotionally ready to do so."

I smiled. "That's sweet of you, but I know how to put my emotions aside for a job. You know the kind of work I've done all my life."

"You've done it with your family."

That shadow crossed my heart again. How could it be that Toby was gone?

"I know," I said softly. "But I'll be doing this for Toby, which is nearly the same thing."

His eyes met mine. "Once we commit to this, we're going to have to move quickly. Are you absolutely sure?"

"Yes," I said. "I'm sure."

I remembered the context in which I had used those words last night and felt the flush creep up my cheeks. I think he must have remembered it, too, because I felt a shift in the way he was looking at me.

"It's as I thought," Archie said, coming back to the table.

I looked up quickly, and Ramsey shifted slightly away.

I felt Archie's eyes on my face, and I wondered if he could tell how things had changed between Ramsey and me. I was certain he couldn't have missed it.

Of course, he wouldn't mention it. But I was still accustoming myself to the idea of having a lover; I didn't quite feel like having something so new and fragile and intimate out in the open.

"There's been chatter," he said, taking his seat. "We decoded a message only this morning about recalcitrant prisoners. We interpreted it to mean they are asking for a . . . professional interrogator."

I felt a bit sick at the words, but it also gave me hope. "Then it's not too late. But we'll have to move soon."

Archie nodded then turned to look at Ramsey. "What do you say, sir?"

Though Archie was technically in command of the operation, this was a bit outside of what we had expected.

I looked at Ramsey. He turned to glance at me before looking back to Archie. "As Electra says, we'd better act quickly."

Archie nodded, as though he wasn't surprised at Ramsey's agreement. "I'll need to gather some intelligence. Shall we meet again in the morning?"

"Yes," Ramsey said.

"Let me drop you back at the hotel," Archie said. "The rain seems to be getting worse. When I phoned about that intercepted message, I asked Simon to pick me up."

We finished our drinks, and then Simon Woods arrived with Archie's car. Ramsey sat close to me in the backseat, and I leaned against him ever so slightly. It was a relief—especially given the news of today—to not have to hide my feelings.

I did wonder what Simon Woods thought of it all. He had, after all, believed me engaged to Archie only a few evenings ago. I thought I detected a few curious glances, but, naturally, he didn't comment.

We parted ways with Archie and walked back upstairs together. Ramsey had the key to my room now, and he opened the door and helped me out of my damp coat.

"I have a bit of work to do on my other cases and some telephone calls to make," he said as I took a seat on the sofa. "I'll order some dinner sent up to you. Do you think you can eat some of it?"

"I'll try."

"You'll need your strength for tomorrow."

I nodded. "Yes. I'll eat."

"Good girl." He gave me a faint smile and then turned toward his room. "I'll check back in with you later."

"All right."

I didn't know if this was his way of putting some distance between us, but I was too tired at the moment to think about it. I felt like one of Nacy's dish towels that had been wrung out.

He closed the door to his room, and I went and lay down on the freshly made bed. I didn't have any intention of falling asleep, but I did and woke sometime later to the knock at my door as dinner was delivered.

Ramsey had ordered me another delicious soup with warm, crusty bread, and I managed to eat a good bit of it.

My laundry had been delivered during the day, too, and I decided there was no choice but to go back to my comfortable pajamas. The silk nightgown was dreadfully rumpled. Besides, I wasn't even sure Ramsey intended to . . . continue our liaison. Perhaps last night had merely been the result of a moment of weakness on his part.

I had finished preparing for bed when there was a tap on the adjoining door. My heartbeat sped up.

I moved to the door and opened it.

Ramsey looked down at me through the wide crack.

For a moment, neither of us said anything. It felt like a very long moment.

The hesitation on my part was due to not knowing what his intentions were. My first instinct had been to pull the door open wide and step back to allow him to enter. But if he didn't mean to spend another night in my room, that action on my part would make things embarrassing for both of us.

Then again, perhaps he thought I regretted last night and was hoping he would make no overtures this evening.

I sighed. We were going to have to be direct about things, it seemed. "We didn't finish our discussion this morning, about where things might go," I said.

"No," he agreed. "And you've had rather a stressful day."

"That doesn't change anything," I replied.

"No regrets?" he asked, his eyes on my face.

"None at all."

"Tell me honestly: Would you rather be alone tonight?"

"No. But if you would rather not . . ." I felt myself flush even as I tried to find the right way to word things. ". . . stay with me tonight, then I understand."

Having had my say, I forced myself to meet his gaze as I waited for his answer.

"Do you suppose," he said, a hint of warm amusement in his voice, "that after last night I would prefer to sleep in my own bed?"

I felt a rush of relief—and anticipation—at this confirmation. It wasn't just that I didn't want to be alone tonight—it was that I wanted to be with *him*.

"We will, of course, need to talk about this at some point," he went on, stepping into my room. "But . . . perhaps, not tonight?"

"Yes," I agreed. "Not tonight."

CHAPTER TWENTY-EIGHT

It was still dark when I woke up in his arms in my bed, the memory of the news about Toby hitting me like a fresh blow. I closed my eyes tightly, pushing down the wave of sorrow.

I lay still, enjoying Ramsey's warmth, the heavy weight of his arm across me. It felt so safe. I wasn't sure how I would have faced my grief without him.

I had begun to rely on him emotionally. I understood the danger of it, the heartbreak it would lead to. But I couldn't think about that now. I couldn't think too much about Toby or about a future without Ramsey; I wouldn't be able to do this job. The job I knew needed to be done.

The two prisoners who were with Toby would know details about the route from France to Lisbon. If we didn't free them before they were forced to tell what they knew, then other escapees fleeing France would walk directly into German hands. The people who had helped them would be murdered—or worse. We simply could not allow it to happen.

Ramsey stirred, opened his eyes. "Good morning."

"Good morning."

"What time is it?"

"I'm not sure. Early, I think." Neither of us made a move to look at the clock.

"Then we needn't get up just yet."

"No." I wished we could stay in this cocoon of sleepy warmth forever.

I loved looking at him like this, rumpled from sleep, unshaven and relaxed. My heart swelled with affection.

Hesitantly, I reached out to gently touch the two bullet-wound scars on his shoulder. "Have you been hurting?"

He shook his head. "Not in your bed. You're better than morphia."

I blushed and laughed. "Why, Major Ramsey, I never would have imagined you a sweet talker."

The corner of his lips twitched. "I'm a man of hidden depths."

"So it seems."

"I think the slightly warmer weather has helped, too," he said. "The ache isn't constant like it was in London."

"I'm glad."

He brushed the hair back from my face and kissed me. Then, his hand still on my cheek, he looked down at me. "You're absolutely certain you want to do this?"

"Yes. We have to get them out. It's simple, really."

He smiled down at me, a bit ruefully, it seemed. "Nothing is ever simple with you, Electra. But I suppose your complexity contributes to your allure."

"Am I alluring?" I teased.

"Bewitching," he murmured, leaning to kiss my neck. His stubble scratched my skin and raised gooseflesh along my arms.

He lifted his head suddenly and looked over my shoulder at the clock. "We don't need to meet Blandings for another two hours. Do you want to go back to sleep?"

I lifted a brow. "Do you?"

He brushed his thumb across my lips, his gaze hot. "I could think of more constructive uses for our time."

I shifted closer, slipping my arms around him. "By all means."

We were nearly late to meet Archie in the lobby, but we got there just as he was walking in the door.

"The car is waiting," he said. "I thought, since this is rather a sensitive conversation, that we'd go to a restaurant I know with a private room. We'll be able to talk there without being observed."

We went out to the car, which was waiting at the curb. Ramsey's hand rested lightly on my back as he helped me in. I was aware of how much he touched me now, and it brought a pleasant flutter to my stomach.

"I'm going to bring Simon in on this," Archie said as we got in. "I thought another man might prove useful."

"I was able to get a sort of blueprint of the castle," Simon said, looking at us in the mirror. "At least a rough one. It should be helpful."

"Helpful, indeed," I said. "It sounds like you're just the man for the job, Simon."

He smiled, flashing a dimple.

The restaurant was crowded and clearly popular, but Archie led us into a private room in the back. There was a wide oak table, and Simon put the map and blueprint side by side. We all moved to look at them.

"The prisoners are being held in Castelo de Vento, here," Archie said, pointing at a place on the map. "The castle is set on a hill, and the surrounding terrain is rocky, with very few trees for cover. There are outcroppings of rock that we can move amongst, but, obviously, those won't be listed on any map. We'll just have to move carefully."

"What about the building itself?" I asked. "Where will they be keeping the men?"

"As far as we can ascertain, there are the remains of medieval prison cells in the cellars," Archie said.

"A dungeon, you mean." I felt cold at the thought of it.

Archie nodded. "Do you think you can get us in?"

"I don't imagine dungeon doors will prove much more difficult than modern locks," I said. In truth, I wasn't entirely confident. I didn't have much experience working on locks that were hundreds of years old. Of course, mechanisms hadn't changed that much over the years, and I'd played with older locks in Uncle Mick's wizard's workshop.

"Breaking into a prison is something new," I said, trying for a bit of joviality in the tense moment.

Archie offered me a smile. "You enjoy a challenge."

"She's her uncle's niece," Ramsey said. There was, I thought, the slightest note of something like . . . pride? . . . in his tone.

I smiled up at him, and I noticed Archie's eyes flicking between us. A small smile appeared on his lips.

I looked down again at the map of the area and the rough drawings—though not quite blueprints—of Castelo de Vento. "It seems as though we're in a film or an adventure novel. It's absurd. We're going to break someone out of a castle dungeon."

"You needn't pretend you're not excited at the prospect," Ramsey said dryly.

He was right, of course. I flashed a smile at him before turning back to the map. He came up beside me to look at it, his arm brushing mine. He didn't bother to move it away, and we stood side by side, our bodies leaning slightly into each other. It might have distracted me before, his casual nearness, but it was, somehow, easier now that we had acted upon our attraction. Giving in to passion had eased the tension and allowed us to focus on the work.

There was no denying that things had changed between Ramsey and me since we'd tumbled into bed together. It wasn't just the physical side of things, the ease with which we touched now. I felt a shift in the dynamic of our professional relationship, the way this felt more like a partnership than a mission where Ramsey gave the orders.

I supposed what was really different was the personal. Ramsey was letting me see the side of him that he didn't show to many people. He teased me. He confided in me. He touched me as often as he could without being too obvious about it.

There had been no talk, of course, of what would happen when we returned to London. I had to imagine that Ramsey was avoiding thinking about it. I, meanwhile, thought about it far too often.

Though it was a dreadful prospect to contemplate, I intended to keep my word. I had told him that our affair in Lisbon needn't have any impact upon our lives when we returned to London. If he wanted to forget everything that happened here in Portugal, then I would have to live with his decision. At least I would have the memories.

Perhaps that was melodramatic. I was sure that, in time, I would get over my love for Ramsey. I would have no choice. But the idea of it was incredibly depressing.

I realized that I was not quite as immune to distraction as I had thought as Ramsey said, "Electra?"

"I'm sorry," I said, to cover my momentary lapse in attention. "I was counting how many doors we'd have to go through." Not a complete lie. I'd managed to count at least three doors, if we were going to be as surreptitious as possible. Three locked doors was not an impossible task by any means, but it would require a lot of focus to get through them all in a timely manner.

"Are there guards?" I asked.

"I don't have good intelligence on that," Archie said. "We haven't had any reason to surveil the castle until now. Nothing had indicated to us that it was even inhabited. We'll go armed against the possibility, of course."

"Do you know who owns it?" I asked.

Archie looked at Simon.

Simon shook his head. "I haven't been able to link it back to whoever bought it most recently. It wouldn't have drawn attention at the time, but now, looking at the channels the deed has gone through, it's clear someone took pains to conceal it."

"Well, that doesn't really matter, does it?" I said. "We know what we have to do. It doesn't make any difference who owns Castelo de Vento. We've only to get in and out."

Archie smiled. "In and out. You make it sound so simple."

I shrugged. "That's what it boils down to."

"Is there anything else you need?"

I considered. I had my lockpicking kit with me, of course. But there was a good chance we might need something a bit more heavy-duty. "Do you suppose you can bring some bolt cutters, just in case we encounter chains? And perhaps a thick-bladed knife. It may come in handy if any of the locks are rusted."

Archie smiled and looked at Simon. "You hear that?"

"Check, sir."

"Anything else?"

"Not unless you think it advisable to bring some dynamite."

Archie laughed. "I don't think it advisable. Not if we want to get quietly in and out."

"I thought as much," I said. "Then I suppose we'll have what we need."

"Then it's settled. We'll pick you up at six o'clock and start for Castelo de Vento."

CHAPTER TWENTY-NINE

Simon dropped Ramsey and me back at the hotel. My mind was spinning with different elements of the plan. I felt that familiar sense of anticipation that always came before a big job. This was perhaps the biggest, most dangerous job we had yet to attempt, but I knew that I was ready for it.

What was more, I felt the rightness of it. The jobs I'd done with my family had always been exciting, and I'd never thought too much about the people on the other side of it, the people we stole from.

But with this job, the lines were clearly drawn. We would be thwarting our enemies, the people trying to destroy all that was good and right in the world. That sense of purpose gave me added strength.

We had just walked into the lobby, and I was still lost in thought, so it was a moment before I recognized the familiar figure walking toward me. I blinked, not believing my eyes.

But the figure was still there, getting closer.

"Colm!" I cried, staring at my cousin.

"Hello, El," he said with a grin.

I ran and flung myself into his arms, immeasurably glad to see him. Colm hugged me tight, and, enveloped in his strong arms, I felt tears come to my eyes.

"What are you doing here?" I asked against his shoulder. He had been stationed at the RAF air base in Torquay. I'd seen him only a handful of times since the beginning of the war.

"Ramsey pulled some strings yesterday to get me sent here first thing this morning."

I pulled back to look up at him, suddenly afraid I would have to be the one to tell him. "You . . . you know . . . about Toby?"

He nodded, his expression tight with restrained emotion. "Ramsey told me."

He wanted to say more, but we both felt the constraint of our surroundings and the danger of giving our emotions free rein. There would be time for that later.

I swallowed hard, pressing down the tears that had been threatening to spring to my eyes. "But you agree we should get the others out?"

He nodded. "Yes. Toby would've wanted it."

"Oh, Colm," I said, embracing him again. "I'm so glad you're here."

Things were getting difficult now that we were on the cusp of this mission, and I had been missing the support of my family. I trusted Ramsey, of course. I'd put my life in his hands on more than one occasion, and I'd do it again in a heartbeat.

But, as he'd said, it was a different thing with family. That bond wasn't one that was easily replicated, and having Colm fighting at my side would give me the added boost of strength I hadn't known I needed.

Then another thought occurred to me. "Maybe we shouldn't risk both our lives doing this," I said. "If something happens . . ."

He shook his head. "Nothing's going to happen. Dad and Nacy need never know."

I wondered if he was right. If something happened to either of us in addition to Toby, it would kill Uncle Mick and Nacy. Then again, I had my mind made up about what we needed to do, and I assumed that Colm did, too. He had come all this way, and nothing would stop him from honoring what was certainly one of his brother's final wishes, that his friends would escape to freedom.

Besides, there was no way that he would sit by and let me do it without him. He would want to keep an eye on me. I wondered if that was part of the reason Ramsey had brought him here, because he knew it would be another person to stand between me and danger.

Ramsey approached us then. He and Colm shook hands.

"Thank you for bringing me in on this," Colm said.

"I'm sorry about your brother," Ramsey told him.

"Thank you." I saw a glint in Colm's eyes. "If the chance comes to repay his death in kind, I'm ready."

I didn't blame him for the sentiment. The thought of someone killing Toby—Toby, with his laughing eyes and lopsided grin—filled me with white-hot fury.

I thought again how glad I was that Colm would be with us on this.

"Are you staying here?" I asked.

He smiled. "This place isn't exactly my usual turf. But I've got a comfortable room not far from here."

We had lunch in the hotel dining room, and we caught up on the latest news. Colm had been busy working at the RAF air base in Torquay. He wrote frequently, but that wasn't the same as sitting side by side and talking. I caught him up with what Uncle Mick and Nacy had been doing and told him about Burglar, the newest addition to the family.

We fell into that easy rapport that exists between siblings, but, despite the laughter, there was a sense of an empty place in our trio. An empty place that would never be filled.

Ramsey lunched with us, though he let Colm and I do most of the talking. He had offered to leave us alone, but we had both insisted he stay. Perhaps it was that we were accustomed to having a third person with us. Perhaps it was also easier to keep our emotions in check with an outsider there. Whatever the case, the meal passed pleasantly enough, and then Colm was rising to go.

"What time shall I report?" he asked Ramsey.

"Eighteen hundred hours," Ramsey said. "We'll meet you in the lobby."

He nodded. "Until then."

I gave him another tight hug, and then he took his leave.

As Ramsey and I went into the lift together, I turned to look at him. "You . . . didn't tell Colm that we'd had to marry, did you?"

"No."

I nodded. "I think it's best we don't tell him about . . ." I waved my hand. "All of that."

"Whatever you want."

"Thank you." If we meant to go back to our separate lives when we returned to London, it would be simpler that no one ever know what had happened between us here. There was no sense in complicating things, especially as Colm's protective streak where I was concerned was liable to make him less than understanding about the situation.

I knew Ramsey probably felt the same way, and it made me appreciate the gesture of his involving Colm all the more. "Thank you for bringing him."

"I knew we could use him."

"You knew *I* could use him." I reached out and squeezed his hand.

He looked down at me. "Things have been difficult for you. I thought perhaps it would be good to have a familiar face. Besides, it's good to have allies one can trust in tricky situations."

"Yes," I said, smiling up at him. "It is."

And then, because I couldn't help it, I kissed him.

The lift doors almost closed on us again before we realized we had reached our floor.

CHAPTER THIRTY

We had an early dinner in my room—our room, lately—and then we began to prepare for our evening's adventure.

Ramsey watched as I ran a brush ruthlessly through my hair.

"It refuses to be tamed," I said.

"Almost allegorical, isn't it?" he said with a smile.

It did something strange to my stomach, that smile of his. He seldom smiled, but I'd seen more of them in the past few days than I had in all of our previous acquaintance.

It was as though he was purposefully making an effort to be softer with me, to reveal more of his emotions. Perhaps that was natural in a relationship like this—I had little experience on which to gauge such things—but I didn't think it was only that. He wanted me to be comfortable, to know how he felt.

I kept reminding myself that this was temporary. I absolutely could not anticipate that any of this would continue once we returned to London. We were from two entirely different worlds, and it would be foolish to think they could ever align.

I would have to accustom myself to living without him again. So I would just enjoy this little slice of life with him while it lasted.

I finished pinning my hair into a tight bun. That would keep it out of the way tonight.

When I was done, he came and dropped a kiss on the back of my neck. "I shall look forward to removing those pins at the end of the night."

I turned into his arms. "Just the pins?"

"No. Not just the pins."

I felt the heat of his look sizzle through me.

I dressed in serviceable clothes, glad I had thought to bring them. I wore a black wool turtleneck and black trousers. I also brought a pair of leather gloves and tucked them into the pocket of my black coat. I had a black beret if the wind got cold, but my own hair was black enough that it wouldn't call any attention to me in dark places.

Colm met us in the lobby. He was dressed similarly to Ramsey and me, all in black. We stood out a bit amongst all the bright clothing of the women prepared to go out for the evening, but no one looked at us askance. The lobby had seen much more unusual things in the past year.

Archie and Simon Woods picked us up, and we began our drive toward Castelo de Vento, near the Spanish border. It was a journey of a few hours, and, though we talked a good bit about the mission, there were long moments of silence, each of us lost in our own thoughts.

I sat in the backseat, between Colm and Ramsey. More than once, I caught myself leaning into Ramsey's side, my leg pressed against his, and pulled away, wondering if Colm had noticed. At least I had remembered to slip off the wedding ring before I'd left my room.

Simon put on the radio at one point, and the strains of orchestra music filled the car. I thought of Felix, wondering where he was and what he was doing tonight. I hoped he was safe.

We stopped to stretch our legs and drink some tea that Simon had brought in a thermos.

For a moment, Ramsey and I found ourselves off to the side of the group. He took the opportunity to coddle me.

"All right?"

I nodded.

"I want you to tell me if you're not."

I frowned at him. "Don't fuss. Isn't that what you always tell me?"

"Yes, but—"

"I'm all right. Really. Perhaps I won't be when this is over. I haven't allowed myself to think about . . . to think about what Toby being gone really means. But for now I'm fine. I'm focused. I know how to prioritize."

"Be that as it may, *you're* my main priority at the moment, Electra."

I felt a lump in my throat at the words. I looked up at him with glittering eyes.

"You should keep your coat buttoned," he went on, his fingers deftly beginning the work. "It's colder here at higher elevation."

He was fastening the top button when I noticed Colm watching us.

I wasn't sure what my cousin would think about a relationship between Ramsey and me.

When I'd first begun working with Ramsey, Colm had warned me in his big-brotherly way that the major was not the type of man who would have a long-term interest in a woman of my background and social status. He had meant it kindly, of course, but the words had been haunting me as of late. Because I knew that, while we were here, away from everything and everyone we knew, it was easy for Ramsey and me to be together. When we returned to the real world, it would be a different story.

I had noticed more than once this afternoon the way Colm watched Ramsey. He was, I assumed, suspicious that there was something between us. Ramsey treated me as professionally as possible when we were working, but there was a certain sort of physical ease between us now that might be perceptible to anyone who knew me well. I would have to try harder to hide it.

My romantic life was, of course, really none of Colm's business. But he had been overprotective of me since we were children, and I didn't want to make any sort of waves if I didn't have to. We had more important things to think about.

For the rest of the car ride, I felt my cousin's eyes drift to me occasionally. He and Toby had always been overly defensive about me where men were concerned. I assumed, however, that he would shift his focus to the mission once we got to Castelo de Vento.

We arrived near the location, and Archie instructed Simon to park the car in a copse of trees at the edge of the village. We could see Castelo de Vento from here. I looked up at it in the distance, the black silhouette against the night sky.

This was the first time I'd ever tried to break someone out of a place. Then again, I supposed it wasn't much different from breaking in. The process would be much the same. We'd have to get through the locks either way. And in every robbery I'd committed, we'd had to make our escape. This was nothing new.

There was a bit of me that felt the familiar thrill of the chase, but I knew that the stakes were far greater than anything I had done before. Even the dangerous things I'd done working with Ramsey didn't compare to this—because it wasn't just my life that might hang in the balance this time.

We were all that stood between the prisoners and near-certain death. All that stood between the Nazis and the escape route, where escapees were no doubt making their way toward Portugal even now, trusting in the viability of the passage to bring them to freedom. We had to succeed. There was no other choice.

We proceeded on foot. Archie led the way, followed by Simon. Ramsey and I walked in the middle, and Colm took up the rear. Colm was a good man to have at your back.

It was fully dark by the time we reached the base of the mountain. We'd all been keeping a close eye out for any sign of searchlights or the glow of torches from patrolling guards. But everything was dark and quiet.

The castle was magnificent in the moonlight. It looked like something out of a fairy tale. No, that wasn't quite right. It looked more like something from the early days of lore, King Arthur and the Knights of the Round Table—all dark gray stone, with turrets and towers and small windows allowing for long-ago archers to shoot at approaching enemies.

It had been built to keep people out, and it had no doubt succeeded for centuries. Then again, it had yet to meet a McDonnell.

It was built on the high ground, giving it a view of the land spread out beneath it. That's why it had been necessary to approach under cover of darkness.

The hill was dotted with rocky outcroppings. None of them was especially large, but there was certainly enough cover to keep us concealed as we made our way up the hill. If we moved slowly, I thought we had a very good chance of getting to the top without being detected.

I knew that Archie and Ramsey were armed. It seemed likely that Simon also carried a gun. And, if I knew Colm, he wasn't likely to be the only unarmed man on the mountain.

That left me, of course. No one had offered me a gun. Not that I would have taken it. I had never shot a gun before, and I didn't intend for tonight to be the first time. I would just have to rely on other skills if push came to shove. As a precaution, I had tucked a knife into my boot. I would use that as a last resort.

We stopped at the bottom of the hill in the shadow of a rocky outcropping. Archie turned to us. "Let's make our way up in pairs."

"I'll go with Ellie," Colm said.

I looked at him. I had assumed that I'd be going with Ramsey. I was accustomed to partnering with him. Then again, Colm was accustomed to partnering with me. We'd been doing jobs together for a decade.

I nodded, though I felt Ramsey tense beside me like he was about to object. But Archie had already moved on. "Simon and I will make our way up first. Ellie and McDonnell, you can come up behind. And, Ramsey, if you'll take the rear, you can watch our back trail."

Ramsey nodded, and I was glad there wasn't going to be any additional tension. I knew Ramsey wanted to be with me, to protect me. I appreciated that instinct in him, but I think he understood that Colm was like a brother to me. And we had just lost Toby. Colm wanted to be sure that I was all right.

"We'll meet at the tower on the east side, as we discussed," Archie said. "And then we can proceed from there."

I nodded. I knew that I would be the one proceeding. Colm could pick locks, too, but I was perhaps quicker than he was. He had a good mind for machines and the intricate pieces from which they were compiled, but that knowledge sometimes made him think too much rather than react to the mechanisms.

We were on the south side of the mountain now, the side with the most ground cover. We would have to make our way up to the castle and then slightly around it to the east side. Archie and Simon went ahead, disappearing into the shadows, and after a few minutes, Colm and I moved up behind them. There was still no movement or sign of life from the castle. There was, I saw, one light in a window high on the south side of the building, but we knew the castle was occupied. That was no surprise. What was surprising was that no one seemed to be on the alert.

Then again, they didn't know we were coming. They thought they had pulled it off, captured two escaped POWs who would give them the information they needed to capture anyone else who followed in their footsteps.

Colm and I moved together with the ease of long practice. He was much bigger than me, as tall as Ramsey and even brawnier. But he moved gracefully in the darkness, and we kept pace together, moving silently over the rocks and damp wild grass and undergrowth. There were places where the rain from the storms earlier in the day had collected in puddles, and we dodged them even as we dodged the open places where we might be spotted.

"What's going on with Ramsey?" he asked me as we paused behind a clump of rock to survey our next movements. Every so often I would catch sight of a dark shadow ahead of us as Archie and Simon moved across an open patch of ground. Unless one was looking directly at them, I didn't think they would be easily observed.

"What do you mean?" I asked as casually as I could, my eyes still on the landscape.

"Does he fancy you?"

I frowned at my cousin in the darkness. Now was not the time for this. "What makes you ask that?"

"I've got eyes in my head, haven't I? And you fancy him, too. But I warned you once to be careful with him, El. He's not from our world. If you're messing about with a toff, you're only going to end up hurt."

"I can take care of myself, Colm," I said. "I think we can move now."

I started out of our spot before he could say anything else, and he came along silently with me. That answered my question about what Colm might think. Ah, well. Worries for another time. I needed to focus.

He didn't bring it up again, thankfully.

The castle was enormous up close, towering stone walls and ancient battlements. I put my hand against the stones, feeling the history of it, how long it had stood there.

"Be friendly to us," I whispered, brushing my hand along the rough wall.

Colm and I moved around to the east side of the building.

Archie and Simon were already there, hidden in the shadows. There was still no sign of light or movement.

The door that we'd elected to use to enter the castle was set in a massive stone tower. The door was thick wood, worn smooth with the passage of time, with an old iron lock plate.

I took my lockpicking kit from my pocket and removed a pick and a file. I knelt on the ground, my trouser knees going damp from the rain on the stones.

"Simon, block the light," Archie instructed. "I'll turn on my torch."

Simon stood close, his back to us, keeping an eye on the landscape while shielding the torchlight from any onlookers. Colm stood close enough to watch, but not so close that he would distract me.

Ramsey hadn't arrived yet, but I wasn't alarmed. He was probably taking his time, making a survey of the castle. I wouldn't be surprised if he decided to circle it before making his way to the east tower.

I pushed the pick into the lock. It was old and slightly rusty, but the feel of the mechanism was familiar enough. I could do this.

Blocking out the expectancy I felt in the men all around me, I concentrated on the feel of the pick and the components of the old lock. Mentally, I willed it to give in to me. This was just the first of many, and time was of the essence.

Slow and steady, Ellie girl. I heard Uncle Mick's voice in my head, and I slowed my breathing. Focused. For one fanciful moment, I felt as though he were there with me in spirit.

The lock clicked.

"There," I whispered.

"Excellent work," Archie said. "Brava."

"It's only the first one," I said as I rose to my feet. "Don't congratulate me too early."

"In and out. Nothing to it." Archie grinned.

"Where's the major?" Simon asked.

Archie turned around to look, seeming to realize for the first time that Ramsey hadn't arrived. Colm had already taken note of his absence, of course. Colm always took note of the details.

Archie looked at me expectantly.

"I don't know," I said. "I assume he's . . . reconnoitering."

"Exactly so," Ramsey's voice said as he materialized out of the darkness. I saw Simon start a bit at his sudden appearance.

"Electra's got the first lock done?" he said, looking at the door.

Archie nodded. "Are you ready to proceed?"

"Yes," Ramsey said. "Though I think perhaps someone ought to wait out here and keep a watch."

"Simon will stay," Archie said.

Simon didn't look exactly pleased at being left out of things, but he nodded his acquiescence.

"I'll stay with him," Colm said. For some reason I couldn't name, I was glad of it. I knew that he would keep things safe here aboveground while we descended into the depths.

"Whistle if you need me?" I asked him. In our childhood, my cousins, Felix, and I had created a series of whistled signals to alert the others. My cousins and I had used them occasionally in our thieving work, and Felix and I had used them on a previous mission with Ramsey. It might come in handy.

Colm nodded. "Be careful, El."

"I will."

And then we opened the door and stepped into the castle.

CHAPTER THIRTY-ONE

We were inside the eastern tower. For several moments, we stood in a silent group in the dark, listening. There was nothing, no sound, save the occasional drip of water somewhere in the stairwell. Finally Archie switched on his torch, and I could see that there was a narrow, curving stairwell along the outer wall that both rose above us and descended into the darkness. The small landing we stood on was barely wide enough for the three of us.

Ramsey pulled the door almost all the way closed behind us, shutting out the moonlight. The little alcove we were in felt cold and close.

I looked at where the stairs descended into blackness. The stairwell was narrow, dark, and winding. In short: just the sort of stairwell one would expect to lead to a dungeon.

Ramsey switched on his torch and angled it down the tower staircase. I drew in a breath, ready to be on the move.

"Let me go first," Ramsey murmured.

He slid past me, the narrowness of the opening causing our bodies to brush against each other. For just an instant as he passed, his hand rested on my shoulder and squeezed, reassuring. Then he was before me, the light in one hand. He removed his gun from the holster.

"Stay behind me," he said.

I didn't argue. It wouldn't do me any good.

He began making his way silently down the stairs, and I followed after him. I was glad for his solid, reassuring presence. Archie was quiet and light on his feet behind me.

I had never been afraid of the dark. Even as a child, it hadn't bothered me. But something about being encased within the bowels of this castle made the back of my neck prickle. That and the fact that, if we were discovered, it might very well mean we would be added to the group currently cooling their heels in the dungeon.

Suddenly, Ramsey stopped. He reached back to warn me, but I had already bumped into him.

"It's another door."

I had not expected a door here. As far as I could tell, we were only halfway down the staircase. There should still be a few more turns before we came to the second door.

The beam of Ramsey's light illuminated a thick wooden door with an ancient iron key plate.

I came up beside him, our bodies pressed close in the small space, and leaned in to inspect it. This was a very old lock, and slightly rusted from the moisture down here beneath the earth. All the same, I supposed the mechanism was in working order or it would have been replaced. Especially if they were actively using the dungeons.

I took out my kit again and selected one of the sturdier picks. Pushing it into the lock, I worked the mechanism. It clicked open, and I let out a breath.

Ramsey moved around me to go through the door first, his hand trailing along my waist as he did so, but it was only another small stone landing. The stairs continued downward from here.

Finally, after a few more curves of the narrow spiraling stairs, we reached another door. This one I had expected from the rough drawings Simon had been able to get us.

This door was much as the other had been, old but well-oiled. Or, at least, recently oiled. The lock gave me no trouble.

We went through, and then we were in what had once been the dungeon of the castle—what technically still was, if our information was correct.

Overhead, there were vaulted ceilings strung with cobwebs. The floor was dusty and littered, but there were several sets of scuffed footprints going to and fro, too many to tell if that now-familiar crisscross pattern was among them.

We followed along the dim corridor, listening. There was no sound but the occasional drip of water or the scutter of some animal in the shadows. Rats, probably.

At last, we reached the final door. If the plans were right, the old cells were behind it. This one had a new padlock on it. Very new, by the looks of it. It was still shiny.

This was the most easily opened, though it was the newest. Obviously, whoever was using this dungeon had assumed it would be good enough to keep the prisoners in. Besides, they were probably being kept in locked cells. They wouldn't have been able to break out through so many doors.

We entered the room and found ourselves in a tight, narrow corridor. On either side, there were cells. Most of them had fallen into disrepair, with stones crumbling into little piles on the ground.

Only one, toward the far end, had a fresh row of iron bars. They glinted dully in the torchlight. From the entryway, I couldn't see inside. The light from Ramsey's torch penetrated only so far.

We started forward slowly. At first, I was afraid that there was something wrong, that the men weren't here. Then I realized they were probably sleeping. It was the middle of the night, after all. Though there was no light from the outside, I saw recently burned torches in sconces along the wall that probably lit the space during the day. How very medieval.

At the shifting of our torchlights, we heard movement in the cell, and I wondered if we had roused the prisoners. Perhaps it was only rats.

And then I saw a pale face squinting at me from the darkness.

"We're English," I whispered. "We've come to get you out."

"English!" the man said. "Well, ain't that a sound for sore ears."

And then I heard something I'd never thought I'd hear again.

"Ellie?" The voice was familiar. Then Toby's face materialized on the other side of the bars.

My vision swam for just a moment as my heart lurched. Then I felt Ramsey beside me, his hand on my back. I drew in a breath and stared at the cousin I thought dead.

"Ellie, what in the blazes are you doing here?"

I rushed toward the cell. "They . . . they said you had been killed." My voice was a choked whisper.

"As far as I know, they were mistaken," he said. "But how in the world did you get to a castle in Lisbon?"

"I'll explain it to you later," I said, reaching for him through the bars. My hand cupped his face, which was half-hidden behind a long black beard. "It's really you."

He grinned, that familiar lopsided grin. "In the flesh."

I felt the urge to both laugh and weep at the same time.

"Let me get you out of here," I said, pulling back to look at the lock. This one was built into the cell door they'd installed, a bit more difficult than a common padlock.

My hands were shaking almost too hard to open the lock. I fumbled with it a few times, nearly frantic to get him out.

"Electra." Ramsey's voice beside me calmed me as it always did. His warm hand covered my cold, shaking ones for just a moment.

I looked up at him. It was still very dark, but I could see his eyes, silvery-blue even in the shadows.

"Take a breath," he murmured.

I nodded.

"You can do it, El," Toby said. "Just take your time."

We didn't have that much time, but I drew in a deep, calming breath as Uncle Mick had always taught me, as Ramsey had wisely advised.

Then I focused. It was the work of only a minute or two, but it felt like an eternity. All was silent, except for the scrape of my pick on metal and the pounding of my heart in my ears.

At last, the lock gave, and I pulled open the iron door. Toby came out first, and I flung myself into his arms, the tears I had been holding at bay falling onto the shoulder of his worn and dirty shirt.

I ought to have thought about his condition, I realized, the moment I began to regain some sense. He felt thin—so incredibly thin that it frightened me.

But when I looked up into his face, there was that same expression I recognized, the twinkle of undimmed good humor. There were shadows beneath his eyes, but there was still a familiar sparkle in them.

"Don't cry, Ellie," he said, ruffling my hair in the way that had always enraged me when we were children. "I'm safe and sound. None the worse for wear."

He was lying for my sake. I didn't want to imagine what he and the others had been through all these long months. Their clothes, ragged and torn in places, told part of the tale. How very cold they must have been in the mountains.

"We never gave up hope," I said. "We never stopped believing we'd see you again."

He nodded. "I knew you'd all be waiting for me. It was a great comfort to think about home in the hard times."

I hugged him again, then reached out to squeeze his hands. It was then I realized his hands were wrapped in cloth. Makeshift bandages.

"What happened?" I asked.

"My fingers were frostbitten crossing the Pyrenees," he said with a shrug. "They've mostly healed, but I don't have as much feeling in them as I did. That's why I couldn't do the locks myself—the main reason I couldn't get us out of here. That and they confiscated anything that I might have used as a pick. Any self-respecting lockpick would have been able to make an escape otherwise."

"Oh, Toby!"

"It's all right. Nothing to fret about. I'm sure the feeling will come back eventually."

Maimed fingers were the worst sort of injury for the locksmith, but that was something to worry about once we got him out of here.

He put an arm around my shoulders, eyeing my companions. "And who else is in the rescue brigade?"

"This is Major Ramsey," I said. "He's an intelligence officer I've been working with. It's a long story."

"It sounds like we've both got a bit of catching up to do."

He extended his bandaged right hand to Ramsey. They shook, though I saw Ramsey's fingers close carefully over the bandage.

"Glad to see you, McDonnell," Ramsey said. "Your cousin has been very worried about you."

"It's good to be seen, sir," Toby said. "By English eyes, that is."

Ramsey nodded. "I imagine you've had quite an adventure over the past few months."

"And this is Captain Archie Blandings," I told him. "He's the reason we're here."

"I owe you my thanks, Captain," Toby said.

"Don't thank me until we're clear of this place," Archie said lightly.

"Yes, don't mean to rush you, Mac," said the other voice. "But I'd just as soon be out of here."

Toby turned. "This is Fred Sawyer. He escaped with me. And that," he said, nodding at the third man, "is Frenchy."

"We don't understand him," the man called Sawyer said. "He

speaks only French, I think. We haven't understood a word he says, anyway. But he came upon us when we were making our escape, and we took him along."

I looked to Ramsey.

He turned to the man and said something to him in French.

The man's face lit up, and he began an outpouring of effusive French, in clear relief.

They went on speaking for several moments until Toby held up a hand. "All right, all right, Frenchy. You can talk to him when we're free."

Ramsey translated, and the man looked mollified.

"Let's go then, shall we?" Archie said.

We turned to go, but the Frenchman stumbled.

"He's got a bad foot," Toby said. "The frostbite. I think he may lose a few toes before this is over."

"I'll help him along," Archie said, going to put the man's arm around his shoulder.

So I led the way, Ramsey behind me, then Archie with Frenchy, and Toby and Sawyer in the rear.

"Thank you," I said to Ramsey as we made our way through the corridor back toward the stairs. "I can never thank you enough for all you've done to help me bring Toby home."

"I'm glad we could do it," he said, "and glad that the report of his death was mistaken."

So was I. So immeasurably glad.

It was harder going up the stairs than it had been coming down, and it took a lot longer. The prisoners were malnourished, and we slowed several times to give them rest. Ramsey and Archie took turns helping the Frenchman up the steep stairs.

Several times, I looked back to find myself alone, the rest of them hidden by a turn in the stairwell.

This had happened again as I finally reached the landing at ground level.

I had paused at the door, waiting until everyone arrived to open it, when I thought I heard a rustle above me. I looked up. The stairwell ascended into the tower above us, curving into darkness. I could see nothing.

Perhaps it was another rat, or a bird that had flown in at the battlements. All the same, I felt uneasy.

I heard the approach of the men coming back up and had turned to confer with Ramsey when I felt a hand slip around my waist from behind, dragging me against a hard body as the cold metal of a gun was pressed behind my ear.

"I had hoped we would see each other again," said Max Hager.

CHAPTER THIRTY-TWO

"You left precipitously last time," he said in his perfect English. "That kiss at the casino was only the beginning of what might have been a very enjoyable evening."

I struggled against him, but his arm around my waist was hard as iron, and he pressed the gun a bit harder into my skull.

I gave a little cry, though it wasn't because I was frightened. I hoped that the men coming up the stairs would hear, that I could alert them to remain quiet.

But I ought to have known better.

"Let her go." Ramsey's voice came out of the darkness of the stairwell, and then he appeared on the landing. I knew Archie, Toby, and the other prisoners were behind him. The stairwell was too narrow for all of us to have come up at the same time. Even if they wanted to rush Max Hager, there wasn't room. And if anyone started firing guns in this enclosed stone tunnel, the bullets would ricochet and cut us all to ribbons.

So I stood with Hager's arm around my waist and his gun pressed beneath my ear. Ramsey faced us, his face grim and set in the torchlight.

"I think not," Hager said, his tone amused. "Does this pretty one belong to you now? I thought she belonged to Blandings. Or do you share her? The English must be more open-minded than I believed."

Ramsey's face was cold, but his eyes were blazing. I hoped he would keep his temper in check.

"I don't belong to anyone," I said, to draw Hager's attention back to me.

"You will, I think, belong to me soon enough," he said. He leaned to move his mouth close to mine, and I turned my head away.

He released my waist to grab a handful of my hair, wrenching my head back, his gun hand snaking down to my torso in a perverse caress.

Ramsey took a step forward, and the gun pressed hard into my chest. He stopped, his face white with fury.

"Don't worry, *Liebchen*. I'm not going to hurt you," Hager said, nuzzling my ear. "Not when you've such a lovely body to explore first."

"If you touch her, I will kill you with my bare hands," Ramsey said. His voice was tight with that barely contained rage.

Hager smiled and, with his gaze still on Ramsey, leaned to kiss the portion of my throat exposed by his grip on my hair. "You will be dead when I really begin to touch her, Major, and there is nothing you can do about it."

I felt a surge of revulsion and fear.

We were, I realized, perilously close to being murdered.

Not again. It was the first thought that sprang to mind, and I almost laughed at the absurdity of it. After all, how often did one come face-to-face with people who wanted to eliminate them?

The odds, it seemed, were considerably higher in this line of work.

I looked over at Ramsey. I thought he had been making an effort not to look at me, but, as if drawn by my gaze, his eyes turned in my direction. As they met mine, I felt the force of the emotions he was suppressing: wrath, dread, desperation. Though I was the one in Hager's grasp, my overwhelming instinct was to help Ramsey, to relieve him of those feelings.

Then suddenly I had an idea. I licked my lips and let out a loud, trilling whistle. The sound was magnified in the stairwell, the piercing note repeating itself as it bumped against the ancient stones.

For a moment, there was the silence of confusion. And then the door flew open, Colm silhouetted in the doorway.

Hager had started to turn his gun in that direction, but the moment it was pointed away from my body, I grabbed his wrist, propelling his arm—and the gun's aim—upward. At that moment, Ramsey sprang forward.

I twisted out of Hager's grasp as Ramsey rushed him. The gun was knocked from his hand and clattered down the stairs. For a moment, I feared it would go off. I went to retrieve it, though I wouldn't dare to shoot, not in the stairwell, and not when the men were fighting so close. I couldn't risk hitting Ramsey.

Ramsey and Hager grappled, locked in a brutal fight in the enclosed space. I saw Hager turn sharply, trying to propel Ramsey down the stairs. Ramsey regained his balance, however, and pushed Hager back toward the upward curve of the stairwell as their ruthless struggle continued. I thought of the knife in my boot. Perhaps I could get it to Ramsey. But I didn't think I could do so without distracting him, and even an instant of distraction might prove fatal. Colm, too, stood motionless in the doorway, realizing that there was no room to interfere.

Suddenly, Ramsey swiveled and got behind Hager, his hands on Hager's head. I wondered momentarily why he didn't put his arm around his neck instead, attempt to cut off his airway and incapacitate him.

Then there was a loud, jarring crack that echoed in the stairwell as Ramsey snapped Hager's neck.

Ramsey released him, and Hager dropped, tumbling down a

few stairs before his body came to a stop. I stared at his inert form, the gun still held limply in my hand.

"All right?" Ramsey asked, coming to my side.

I was still staring at the body. I'd been there, more than once, when Ramsey was forced to kill someone. But I had never seen him do it with his bare hands as he had just done with Hager.

"Electra, are you all right?" he asked again.

I looked up at him. "Yes," I whispered.

Ramsey reached to take the gun from my hand, tucking it into his waistband at his back, and shepherded me out into the night where Colm and Simon waited. Archie came up behind us with Sawyer and Frenchy, stepping over Hager's body. Toby was behind them.

I looked around, my eyes searching the darkness around us. Were there more enemies waiting for us? It seemed that they would have rushed us during the struggle, if so. But why had Hager approached us alone? Surely he wasn't the only one here.

We needed to leg it.

And then I saw Colm's face go white.

I turned, wondering what was wrong. That was when I saw Toby emerging from the tower.

Colm took two quick strides forward and grabbed Toby in a crushing hug.

Suddenly, I was crying. I went over and hugged them both, their arms coming around me, too, and it felt, for one wonderful moment, as though all was right with the world. The McDonnell brood all together again.

It was surreal that I had come here to break out two strangers only to find out that Toby was still alive. The intelligence had been wrong. What if we had given up on the idea and turned around and went home? I would never have known that I might have saved him.

When we broke apart, there were quick explanations as there had been in the dungeon.

I looked around at the others as my cousins spoke. Archie and Ramsey were both watchful. Simon looked uneasy. Frenchy looked dead on his feet. We needed to get out of here.

Ramsey's hand reached down and squeezed mine. Then he let go. "We'd better get going."

"Yes," I said.

Archie nodded. With his usual brisk efficiency, he brought everyone into quick order.

We broke off, more or less, into groups of two as we made our way down the mountain. Archie and Simon went first. Colm was with me. He stuck close, keeping a protective eye on me as he had done all my life. Toby followed a little behind us with Ramsey and the other two escapees. They were helping the injured Frenchman.

I would have liked to keep pace with them, but Ramsey had insisted that larger groups would be easier to spot in the darkness, and I had relented.

We were about halfway down the hill when everything went to blazes.

I had just made my way over a clump of rocks and had reached the ground beyond when there was a sudden loud crack, and then Colm was pushing me down into the soft earth.

"What—" I started to protest.

"That was gunfire," he said. He was already crouched near me, pulling his gun from his waistband.

Then Hager did have reinforcements. They'd just arrived too late to help him. They must have come from somewhere else in the castle to find their leader dead in the stairwell. Now they would be out for blood.

"Where's Toby?" I asked him, looking around pointlessly into the darkness around us.

"He and Ramsey are still behind us," Colm replied.

I turned to look up the hill, but I could see nothing. Even with the light of the waxing moon, there were too many rocky outcroppings on the hill. Hopefully, Toby, Ramsey, Sawyer, and Frenchy had managed to hide behind one of them after that shot. I wouldn't let myself think about whether the bullet had been meant for anyone in particular or if it had found its mark.

"What about Archie and Simon?" I asked.

"They're quite a bit farther down than us, I think. I lost track of them."

Colm was still staring back in the direction of the castle when I saw a flash of light followed by a second crack of gunfire.

"Are they shooting at us?"

"Who else?" he replied.

He had his pistol pointed uphill now, but I knew he didn't intend to fire unless he could hit his mark. Colm was not the sort of man to waste bullets.

Another flash, another echoing shot.

I felt a surge of anger. We hadn't come this far—hadn't gotten Toby back—only to fail now.

"How many of them are there?" I asked, my eyes searching the darkness for any movement, any other flash of gunfire or searching torches.

"All of those shots have come from different places, so there's at least three of them."

"Don't you think we'd better keep going?"

He considered. "I suppose we'd better. We need to get down as quickly as we can. There's still a chance we can outrun this lot before anyone gets hurt."

I felt a flicker of fear at the words. Colm had given voice to those worries I wouldn't acknowledge, even in my own head.

"We haven't heard anyone cry out," I said. "Perhaps they're just shooting blind, hoping we'll give ourselves away."

"Maybe," he agreed. "Let's get going."

I turned and began making my way down the hill as quickly

and as quietly as I could. There were so many loose bits of rock, and I worried that kicking one of them would draw attention to our location.

Suddenly, there was a loud clatter of something farther down the mountain—rocks, I assumed—and then the gunfire started in earnest. I heard several reports all at once, and, alarmingly, saw the spray of debris nearby as bullets ricocheted against rocks too close for comfort.

"Ellie, go!" Colm said, giving my shoulder a shove.

I started back down the hill again, scurrying over the rocks, staying low to the ground.

I assumed Colm was behind me, but I didn't hear his movement. I turned to look over my shoulder and saw that he was covering me, his gun aimed up the mountain.

"Colm!" I whispered loudly. "Come on."

"Go!" he yelled.

I turned to continue down the mountain when there was the sound of another shot. I looked back again, and I saw Colm jerk with the impact of a bullet and then crumple to the ground.

CHAPTER THIRTY-THREE

"Colm!" I cried, turning to run in his direction.

There was a gunshot and a cry from farther up the hill.

And then, as if out of nowhere, Ramsey was in front of me, blocking the way. "Get down." He grabbed me by the arms and pushed me to the ground.

"Colm was hit." I could barely catch my breath.

"We're under heavy fire," he said into my ear. "You can't go to him now."

I swore at him, pushing up from the ground, and tried to move toward Colm. Ramsey rose to block me again, that big body of his directly in my path, and so I went in the other direction.

He caught me in his arms this time, preventing any more movement.

"Let me go!" I pushed against his chest, but it was, of course, like trying to move a boulder. Useless. "I've got to go to him!"

"You can't," he said.

And then he picked me up and carried me as easily as one might carry a rag doll—if the doll were kicking and fighting—to the outcrop where he had been taking cover.

Ramsey set me down, and I shoved him with no impact. "Don't you dare try to stop me."

"Listen to me," he said. His hands grasped my arms, and his voice was clipped and stern. It was his commanding officer voice. The one I hadn't heard since we'd started sharing a bed. "You will not put yourself in danger. Do you understand me?"

"I've got to help Colm," I pleaded.

"I'll go back for him," he said. "If you swear to me you won't come haring up the hill after me."

I clenched my teeth in frustration. I didn't want him to put himself in danger.

"Where are Toby and the prisoners?" I asked.

"They're a little to the east, out of the line of fire for the moment. Your cousin is helping the others down."

They'd still have to come west, through the gunfire, to get to the tree line where the car was parked. My heart clenched at the thought of Toby in danger, but the escapees had made it this far. They would make it the rest of the way.

"Blandings and Woods are at that outcrop there," Ramsey said, pointing to a distinctive rocky formation down the hill. "You should be able to get to them without being seen. I want you to go."

"But . . ."

"Electra." His tone brooked no argument.

"But what if they see you . . ."

He shook his head. "I hit the one who shot your cousin. The other two aren't as close. I can be careful if I'm not having to worry about you. Will you do as I say?"

We were losing time. I had to trust him. "Yes."

He looked into my eyes for a long moment. Then he gave me a short nod and turned and disappeared into the darkness.

I looked farther down the hill and saw a flash of light where Archie and Simon were hiding. What was that?

There was moonlight glinting off of something. If they weren't careful, it would be seen from above. I supposed I ought to try to get to them to tell them, but I wasn't certain if that path would put me in the line of fire.

I worked my way quickly and stealthily down the rock face, moving erratically to keep from making an easy target. There was still the occasional sound of gunfire, though it was not as rapid as it had been moments ago. Ramsey had put one of the shooters out of the game, and I thought it likely the other two, after seeing their compatriot hit, were holding their fire until they could better gauge our locations.

After what seemed like forever but couldn't have been more than a minute or two, I dropped into the depression near the out-cropping where Archie and Simon were hiding.

"Everything all right?" Archie asked.

"No," I said. "Colm's hit."

"How bad?"

"I don't know. Ramsey went back for him."

Archie swore. The first time I had heard him do so.

"Better wait here with us. When the coast is clear, we'll make for the car."

I looked over at Simon. He was looking over the cusp of rock back toward the castle. I saw the sheen of sweat on his forehead and felt sorry for him; this was likely more than he had bargained for.

He didn't appear to have a gun. Perhaps Ramsey and Archie hadn't provided him with one, after all.

Another barrage of gunfire drew our eyes upward, and I searched the darkness for any sign of my cousins or Ramsey. My heart was in my throat. We had to get out of here.

Archie, gun in hand, was looking over the rock that concealed us. He was cool and steady, and I thought again how easily he concealed this side of himself behind his façade of easygoing boy-ishness.

Simon shifted beside me then and dropped something. He leaned to pick it up, and my gaze followed his hand to the ground.

I felt a cold chill move through me as I noticed, in the faint moon-light, the footprint on the wet earth.

It was a crisscross pattern. It was the same print I had seen in flour at Fernando Estrada's flat . . . and in blood at the home of Carlos Motta.

Simon? Simon was in league with Hager? He couldn't be. But it made sense, the pieces clicking rapidly into place in my brain. No wonder Hager had always been one step ahead of us. No wonder he had been expecting us tonight. No wonder he had felt confident enough to approach us alone. He had assumed that Simon would be in the stairwell with us to back him up. Only Simon had been left outside with Colm, unable to make contact, unable to help when the fight broke out.

I looked over at Archie, who was still looking back toward the castle. I stood for a moment in indecision, trying to decide what I should do, how I could draw Archie aside to inform him without alerting Simon.

It was then I saw Simon slowly drawing something from his pocket, his eyes on Archie. He was pulling out a knife, I realized. If he killed Archie, he could take Archie's gun. From that point, he could shoot me and then the others as they came down the ridge, one by one.

All of this crossed my mind in the space of an instant, and even as it did, I cried, "Archie! Look out!" as I ran full tilt toward Simon.

Archie had turned toward me and didn't see Simon behind him with his knife raised. He stepped in my direction, assuming I needed him, but he wasn't paying attention to the right person.

There was no choice. I hurled myself directly at Simon. Luckily, with his attention focused on Archie, he hadn't taken much notice of me. I hit his torso hard with my shoulder at full speed, propelling him backward with a grunt of surprise.

He hit the ground, and I landed on top of him, my arm reaching up to grab the wrist of the hand that held the knife. I had the advantage of surprise, but Simon was bigger and stronger than me, and in the space of a moment, he had pulled his arm free.

He slashed at me with the knife even as he rolled to push me away from him. I deflected his blow by using my forearm to block him, but I felt the sting of the blade along my upper arm and knew I had been cut.

Archie had come up behind us now. He was armed, but he couldn't make a clean shot with Simon still wrestling me in the dark as I tried to gain control of the knife. Besides, a shot would draw attention to our spot on the hill.

All the same, I hoped he would do something quickly, because I realized as I struggled with him that Simon had a good chance of overpowering me.

Archie came up behind him and tried to pull him back. Simon whirled then, slashing at Archie with the blade. Archie was too quick, however. The time he'd spent at a desk had not dulled his instincts, and he darted just out of reach of the knife. Simon had turned his back to me to do this, and I jumped on him, my arms moving around his neck in a choking hold.

He reached back, trying to cut me with the knife, but I deflected the blow with one arm while still holding tight to his neck, trying to cut off his air supply.

And then Archie swung out with the butt of his gun. There was the crack of steel against bone, and Simon slumped in my arms. I let him go, and he dropped to the ground, unconscious.

For a moment, neither of us said anything. I stood frozen, trying to catch my breath.

A shot ricocheting off a nearby rock brought us back to the present, however, and we crouched at the same time.

"I can't believe it was Simon," Archie said, looking down at him. "It's a good thing you were watching him. How long have you known?"

"Just a few minutes," I said. "It was the footprint he left in the mud. It matched the one in flour at Estrada's flat and in blood at Carlos Motta's house. It seems he's never been too careful about where he steps."

Archie smiled. "You're a marvel, Ellie McDonnell."

"I'm just glad we were able to subdue him," I said. "But what do we do with him now?"

Archie considered. "We can't risk him attacking us again or giving away our location."

I was worried for a moment that he would suggest killing him. I knew such things probably happened in the course of war, but the thought made me sick to my stomach.

"Can we tie him up?" I suggested.

"And carry him down the mountain?"

I tried to think. We still didn't know where Ramsey and Colm were, or what Colm's condition might be. If we were going to carry anyone down the mountain, it would have to be my cousin.

There was a shuffle of movement in the darkness just above us, and Archie raised his gun.

Then I heard a low whistle.

"It's Toby," I told Archie. He lowered the gun just as my cousin slid over the rock and into our little hiding place.

"What's happening?" I asked. "Did you see Colm and Ramsey?"

He shook his head. "I didn't see anything. I was pinned down by fire as we made our way west and only just managed to climb down here. Sawyer and Frenchy aren't far behind."

"Colm was hit," I said.

Toby's eyes flashed in the moonlight. "How bad?"

"I don't know. Ramsey went for him, but we . . . we haven't seen them."

Toby swore. "I thought I saw a glimmer of light down this way. Someone must be wearing something reflective and it drew their fire."

I realized then what it had been that Simon had dropped. I looked down at the ground and saw it lying in the dirt. A mirror. Simon had been signaling our location to those above and then ducking for cover while we were getting shot at.

If that was the case, we might be in danger here. We needed to move.

"I don't think we're safe here," I said. "We should start down."

As if on cue, there was another barrage of gunfire, and I flinched.

"You start down," Toby said, looking back up the hill. "I'll go look for them."

"No, wait!" I caught his arm. Colm and Ramsey were already missing in the fracas. I didn't think I could bear worrying about all three of them.

"They might need help," Toby said.

"We need help," I told him.

He glanced at Archie, then reached out to squeeze my arm reassuringly. I winced. His hand came back wet, and it was then he realized I'd been cut. I had forgotten about my injury while we were at sixes and sevens, but now I felt the warm trickle of blood beneath my sleeve.

"You're hurt," he said, taking my elbow in his hand and looking down at the slash in the arm of my coat. "A bullet?"

I shook my head. "Knife."

"What? How?"

Simon stirred on the ground, and Toby turned to look at him, noticing him for the first time.

"What's happened?" my cousin asked in a tight voice.

"He's a traitor," I said. Archie had taken the handkerchief from his pocket and was tying it around my arm to staunch the bleeding.

"Did he cut you, El?" Toby asked.

With alarm, I recognized that tone. It was the one that had always prefaced a brawl with any of the neighborhood boys who had dared to look sideways at me. It always preceded violence.

My hesitation was enough. Toby turned toward the inert figure.

"Toby!" I said sternly. "Now is not the time!"

"I'll wring his neck," Toby growled. "He tried to kill you? Then he can die on this hill."

"Toby!" I said again, more harshly, reaching out to grasp his arm and give it a little shake. "Listen to me, will you? I know you've been through a lot, and you're on edge. But I need your help, and this display of temper is not in the least helpful!" It was as if Nacy had spoken directly from my lips, and it did the trick.

Toby looked back at me, his expression dark and sulky. "I'll teach him a lesson yet, Ellie. So help me I will."

"Later," I said. "Right now we need to figure out where Colm and Ramsey are and get out of here before whoever's on our trail arrives."

Archie pulled hard on the handkerchief then, and I winced.

"Be careful," Toby snapped at him.

Toby's temper was up, and that was never a good sign. I needed to get him out of here.

"I've got some rope in my pack," Archie said. "I'll tie him up."

He rolled Simon, who had begun to stir but hadn't fully regained consciousness, onto his stomach and tied his arms tight behind him, while Toby and I looked up into the darkness.

A moment later, there was another sound, and Sawyer and Frenchy slid into our hiding place. Now we just needed Colm and Ramsey.

"We need to go," Sawyer said. "Reinforcements have come from where they were searching the north side. They're everywhere on the mountain now. I counted shots from five locations."

I felt the clench of fear in my stomach, but I ignored it.

I had promised Ramsey that I would try to keep myself safe, and I had to keep my word.

Archie was dragging Simon to his feet. "Get going," he said, that normally cheerful tone of his underlaid with steel. "And if you try anything, I will shoot you without a second thought."

Simon gave a little moan in reply.

Archie looked to our group then. "Start down, Ellie. McDonnell and Sawyer, take Frenchy between you so you can move faster. I'll follow with Woods."

"Be careful," I told them.

I looked at Toby, and he gave a short nod. "It'll be all right, El. Just get going."

And so I turned out of our hiding place and began making my way down the mountain.

A shot rang out in the darkness, and I heard it hit the rock not five feet away from me. I'd been spotted.

I moved quickly, trying to zigzag down the slope in order to make myself a more difficult target.

I had to hope that the others were following suit. I heard the movement of rocks on the paths behind me and assumed they were still coming. I had to believe that they would all make it. I couldn't bear to think otherwise.

It felt like hours, running from outcropping to outcropping, sometimes across wide patches of land. I waited for the sting of a bullet, but, finally, I reached the bottom. Now it was only a clear patch of land to the woods.

I took off at a run.

CHAPTER THIRTY-FOUR

Gasping from the long run, I slipped into the shadows of the trees. It was dark, and I couldn't see anything. For a few minutes I stood alone, trying to catch my breath, listening for movement and searching the darkness behind me.

And then there was the rustle of approaching footsteps. Toby and Sawyer broke into the trees, supporting Frenchy between them.

A moment later, Archie and Simon followed. I felt an immense relief that we had all made it. Now we just needed Colm and Ramsey to arrive.

"Let's get to the car," Archie said. "They'll likely pursue us."

I wanted to wait for the others, but I knew he was probably right. We needed to be ready to leave at the earliest opportunity.

We hurried through the trees and back to where we'd left the car. We'd anticipated putting two escapees in the large boot where they could be concealed from the villagers. Now we had three of them.

I realized then that it had likely been Simon who had given Archie the false intelligence that Toby was dead. He had wanted to put us off the case, had believed that we would give up if the personal stake were gone. He hadn't known that we McDonnells were made of sterner stuff.

We reached the car, and it was Simon whom Archie put into the boot. I was glad. He couldn't cause trouble there. I got in the backseat with the three prisoners. It was a tight fit, but they were all thin from their long trek across the Pyrenees.

Archie drove the car back in the direction of the mountain. He had just rounded the copse of trees when he stopped. There were two figures in the road.

Then I recognized them. Colm and Ramsey. I jumped out of the car.

"Colm," I said, moving to his side. He was on his feet, but his face was white, and though his shirt was black, I could see it was saturated with blood.

"I'm all right," Colm said, reaching out to squeeze my arm with a bloody hand. "Really, I am. Just a graze."

I looked over at Ramsey's face. I knew I would be able to tell, from how stoic his expression was, whether Colm was on death's door. Only when I saw that his face was grim and not impassive did I feel like I could breathe again.

"All right?" Ramsey asked me as we helped Colm toward the car.

I nodded.

"Where's Woods?" Colm asked as we slid him into the front seat. He'd quickly taken in the missing member of our party.

"He was the traitor," I said. "He was signaling the shooters the entire time. That's how they kept picking up our location."

"He came at me with a knife," Archie said. "But Ellie stopped him. Prettiest smother tackle you've ever seen. He cut her, though."

I saw the fury flash across Ramsey's face, and for just the briefest moment there was some kind of shift in his posture, as though he actually thought about going to the boot and dragging Simon out.

Then he reined in his temper. "Let me see."

"Archie's bandaged me," I said, lifting my arm. "It's all right. But we'd better get going."

He looked down at my arm, then nodded. "Let's go."

Archie drove for perhaps an hour at what seemed like a reckless pace. It appeared that we weren't being followed, but I knew we were also racing toward safety and medical help for Colm.

I squashed myself into the front seat between him and Ramsey, so I could keep an eye on him. I was half sitting on Ramsey's lap, but I didn't object. Nor did he.

Colm leaned back against the seat, his face white and covered in sweat. Every so often, however, he would look over at me and give me the faintest smile to reassure me.

Ramsey, either unconscious of where we were or not caring, kept a hand on my thigh as the car rattled over the dusty roads. The warm, reassuring hand felt like an anchor in the storm of my emotions, and every so often I would press my own hand against it in silent thanks.

Finally, Archie pulled into a barn that stood beside a cottage. There was another car inside, free of dust, I noticed. It had been recently used.

"This is a safe house," he told us, cutting off the engine. "I can get a doctor from the village."

We all bundled into the cottage, which was decorated in a rustic but comfortable style, and Archie, after placing a telephone call in brisk Portuguese, set about building a roaring fire in the fireplace.

I settled Colm on the bed in one of the bedrooms and found a clean towel to press against his wound. Archie had put a protesting and still-woozy Simon, trussed up like a chicken, into the other bedroom.

The doctor was there within fifteen minutes, and I chewed my lip as he examined Colm in the bedroom. Toby was there, too, and every so often I could hear his voice, louder than the other two, asking some sort of question.

"He's going to be all right," Ramsey told me, more than once. I knew I should be reassured by this, for I knew he wouldn't lie and give me false hope. All the same, it was possible that he might be mistaken.

At last, the doctor emerged and closed the door behind him. We all stared at him expectantly. He spoke in Portuguese, and Archie asked a few questions of his own.

I didn't realize that my hand had slipped into Ramsey's until he squeezed it. "He's going to be fine," he translated in a low voice. "The bullet passed through the flesh in his side. The doctor was able to stitch the wound, and there shouldn't be any lasting damage."

Toby came out of the room then, and Ramsey and I released each other's hands at the same time.

It was the first chance I'd had to see Toby in good lighting, and I realized suddenly how very gaunt he was. He'd always been a big lad, not as big as Colm or Ramsey, but tall and sturdy. Now he was thin, his clothes hanging loosely. The beard on his face was long and thick.

"Toby, come sit down," I said. "You look all in."

"I am a bit tired," he admitted.

As was common with my cousins, I knew that any sign of weakness was always vastly underplayed. Toby was, no doubt, positively knackered.

"Is there anything here to eat?" I asked Archie.

He nodded. "Some canned goods, I think."

"I can make something," I offered.

Archie shook his head. "Let me. You're wounded, too, remember."

"About that," Ramsey said. He turned to the doctor and spoke to him in Portuguese.

The doctor's eye traveled to my bandaged arm, and he motioned me into a chair so he could examine it. Half an hour later, I had my second set of stitches on this brief holiday.

"Not only am I bringing you home, Toby," I said, "but I'll have two new scars to show for it."

"Two?" he asked.

I lifted up the curls on my forehead and showed him the nearly healed wound there.

He let out a whistle. "That's a corker, El. How did you get that one?"

"Bottle to the head," I said.

I saw the flash of anger in his eyes and hurried to change the subject.

But it brought up another question. What had become of Velo? Had he been a coconspirator in all of this, or had he simply run because of the dodgy work he did? I thought it likely he'd evaded my pursuit for reasons unconnected with this case, and I wished he might have done so without walloping me on the head.

A short while later, Archie was serving us a dinner of tinned meat and vegetables. It was delicious, and it worked like a tonic on all of us. I saw the color slowly returning to all the escapees' faces.

More than once, Toby looked up to find me watching him eat and frowned at me. He didn't want to be coddled, not by his little cousin. But he might as well get used to it, because if he thought I was bad, he was going to be positively smothered by Nacy.

There was the sound of movement in the other room, and it was only then that I remembered Simon.

"What will happen to him?" I asked.

"I'll bring him back to Lisbon for questioning," Archie said. "He's worked with me for years. I want to know how long he's been in league with Hager. I don't have answers now, but I'll have them soon enough."

"The man who followed us—who was watching you at the hotel—was one of the men shooting at us tonight," Ramsey said. He didn't say so, but I knew if Ramsey had been near enough to identify him, the man would not be following anyone else.

Finally, our stomachs full and the wounds tended to, it was time to finalize our plans.

"I think it best we take the escapees from here to Sintra in the morning, rather than go back to Lisbon tonight," Archie said. "I've telephoned someone to come and pick up Simon. You two go back to the hotel and collect your things. I'll stay here tonight with your cousins, Sawyer, and Frenchy. We'll meet you at the airport in the morning, using the other car in the barn."

I looked at my cousins. I didn't want to be separated from them, but I also thought Archie was right. They needed the night's rest rather than the long journey back to Lisbon. They would be safe here. Taking them to Lisbon might prove dangerous.

And so the decision was made. I bid my cousins farewell, and Ramsey and I got back into the car.

We didn't talk much on the drive back. We were, I assumed, both lost in our own thoughts. I sat close to him as he drove, though, occasionally resting my head on his shoulder.

It was very late when we got back to Lisbon. There were people coming and going in the lobby as we made our way into the hotel, as there had been every night, and it seemed strange that none of them had been through the life-threatening adventure we'd had tonight, that none of them could sense the danger that had hovered around us. We barely merited more than a glance as we made our way to the lift and upstairs.

Ramsey came into the room with me and closed the door behind us.

"Are you sure you're all right?" he asked, brushing a curl behind my ear.

I nodded. "I've got Toby back. I thought it impossible."

"I'm very glad for you, Electra." He looked into my eyes for a long moment, then he stepped back. "We'd better get cleaned up."

"Yes." He went into his room, and I went to my own bathroom. I bathed and changed into my pajamas, brushing out my freshly washed hair. Ramsey hadn't gotten to remove the pins, after all.

I had left the adjoining door between our rooms open, and he came through it in his robe. My heart fluttered at the sight of him.

Tomorrow we would be going back to London. This was our last night together.

He came to me and pulled me into his arms, but he didn't kiss me. He just held me close. I rested my head against his chest and closed my eyes, savoring the warmth of him, the security I felt in his arms. It had been a trying night, a night rife with dangers, and it felt wonderful to know that we had made it out. That my cousins—both of them—were safe.

"It's late," he said after a while, though he still hadn't released me and his fingers toyed with my damp hair. "You'll want to be rested for the flight tomorrow."

I understood the consideration of what he was saying, suggesting we forego any romance in favor of sleep. But I knew he didn't truly want that, and nor did I.

I looked up at him. "This is our last night in Lisbon. I think we should make the most of it."

His eyes met mine, and I wondered what he was thinking. Was he, too, feeling this moment was bittersweet?

He lowered his mouth and kissed me, and I tried to forget everything but this last night in the arms of the man I loved.

CHAPTER THIRTY-FIVE

I woke early.

Ramsey slept soundly beside me, his breathing slow and even. I took a moment to study him in the dim predawn light. He looked younger asleep, his stern features relaxed. In that moment, I loved him so desperately it took my breath away, and after today I would lose him.

As if sensing my inner turmoil, he shifted toward me, his arm moving to draw me closer.

I settled against him, his warm arm across me, and watched the dawn rise through the curtains, knowing that tonight I would go to bed alone in the darkness of London.

We made it to Sintra and onto the airplane without incident. Archie tended to our luggage, while I paced, hoping everything would turn out all right. We had overcome so much that some part of me feared there would be more obstacles ahead.

Toby had found a razor and was clean-shaven this morning, his pale, thin face emphasizing the effects of his ordeal. I couldn't wait to get him back for Nacy to fatten him up.

I fretted about getting him, Sawyer, and Frenchy onto the flight. It was possible that there were still people who were looking for us, and who might be willing to kill them if they couldn't recapture them. Archie seemed to think that Hager's death would have their group in disarray, but I still felt the sooner we were off the ground, the better it would be.

"I was able to get a bit of information out of Simon last night," Archie said when he'd returned to my side. "He tells me that he's been working with Hager for about a year. They knew that escapees and refugees were making their way to Lisbon using the route your cousin took, and they've been desperate to root out the operatives involved. Simon, of course, knew a good portion of my movements, and we've been neck and neck with them in the race for information."

"Who killed Mr. Suvari?" I asked. "Was it Simon?" Though I knew he was a traitor, though I had seen him wield a knife against Archie, I still found it difficult to picture the dimpled Simon Woods doing the killing.

"No, that was Noack, the man who was watching the hotel and following you. He killed Carlos Motta, too. Simon was with him on that job, as evidenced by his footprint left at the scene, but Simon didn't do any of the actual killing."

Noack was the man Ramsey had shot on the mountain. Perhaps it was wrong of me, but I was glad that such a ruthless man was no longer on the loose in Lisbon.

"What about Toby and the others?" I asked. "Did they give you the information you need?"

Archie nodded. "A good deal of it, anyway. They'll need to be thoroughly debriefed in London. Ramsey will see to that. But your cousin and I talked most of the night, and I learned a great deal that will prove invaluable. I didn't let the poor boy sleep much, I'm afraid."

I smiled. "He can rest when we're safely back in England."

"I have a few things to tend to here," Archie told me. "I'll be back in London in a month or so. I'll come to see you."

"Thank you, Archie," I said, my throat tight with emotion. "For everything." I hugged him, and his arms came around me, returning my embrace.

"It was entirely my pleasure, Mrs. Ramsey," he said into my ear, a smile in his voice. "Keep that husband of yours in line."

I didn't answer, but I managed a smile as I bid him goodbye.

My gold wedding ring was already tucked away, a souvenir of an adventure I would never forget.

Somehow, we managed to get onto the plane without drawing any particular notice. Once we were in the air, I breathed a bit easier, but I knew I wouldn't truly be able to breathe a sigh of relief until we landed on English soil.

Despite our anxieties, we all dozed for most of the flight, except for Ramsey, who spent the time reading documents related to one of his other operations. I longed to snuggle up at his side, to rest my head on his shoulder as I drowsed, but we were beyond that now. We had left that sort of easy intimacy in our bedroom at the Avenida Palace.

So I curled up as best I could in my seat, my jacket draped over me for warmth. I woke up as the plane bumped onto the runway in Bristol.

I looked at my cousins as the plane rolled to a stop. I couldn't believe we had done it. I could not believe that I was back in England with both of them in tow. It felt like a miracle.

"How long can you stay?" I asked Colm as we exited the plane.

"I believe Ramsey got me leave for a week, so I have a few days left before I need to go back to Torquay."

"Oh, good. I'm so glad. We'll have time to spend together as a family."

I was exhausted—physically and emotionally—after everything we had been through, but I also felt happy enough that I thought, if the plane hadn't taken us home, I might have been able to fly us here myself.

We took the train back to London. My cousins, buoyed by our escape and being together again after eight long months, talked nonstop and fell back into their old pattern of boisterous laughter. My heart swelled as I watched them.

Ramsey was quiet. We said very little to each other. Perhaps neither of us knew quite what role to play now that we were home.

We got out at the station, and Ramsey's big government car was waiting for us.

I realized it was Jakub who had arrived to pick us up from the station. He was standing outside the car as we approached.

"Hello, Jakub," I said, greeting him warmly. "This is my cousin Toby, who was missing. He has come home!"

Jakub smiled, and I saw the glitter of tears in his eyes. "Oh, Miss Ellie. I am so happy for you."

"Has there been word on your son?" I asked.

He drew in a slow breath. "We heard . . . that he has been killed in combat."

I felt a wave of sorrow pass through me. Jakub and I had shared similar hopes over these past few months, encouraged each other in the times when it felt difficult to believe that we would ever see our loved ones again. But now I had Toby back, and Jakub had learned that his son would not return to him.

"I'm so sorry, Jakub," I said, tears in my own eyes now. I reached out to embrace him, and after the slightest pause, I felt his hand pat my back.

He smiled down at me, and I could feel the warmth in it. "You are kind, Miss Ellie. So kind. And I am glad for you that the news has been good. For us, perhaps, it has been good, too. We . . . we were told he died quickly. Better, I think, than what the Germans might be doing to him now."

I had felt the same way about Toby at times, clung to that same faint sliver of comfort. But Toby was alive and well. And Jakub's son was dead.

"I'm sorry," I said again.

Then Ramsey and Colm arrived with our baggage, and there was light chatter as we got into the car.

I said a silent prayer for Jakub and his wife and their fallen son.

The car pulled up before our house a short while later, and we got out, Colm and Toby helping Jakub take the bags from the boot and set them on the walk.

I couldn't have a conversation with Ramsey now, not with my cousins here. But perhaps it would be better this way, less painful.

There was a part of me that knew his nobler instincts might lead him to make an offer he didn't truly want to make. We had gone to bed together, and it was entirely possible that he might feel duty bound to suggest that our marriage continue because of it.

While that might get me what I longed for—a life with him—it wouldn't give me his heart, and that would be a hollow victory indeed.

As these thoughts flashed through my head, Ramsey turned to me, leaning in slightly to speak to me so we would not be overheard. "I'll ring you up soon. We have a lot to discuss, I think."

I nodded, my throat tight.

"I don't . . ." He paused. "Well, I suppose we'd better wait to have this conversation."

I managed a smile, though I felt heartsick. "Probably so."

His eyes held mine for a moment longer, and then he leaned down and brushed a kiss across my cheek before he went and got back into the car.

I didn't watch him drive away. I needed to concentrate on the happier moments soon to come.

Nacy and Uncle Mick would be ecstatic to see Toby, and I couldn't wait a moment longer for it to happen.

When I looked up, Colm was watching me. I smiled my brightest smile. "Let's go."

I took Toby's arm and pulled him along toward the front door, Colm in tow.

There was no other method that would suffice: I burst through the front door.

"Uncle Mick! Nacy! Come quickly!"

The three of us tumbled into the sitting room.

Uncle Mick stood from his chair, the pipe in his hand frozen at his side. He stared at us for a long moment, as though making sure that we weren't some figment of his imagination.

Then the pipe fell from his hands, scattering ashes on the rug, and he strode across the room, engulfing Toby in a hug.

"Ellie, is that you?" I heard Nacy's voice as she came from the kitchen. "You're back? What's the—"

And then she stopped in the doorway, let out a cry, and rushed toward Toby.

Colm and I stood behind for just a moment, watching the reunion. And then, at the same time, we both moved forward to join in.

"All my little chickens, back in the nest." Nacy was weeping, tears streaming down her face as she hugged Toby again, her hand caressing his thin face, then Colm, then me. Then all of us at once.

There were tears in Uncle Mick's eyes, too. He didn't try to wipe them away.

It was, perhaps, the happiest night of my life. We reminisced, laughed, and told stories, and Toby told us about his harrowing escape from France.

It felt wonderful to all be together again. All my prayers had been answered.

And if there was a little ache in my heart, I would just do my best to ignore it. I couldn't ask for too much, after all.

I spent a lonely night back in my own bed, once again tossing and turning. I hadn't realized how well I'd slept with Ramsey beside me. It had been, I thought, the sense of security that made me feel safe enough to sleep. I hoped I would someday be able to rest that well again.

At least I was home, I reflected. Home in my comfortable flat with my kitten, who was thrilled to see me, and both my cousins sleeping in the big house.

I ate breakfast the next morning with the family. Nacy fussed over the boys and me, clearly plotting to fatten Toby and me up and help Colm heal more quickly with an abundance of good food. I had no doubt she would succeed in her goal, rationing or no rationing.

She loved the gifts I had brought her from Lisbon: a lovely silk scarf and a cookbook of Portuguese recipes. "I can't wait to cook some of these things," she said, beginning to flip through the pages.

Uncle Mick's eyes gleamed with interest when I presented him with the Roman key for his collection. "A pretty specimen," he said, examining it.

"What do you suppose it opened?" I asked.

"I would say it's a bit small for a door. Perhaps a chest of some sort."

"The merchant told me he found it at the seashore. Perhaps it was a treasure chest, lost beneath the sea," I suggested.

Uncle Mick smiled. "A treasure would be well and good, Ellie girl, but you've already brought me home the best treasure I could ask for."

"He means me, of course," Toby said with a grin.

"We knew you'd be insufferable once we got you home," Colm retorted.

I laughed. "Well, he has earned the right to be treasured, you must admit."

"I mean *all of you*, home together again," Uncle Mick said, quelling our bickering as he had always done. "It does my old heart good."

My cousins and I looked at one another, thinking the same thing: it had done our hearts good, too.

It was the jolliest breakfast in recent memory, all of us lingering over the table until Uncle Mick finally excused himself for a job.

"Colm and Toby, you're both to rest," Nacy instructed them as we got up from the table. "You can lie on the sofas and listen to the radio and read the newspaper, unless you want to go back to bed. Those are your choices."

Meekly, they retired to the sitting room.

"You've a stack of mail here on the table, Ellie," Uncle Mick called before he left.

I went to the foyer and sifted through the post.

I stopped suddenly at one of the letters. It was from the Chambers Flower Shop.

I tore it open and found the message inside:

Meet at the shop on Sunday at 10 p.m. Come alone.

My heart pounded in my throat. The postmark was from two days ago. And today was Sunday. I'd arrived home just in time.

Another thing occurred to me then. I'd given them the address of my postbox, but they'd sent the letter to my house. They knew where I lived, then.

I took the letter back to my flat and tried to decide what to do.

My instincts were to keep it a secret, to do as the letter instructed and meet with them alone. I had spent my whole life obeying those instincts, had sharpened and honed them in an existence built on secrecy. But I knew that such a thing would be foolhardy, dangerous.

I needed help, and I knew who could give it.

Besides, I owed him the truth. I owed him honesty, open doors and an open heart. No concealment. If he decided that my family skeletons were too great an obstacle to any sort of future, so be it. I had betrayed his trust once, and I wouldn't do it again.

I pulled on my coat and started for Belgravia.

CHAPTER THIRTY-SIX

A chill rain was falling as I rang the bell at Ramsey's town house.

I expected Constance, his secretary, to come to the door, but it was Ramsey who pulled it open. He was in trousers and his uniform shirt, no tie or jacket, and I fought the urge to press myself into his arms. *Things are different in London than in Lisbon,* I reminded myself.

"Electra. Come in." He ushered me into the foyer, his eyes on my face. "What's wrong?"

My tense expression had, I supposed, given away the fact that this was not a social call.

"I . . . need to talk to you," I said.

He nodded, his expression giving no hint of what he was thinking.

He helped me out of my coat, and then, without a word, his hand on my back, guided me toward his office.

The room was warm, a fire crackling in the fireplace, and it smelled of coffee and the faintest hint of Ramsey's aftershave. My chest ached with the familiarity of it, and I wished I had come to spend a cozy afternoon with him rather than make a confession that might end things between us once and for all.

I took a seat in my usual chair. He took the one beside me and turned so that we were facing each other. I wasn't sure if this made it harder or easier than if he had been on the other side of that massive desk.

I looked down at my hands, clenched in my lap. "I have to tell you something that I've been . . . keeping from you."

"Oh?" The single syllable was toneless.

I licked my lips. My mouth felt dry, and my heart was pounding in my throat. My hands were shaking so badly that I had to clench them in my lap.

He reached over and placed a hand on top of mine. "Electra."

I looked up at him.

"You can tell me anything you need to. You can trust me."

His voice was warm and gentle, and tears pricked my eyes. Still, I couldn't seem to find the words. Though I had rehearsed a variety of speeches in my head all the way here, I still didn't know where to start.

A tear slid down my face. He leaned forward and wiped it away. "Just tell me, darling."

Darling. The word made me catch my breath. *Darling* from Ramsey, who "disapproved of diminutives" and used only my full name.

I looked up into his eyes. There was warmth and understanding in them, and in that moment, I felt the barrier of secrecy I had carried around me all my life crack. Or, perhaps, it wasn't cracked. Perhaps it was just that I was willing to hand this man the key.

I drew in a shaky breath. "You know about my parents." He was well acquainted with the details. He'd read the trial transcripts, he told me once. How my mother had been found bloody and holding a knife, my father stabbed to death.

He nodded.

I licked my dry lips again. "I . . . I found out, on my way back from Sunderland, that it was possible my father was spying for the Germans in the last war."

Ramsey's expression didn't change at this revelation. His hand still covered mine. I pressed onward.

I relayed to him the story of my visit with my mother's dearest friend, Clarice Maynard. How she told me my father had been a German spy. I told him everything I had done and learned, laid it all on the table. If I had any hope of a future between us, he needed to know. Even if there wasn't hope, I felt he deserved my full honesty. After all we had been through together, there should be no secrets left between us.

When I had finished, he sat back, appeared to consider. "So you left a message at the flower shop before you left London. And now you've received word that you're supposed to meet this unknown person tonight?"

I nodded, my heart in my throat. It felt as though everything hung on this moment.

He squeezed my hands. "Then we'd better go."

"You'll come with me?" I whispered.

"Of course." He rose from his chair, and I stood with him. "Let me ring up Kimble. He's a good man to have in a pinch."

Kimble was one of Ramsey's most trusted associates. A former Scotland Yard man, he'd worked with us before and had always proven reliable.

I could have asked Colm and Toby to come, of course. But I had, somehow, wanted to protect them from this part of my life, as I had wanted to protect Uncle Mick. My father was his brother, and I knew that it would be hard for him to learn that he had been a spy.

"They told me to come alone," I said.

"But you didn't."

I met his gaze. "No. I didn't. I . . . I wanted you to know, and I . . . I knew I needed your help."

He nodded, his eyes still on mine.

I drew in a deep breath and then said the rest of it, the words that felt almost as difficult as a confession of love, perhaps because they were harder to earn. "I trust you, Gabriel. I should have trusted you before. I understand that now."

He stepped closer and leaned to kiss me. He'd been drinking coffee, and I found I didn't at all mind the taste of it on his lips.

All too soon, he drew back. "All right," he said, his tone back in military formation. "Let's prepare ourselves for what lies ahead."

We arrived at the Chambers Flower Shop an hour early. It felt so good to have Ramsey at my side. My family had always supported me, but it was because they were my family and they loved me unconditionally. This felt different. He had made a conscious choice to accompany me, no matter what we learned, no matter the danger. I needed him, and he was here.

As this street was made up mostly of shops, it was fairly deserted at this time of night, and especially on a Sunday. I was able to pick the lock into the shop without notice.

I pulled open the door, and Ramsey and I slipped inside. I had been in this shop once before, but it looked entirely different now. It had been deserted, and the air smelled of dried and decaying flowers. All the arrangements had been left to wither in their vases, and the floor was strewn with shriveled leaves and petals that crunched underfoot. It appeared that not much had been taken or cleaned up. The shopkeepers—the German spies who had kept this front since the last war—had clearly left in a hurry.

We moved to a shadowed corner, where we would not risk being seen from the door.

"Now we wait," Ramsey said.

I was accustomed to waiting. Burglary and safecracking were occupations that required it. But this felt different. It felt as if I had been waiting for this moment all my life, waiting to unlock this final mystery. Could it be that I would finally have the answers I'd been seeking?

Mercifully, we didn't have to wait long. About twenty minutes later, there was a noise at the door. I looked to Ramsey. He gave me a short nod as he drew his gun from his holster and slipped behind a table with a tall, dead arrangement that would hide him from view.

I drew in a deep breath and moved to face the door. It opened, and I found myself looking at perhaps the last person I would have expected.

"Mrs. Maynard," I said.

Clarice Maynard. She had been my mother's dearest friend. It had been she who had broken the news to me that my father had been spying for the Germans. I had a photograph my mother had given her, of my parents in the Bavarian Alps. What connection my parents had to Germany, I had yet to ascertain.

"Hello, dear," she said with a smile.

My lips parted to speak to her, but too many questions vied for my attention and I couldn't decide what to say.

"I know this must be a surprise, but I thought that this might be the best way for us to meet. I received word from my associates that you've been asking a lot of . . . inconvenient questions."

I stared at her, not quite comprehending. "Your associates?"

"The lovely people who owned the shop." She looked around the room, shook her head sadly. "This shop has been in business for three decades, and now they've been forced to close it. Thanks to you."

"I . . . I don't understand."

Her eyes came back to me, colder now than they had been a moment ago. "When I told you that your father had been a spy, I thought you would have had the good sense to leave it, to stop pursuing answers."

"I had to know," I said simply.

She sighed. "It would have been better for you not to."

"Tell me," I whispered.

Mrs. Maynard moved to a tall table, previously used to display flower arrangements but now coated with dust and dried petals. She took a handkerchief from her handbag and dusted off the table, crumbled bits of flowers falling to the floor. Then she leaned her elbow on it and turned to face me.

"Your father *was* a spy," she said. "A British spy, as it turns out. He did link up with German operatives, went as far as Germany at one point to do so, but it was only to plant false information."

I blinked at her.

"You . . . you mean, he was a double agent?"

"Yes."

"He . . . he wasn't in league with the Germans."

"No," she said. "But I was."

I felt the cold spread through me as the pieces began to come together.

"He found out about you," I whispered.

She nodded. "We had information that your father might be a double agent, and I was tasked with finding him out. To that end, I befriended your mother. She didn't really like me, didn't quite trust me. But I can be very persuasive."

I thought suddenly, unaccountably, of the time Colm and Toby had talked me into riding a wagon down a steep hill. I had felt instant regret as I careened down the incline with no way to steer and no way to stop myself.

I had the same sensation now.

"Unfortunately, once I was certain of what your father was doing, I was forced to take action," she said. "I went to visit your mother that day, but she wasn't there. Instead, I found your father in great haste preparing a document. I got a peek at it. It was information that could not be shared. It was something called Operation Electra."

My stomach clenched.

"It was a plot to assassinate Constantine, the king of Greece, and blame it on the Russians, keeping neutral Greece from joining the Entente," she went on. "That's oversimplifying it, but you understand the implication."

"Called 'Operation Electra' because the king's child, his homeland, would seek revenge, just as Electra wanted to avenge her father, Agamemnon, in Greek myth," I said numbly.

She smiled as though she were a schoolmistress and I a particularly bright pupil. "Unfortunately, the operation did not succeed. I couldn't, of course, have known that at the time. I had no choice in what I did, you see."

My entire body had gone cold. I could see her in my mind's eye, alone with my father in that sunny kitchen.

The knife. The butcher knife that he had been murdered with. It had come from my parents' kitchen.

She saw the look on my face and gave a sad nod. "I'm afraid so. I hadn't wanted to do it, but I had to protect myself from the information he intended to expose. I left the knife there. Your mother made it easy for me by finding him there, dead. In her shock, she picked up the knife and wandered out with it. It was, really, very convenient."

"But she would never confess," I said. "Because she was innocent."

Mrs. Maynard smiled. "She was innocent, yes. That photograph I gave you was taken when she accompanied your father on a secret trip to Germany. But she could not tell the world that her husband had likely been killed because of his spying. Because she worried about the safety of his family."

"You blackmailed her with their safety," I said, remembering how my mother's barrister had told me Clarice Maynard had been in constant contact with my mother. He had assumed they were close friends. But it was because Mrs. Maynard had been holding the safety of Uncle Mick, Colm, and Toby over her head.

"She was a very loyal woman," she said. "She would have gone to the gallows. I think, perhaps, she might even have told the truth, once you were born. She wanted to raise you, of course. She loved you very dearly. But, in the end, the influenza tied up that loose end."

Tears sprang to my eyes at the words even as cold fury seeped through me.

"But she named me Electra anyway," I said, my chin tipping up. "As a warning to my father's associates who knew of the plan. And a warning to you that she hadn't forgotten what you'd done."

Her face hardened. "So now you know the truth. I hope you're satisfied." She reached into her bag. "Unfortunately, you're too inquisitive, dear. Just like your father."

Though tears blurred my vision, I could clearly make out the gun in her hand.

CHAPTER THIRTY-SEVEN

"Put down the gun."

Ramsey had stepped from behind the plant. His gun was aimed at Mrs. Maynard. He could have shot her, but no doubt he needed her for information. After all, she seemed to still be very much involved in the spy game.

He moved to stand in front of me, and I could only think that if he died protecting me, I would never forgive him. And I would certainly never forgive myself.

"We're at an impasse," she said. "I can't let you go."

"You won't be able to kill us both," Ramsey said, though I wasn't entirely sure of that. And anyway, even one of us was too many.

I held my breath, wanting more than anything for this to end well. Wanting us both to walk out of here.

Then, suddenly, there was a shifting of the shadows behind us, a flash of movement, the clatter of the gun as it hit the floor. Clarice Maynard, too, was on the ground, crying out as she struggled against the figure.

It was Kimble, materializing out of the darkness, who had subdued her.

She struggled against him, but it was of no use.

"Easy does it," Kimble said blandly as he pulled a pair of handcuffs from his pocket and secured her wrists tightly behind her back. Too bad she didn't know any lockpicks who might be willing to help her.

"I should be able to find evidence to corroborate her story," Ramsey said, drawing my attention back to him.

"How? What do you mean?"

"I requested additional files related to your father's death recently. I just haven't had time to sift through them yet."

"But why?"

"As you know, the man who attacked us with the knife that night in January admitted that he was after you. He had been paid to give you a warning. That was all he would say. It led me to believe that I should look further into your father's background."

"You already looked into his background when you first hired me," I said.

"Yes," he agreed. "But I assumed your mother really had killed your father. Everything seemed to point to the fact. Her answers at trial were unsatisfactory, her defense weak. It was only recently I began to wonder if there was something else she was trying to hide. I believe, if I look closely enough, I may be able to find proof of your father's work. It will just take time and finesse to get to the classified files."

If anyone could do it, he could. I still couldn't believe this had happened, that this mystery had been solved.

"My mother was innocent," I whispered. "I knew she was innocent."

"I'm sorry I didn't believe you before now," Ramsey said.

I shook my head. "Even though you didn't believe it, you still came. Thank you for that."

We looked at each other, and then Kimble's monotone broke the silence. "Hate to interrupt, but where would you like me to take her?"

Ramsey looked over. Clarice Maynard had been secured, and she was glaring at us.

"Detain her until I've made contact with Colonel Radburn," Ramsey said, referring to his own commanding officer. "We're going to have a lot of questions for her."

Kimble nodded, and I thought I saw, for the first time, a glint in his impassive gaze. "Gladly."

"Come along," Ramsey said to me. "I'm going to take you home."

It was very late when we reached my flat, and the night was frigidly cold, but I felt wide awake and warm. I couldn't believe we had done this. It was as though the weight of the world had been lifted off my shoulders. There was just that one last bit of unfinished business in my life.

"Come in?" I asked Ramsey when we reached my door. The words came out on a puff of steam in the icy air.

He looked down into my eyes. "It's late. Do you think I should?"

I shrugged, trying to maintain my nonchalance when this moment felt so very important. "If you don't want to—"

"Electra," he said in a low voice, stepping forward and backing me into the flat, his foot kicking the door closed behind us. "I think you know what I want."

"Coffee?" I suggested with a raised brow.

In answer, he pulled me into his arms and kissed me with a hunger that left me breathless.

Burglar was sleeping on the sofa. He opened one eye and said "meow" to us as I took Ramsey's hand and led him into the bedroom.

It was early when there was a knock at the door of my flat.

Beside Ramsey in the bed, I froze.

"Stay here," I said, getting up and grabbing my robe. I didn't know who it was, but this was an unusual time of day for visitors.

"Coming!" I called. But apparently, I had left the door unlocked, for it opened, and Colm and Toby came bursting into my flat.

"Roll out of bed, Ellie!" Toby called. "We're going to go to the market. Do you want to come with us, or . . ."

They stopped in the doorway to my bedroom when they saw me, my robe hastily pulled on, and Ramsey, still in my bed, sitting up now with his bare chest visible.

It felt as though all the air had been sucked out of the room, and my face flushed scarlet. I had certainly not meant for my cousins to discover Ramsey and me together in my room.

"So that's the lay of the land, is it?" Colm said, his voice cool. "I thought as much."

"Colm . . . Toby . . ." I said, finding my voice.

I came out of my bedroom, pushing my cousins back a bit and closing the door behind me. At the very least, Ramsey needed a chance to put his trousers on.

"You shouldn't have just barged in," I said.

Colm's arms crossed over his chest. "How long has this been going on?"

"I . . . don't think that's really any of your business."

The door opened behind me. Ramsey had dressed in record time, though he was still buttoning his shirt as he came out. Colm's gaze went from me to him.

"I'll have to ask you, Major, what your intentions are toward my cousin."

"Colm," I said.

Colm didn't look at me; his cool eyes were still fastened on the major.

Toby's eyes, in contrast, were blazing. "And whatever your rank, sir, I'm warning you now that if you give the wrong answer,

I'll knock you into next week and then follow you there and finish the job."

"Toby!" I said sternly. "Might I remind you both that I'm a grown woman, and my private life is not your concern." Despite this assertion, I could feel that I was blushing clear to my hairline. What an awkward situation this was.

"It's all right, Ellie," Colm said. "These things happen. But he'll answer for it, all the same."

"For Heaven's sake—"

"Electra and I are married," Ramsey said, cutting off my protest.

I felt my irritation spike. He had been put on the spot, of course, but now we would have the difficult business of explaining to my cousins why we would, despite what had happened last night, likely soon be getting divorced.

Colm looked to me for confirmation of the news, and, not knowing what else to do, I nodded.

A grin replaced the scowl on Toby's face like sunshine vaporizing rain clouds. "Well, why didn't you say so in the first place? Welcome to the family," he said, shaking Ramsey's hand as though he hadn't just threatened him with bodily harm.

Colm still looked wary, as though he suspected we were pulling a fast one on him.

Toby came and pressed a kiss to my cheek. "Congratulations, Ellie. I know Nacy must be thrilled to have you happily wed. Though I must say I'm gutted to have missed the wedding. When did it happen?"

"In . . . in Lisbon," I said faintly. "It was a civil ceremony. Just the two of us."

"In secret, was it? Dad is going to kill you," Colm said, but there was a good-natured smile hovering on the corners of his lips.

"Boys, please," I said, my mind in a whirl. "I'll be happy to give you all the details if you'll give me time to . . . to get dressed first."

Toby laughed. "I'm sorry, El. And here we are barging into the honeymoon suite. We'll go back into the house and await you at breakfast, shall we?"

I caught the look on Colm's face before he turned away. He didn't quite believe us. At the very least, he knew that something wasn't quite right. He'd always been perceptive.

I'd have to explain things to him sooner or later, but for now I was just glad they were leaving.

"You shouldn't have told them that," I said to Ramsey when the door closed behind Colm and Toby.

"I felt disinclined to get into a brawl with your cousins before I've had my coffee."

"I'm going to have a devil of a time explaining things to Uncle Mick and Nacy. And now we'll have to come up with some reason we're going to get an annulment . . . or a divorce . . . and that isn't going to—"

"I don't want a divorce," he said. "I think we should stay married."

I realized why he was saying it, and my heart sank.

"No," I said firmly. "I know you feel a sense of obligation where I'm concerned, but forget it. It doesn't matter that my family has . . . has seen you here. They know that divorces happen. They know things have never been easy between us."

"Electra . . ."

"And if you feel some sort of silly, misplaced guilt because we . . . because . . . you . . . compromised me or some such thing . . ."

"Electra, darling, be quiet for a minute, will you?" he said dryly.

The *darling* drew me up short.

"I'm not prepared to stay married to you out of a sense of obligation," he said. "I wouldn't do you that disservice."

The sinking feeling deepened, but there was also a bit of relief. I couldn't bear a one-sided marriage.

He stepped closer and put his arms around me, drawing me toward him. "We don't know when or how this war will end," he said. "We could die tomorrow, or we could live sixty more years. All I know is that I don't want to live another day without you. I want to stay married to you because I'm in love with you."

I felt as though all the breath had been sucked from my body. "You . . . you're what?"

He looked down at me, the slightest smile playing at the corners of his lips. "Your fire, your brilliance, your blasted stubbornness. Your infuriating ability to make me lose my temper. I love all of it . . . I threw it all away, and then I cursed myself for losing it. And when you were going to marry Captain Blandings, I had to keep myself every single minute from knocking his teeth out."

I gave a little laugh that was half a sob.

"When it was necessary for me to marry you, I felt only an overwhelming sense of relief that you wouldn't be anyone else's wife, no matter how temporarily. I wanted you to be mine. I fought that realization very hard for a long time." He reached up and brushed my lips with his thumb. "But one war's enough, I think."

Tears were beginning to well in my eyes, and I didn't think I was going to be able to stop them. Sure enough, one rolled down my cheek. "I . . . I'm in love with you, too."

"I'm immensely glad to hear it." He held me tighter and leaned to kiss me.

I pulled back a few moments later, breathless. "But we come from such different worlds," I said. "Our pasts . . . our families . . ."

He kissed me silent before giving me his answer. "I don't care. About any of it. I know what sort of woman you are, and I want you."

"Are you sure?"

"Do you need proof? I'll show you."

He turned from me suddenly and went to where he had left his greatcoat over the back of a chair the night before. He reached into one of the pockets and pulled out a small square box.

"I went out and bought this yesterday," he said, coming back to me. "I had some input from your old friend Pascal LaFleur."

Monsieur LaFleur was an old associate of my family's. Ramsey and I had visited his antique shop on one of our earlier missions.

"You'll remember he told me to come back if I ever needed an engagement ring," Ramsey said. "So you see, I'd already made up my mind yesterday. Long before yesterday, really. I think my mind was made up as soon as I put that wedding ring on your finger in Lisbon. But this one's a bit prettier."

I gasped as he opened the box to reveal the most spectacular emerald ring I had ever seen. It was set in gold, the large center gemstone encased by a frame of brilliant diamonds.

"I love you, Electra McDonnell," he said. "Will you do me the honor of remaining my wife?"

I looked up at him, tears shining in my eyes. "Electra Ramsey," I whispered.

"Yes," he said, slipping the ring onto my finger. "Electra Ramsey."

A week later found me back at my flat, packing some of my things.

I'd been living in Ramsey's house, adjusting myself to the luxury of it, and it was good to spend a few hours in my old home. I would miss this place, but Uncle Mick had said I could keep it and come back as often as I liked.

My uncle had given his blessing to my marriage, of course.

"He didn't have much choice, as we presented him with a fait accompli," Ramsey had told me wryly after their private discussion. "I don't think, however, he was entirely displeased."

My own subsequent conversation with Uncle Mick convinced me that, while he didn't necessarily like the havey-cavey way we'd gone about things, he liked Ramsey a great deal. And, above all, he was glad to see me happy.

Nacy had instantly forgiven Ramsey his past transgressions

where I was concerned—the foolish decisions made by a man in love, she now termed them—and had insisted on making him *ful medames*, his favorite dish from his time spent in Egypt, for a celebratory meal.

For his part, Burglar had adapted to the high life quite readily and had annoyed me by falling instantly in love with Ramsey and pushing me to second fiddle. He seemed to view Ramsey's amused tolerance as mutual adoration and followed him about the house constantly.

It seemed, then, that all was right in my little world. Or almost all . . .

I had just closed my suitcase when there was a familiar knock at the door. It couldn't be. Could it?

I rushed to the door and pulled it open. Felix was standing there.

Wordlessly, I threw myself into his arms, and they closed tightly around me.

"Hello, love," he said against my hair.

"I'm so glad you're all right," I whispered, tears in my eyes. "I've been so worried."

"I told you before. I'm a lucky fellow. I got into a few scrapes in France, but I've more lives than a cat."

When we were settled on the sofa with teacups before us, Felix told me something of what he had been up to. The Official Secrets Act meant there were confidences he would have to keep, but he was able to give me the gist of it.

"I was sent in to pick up one François Marchand, a member of a French Resistance cell who had been denounced to the Germans. I was to help get him out before he was killed and bring him back to London, hopefully to meet with de Gaulle and the Free French."

"Oh, Felix," I breathed. "How dangerous it must have been."

He shrugged, and I knew there were a great many stories contained in that simple gesture.

"You succeeded, then," I said. "You're home."

"Yes, I found him. Only, it turns out it wasn't François. It was Françoise."

"A woman." I looked into his face and knew instantly what he had come to tell me. A smile replaced whatever concern had shown in my expression. "You've fallen in love with her."

Felix looked chagrined. "It's only been a month, I know. You'll think it's some sort of puppy love. But it isn't like that. It's . . ." He looked at me. "Well, I think you know what it's like."

"Yes," I said softly. "I know."

"You'll like Françoise," he said. "She's so clever and brave . . . beautiful, too. Golden hair and big brown eyes. And she doesn't put up with any of my nonsense. I've been thoroughly tamed."

"She sounds a delight!" I said sincerely. "And I'm glad she's managed to bring you to heel."

"We're going to continue working with the Free French here in London. Turns out, I've rather a knack for decoding. And it's an easier job for a man with one leg than running through French fields in the dark."

"I'm so glad. I worried about you all the time. Now you'll be here, where I can see you."

He nodded. "You and Ramsey . . . How are things?" he asked.

"We're married, actually." I hadn't meant to break the news quite like that, but I was afraid if I didn't have out with it, I wouldn't have the courage.

Felix paused with his cigarette halfway to his lips.

"It was part of a mission," I hurried to clarify. "A long story, but . . . but we don't intend to annul it now, as originally planned. We're very much in love, Felix."

Felix, to my relief, grinned. "That part's not news, anyway. Everyone knew it long ago except the pair of you. Well, I'm glad he finally had the good sense to recognize what a gem you are."

"You're not angry?" I asked, searching his face.

His expression was gentle. "No, love. I'm glad. In fact, I was afraid *you'd* be angry with *me*. You see, Françoise and I are going to marry, too."

"Oh, Felix. I'm so happy for you!" I hugged him again, my heart swelling with joy. I couldn't have pictured a better, happier ending for my best friend. "Why would I be angry with you?"

"Well, I did propose marriage to you . . . was it only five weeks ago?"

"It was a time of high emotions," I said. "For both of us."

"I'm sorry, Ellie. I really do love you, you know." The *but* was implied. He loved me, but he had realized he was not in love with me.

"I know," I said. "I love you, too, Felix."

EPILOGUE

Gabriel and I were married again—*properly,* as Nacy insisted on terming it, though we'd had a perfectly proper Lisbon wedding—in a church in Hendon. The road in front of the church was rutted with holes from bombs, and there were buildings reduced to rubble within view, but I still thought London the most beautiful city in the world.

Nacy had worked tirelessly on converting the fabric from my mother's wedding gown, which she'd secretly stashed away, into a breathtakingly lovely dress for me. Even my hair, beneath a netted veil, cooperated for the occasion.

Our uncles met at last. I was nervous, at first, to see Uncle Mick chatting with the Earl of Overbrook, but they seemed to get on splendidly. I saw them laughing together and found I wasn't really surprised. I knew well how Uncle Mick could charm anyone.

Gabriel's parents were lovely and welcomed me to the family with open arms and no pretensions.

All three of his sisters were also there. Noelle, the only one I'd met thus far, greeted me warmly and leaned to give me a light embrace.

"I knew it," she whispered in my ear. "You're going to make Gibby very happy, dearest."

The other two sisters—Lady Nora Blackhurst, the eldest Ramsey sibling, and Rose Ramsey, the younger—were lovely and so kind. I saw Rose and Toby exchanging glances a few times throughout the day and wondered if the Ramseys might be getting more than they bargained for on the McDonnell front.

I also began to think that Colm might be a good match for Constance, who looked charming in a pale pink frock. I was getting carried away with the matchmaking, I knew, but I thought I could be excused for wanting everyone to be as happy as I was.

And Felix came with Françoise. She was even more of a stunner than I'd expected. She kissed me on both cheeks in a very French manner and then proceeded to tell me in perfect English how she felt as though she already knew me well, and she hoped we would be the best of friends. I liked her immensely, and my heart was happy for Felix.

Uncle Mick walked me down the aisle, beaming. When he handed me off to Ramsey at the altar, he leaned to brush a kiss across my cheek. "I love you, Ellie girl."

Nacy cried throughout the ceremony, and Colm and Toby brushed tears away, too.

And when Gabriel and I were once again declared man and wife, when he pulled me into his arms and kissed me, I felt as though I could burst with joy.

It was the happiest ending I could have conceived of. Well, the happiest with war still raging.

There were still battles to fight and hardships to endure. Things would, I knew, be different now as Gabriel's wife. He would try to keep me out of trouble. He knew as well as I did, however, that no one had yet succeeded in doing that.

But, just for today, I would forget all that. *Focus on what is,* Uncle Mick always said. And what a perfect day it was, surrounded by the people I loved best in all the world.

As far as I was concerned, this was my happily ever after.

ACKNOWLEDGMENTS

The end of a book is always cause for reflection, and the end of a series much more so! I'm so very grateful to everyone who saw me through Ellie's journey from beginning to end. I want to offer my deepest thanks:

To Kevan Lyon, my amazing agent. Working with you is an absolute pleasure!

To Kelly Stone, who edited this book with meticulous care, ensuring Ellie's story came to a worthy conclusion.

To Catherine Richards, who has done so much to help Ellie grow throughout the series.

To the team at Minotaur, for every step it took to transform my stories into beautiful books.

To all my wonderful friends, who have cheered me on and who make me laugh every single day.

To Ann Collette, my dear friend and former agent, who believed in me from the start.

To Sabrina Street, who always drops everything to read my latest book before I submit it.

To Clare Oldham, you know Ellie about as well as I do at this point! I so appreciated your support and your insights going into this final adventure.

To my fantastic family: Dan and Dee Weaver; Amelia, Caleb, Larson, and Anders Lea; and Danny and Juliana Weaver. Thank you for your love and encouragement every step of the way.

And, finally, to my readers. Words can't express how much I appreciate you!

ABOUT THE AUTHOR

Amelia Lea

Ashley Weaver is the author of the Amory Ames mysteries and the Electra McDonnell series. When not writing, she works as an elementary and middle school librarian. A lifelong lover of books, Weaver has worked in libraries since she was fourteen and holds an MLIS from Louisiana State University. She lives in Central Louisiana.